A MOST
INCONVENIENT
DEATH

A MOST INCONVENIENT DEATH

Donna Fletcher Crow

MOODY PRESS

CHICAGO

All Scripture quotations, unless indicated, are taken from the King James Version.

ISBN: 0-8024-2710-3

1 3 5 7 9 10 8 6 4 2

Printed in the United States of America

To Ella Lindvall
a gracious lady
a great editor

Major Characters

At Ketteringham

The Boileau Family:
  Sir John—the squire
  Lady Catherine—his wife
  John (Jack) Elliott—
    the heir
  Frank—younger son
  Anna (Ama) Marie—daughter
  Caroline (Carry)—daughter
  Mary—younger daughter
  Theresa—younger daughter
The Rev. William Waynte Andrew[s]

Guests:
Lord Charles Danvers*
Hardy—his manservant*
Her Grace, the Dowager
  Duchess of Aethelbert*
Lady Antonia Hoover*
Nigel Langston*
Hickling—his manservant*
Tommy Frane*
Huntley—butler
Dalling—manservant*
Ringer—Gamekeeper*
Pip—Ringer's son*

At Stanfield Hall

The family:
  Isaac Jermy, Esquire
  Jermy Jermy
  Mrs. Jermy—his wife
  Sophia—their daughter
Cousins:
  Thomas Jermy
  John Larner

Watson—butler
Eliza Chastney—maid
Maria Blanchflower—nurse
Martha Read—cook

At Potash Farm

James Blomfield Rush
Emily Sandford
James Rush, Jr.
Savory—servant

*fictional characters

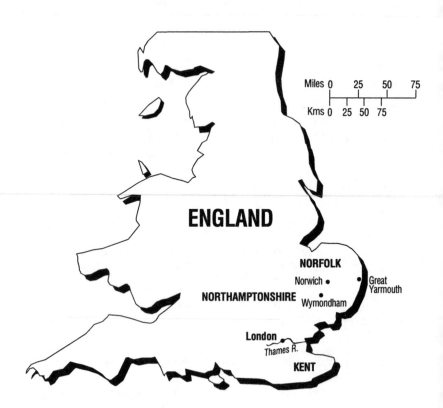

HETHERSETT

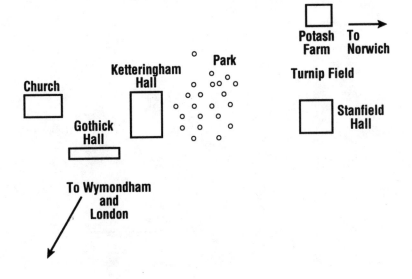

1

The green-gold patchwork of Norfolk farmland rolled past seven hundred feet below. An unusually bright October sky stretched above the red-and-yellow-striped balloon. Its blue pennants waving on the breeze.

The tall, dark man with craggy features in high silk hat and brown frock coat swept his arm to indicate the wide vista, took a deep breath, and began a sombre melody.

"Oft when my spirit doth spread her bolder wings,
In mind to mount up to the purest sky,
It down is weighed with thoughts of earthly things,
And clogged with burden of mortality."

"Ah, sure I am that you're right, your lordship. And good it is to hear you singing again! Even if you must be choosing a gloomy-sounding bit." His stout, sandy-haired companion refrained from referring to the off-key quality of the aria.

Lord Charles Danvers smiled at his man's words. "But that's the joy of poetry, Hardy. Even when life's sorrows intrude, we have the perfect escape."

Only the slightest shadow to the warm, brown, heavily browed eyes and the smallest lines at the corners of the firm mouth showed that the polished Lord Danvers knew anything of life's intruding sorrows as he continued.

"Heart need not wish some other happiness,
But here on earth to have such heaven's bliss."

"It's myself that knows how long it's been since you've sounded so cheerful, m'lord."

"And you, Hardy." He grinned at his customarily gloomy man. "I only hear your Irish grandmother talking when you're profusely content—or exceedingly exercised."

"Ah, and so it is, sir." Hardy removed his hat, and the breeze ruffled the sandy hair that waved back from a receding forehead. His portly build, rosy cheeks, dancing blue eyes, and fondness for green jackets often reminded his employer of a leprechaun.

Danvers laughed. "But then, it's one or the other most of the time with you, isn't it?"

"Aye. And wouldn't my old grannie be amazed if she could see me now!"

Lord Danvers smiled and, picking up the telescope from the wicker and leather gondola of his aerostat, turned the glass to focus. "Ketteringham Hall about two miles to the northeast, Hardy." Danvers pushed his telescope shut and pointed to the great red brick pile of gables, spires, and chimney-pots showing through the trees of the park ahead of them.

"Shall I begin valving, sir?" Hardy reached for the handle on the wooden valve that controlled the gas filling the great balloon.

"Bring her down slowly. I want to enjoy every bit of this rare day. We're unlikely to have many more its equal this fall." Danvers left the mechanics of aeronautics to his trusty servant and leaned against the edge of the gondola to savor the matchless serenity of the flight—the absolute silence, the sense of stillness so suited to his philosophical mind.

Of late he had assiduously avoided such opportunities for introspection. Since outgrowing the youthful religious fancy that had led him at the age of sixteen to consider taking holy orders, for the past eleven years his inquiring mind had taken refuge in the popular philosophers of his day. But since the autumn past, the autumn of 1847, the autumn that was to have brought life's greatest joy to his life, he had found nothing that could bring pleasure or even solace. So he chose the only available recourse—escaping in a balloon. Danvers sighed, and the lines deepened in his forehead. A brooding mood quenched even his melancholy melody of a few moments earlier.

Hardy adjusted the butterfly valve, then tossed a square of tissue paper over the side. The paper appeared to rise, thereby confirming that the balloon was beginning its descent.

"Should be plenty of room in that pasture." Hardy pointed to a green expanse beyond Ketteringham's vast park. "Sure and we wouldn't want to be landing in Stanfield's turnip field." Even from this distance the plowed brown field of the farm below them looked mucky.

The aeronauts skimmed just above the autumn-bright trees. Lord Danver's gaze had just settled on the estate's sun-sparkled lake and small stream winding off in the distance to the River Yare when a flock of game birds rose from the covert and flew almost directly at them. The birds were followed instantly by a volley of fire.

"It's shooting at us they are, m'lord!"

"Get down, man!" Danvers made a grab for his servant who was trying to retrieve a ballast bag. Sand showered through its shot-riddled side as a falling pheasant narrowly missed landing in the basket. A hiss coming from just above his head told Danvers that at least one ball had also punctured the balloon.

The loss of twenty pounds of ballast more than offset the sudden loss of gas, giving Danvers a moment to indulge in relief that the lump of shotgun lead that tore into the balloon had not been hot enough to ignite the gas and send them to kingdom come in a ball of red-yellow flame. Thank God he used the less volatile coal gas rather than the pure hydrogen favored by many aeronauts.

As it was, the situation was serious enough. Danvers looked despairingly at the severed rope that a moment before had secured one corner of the basket to the balloon. Even in such an exigency he spared a thought for the fleetingness of life's securities, then turned his attention to the balloon, which was now hard to navigate, as well as being dashed uncomfortable to stand in. Taking the valve-rope himself, Danvers let out a rush of air, which sent the balloon straight toward a clump of oaks.

As the trees rushed toward them, Hardy grabbed his sheath knife to slit open another ballast bag.

"No!" Danvers shouted. "Throw out the grapnel!"

Hardy obeyed and tossed the anchor-shaped hook out of the basket. The trees shot up at them.

"Flex your knees and hang on!" They hit the treetops to the accompaniment of the fluttering and croaking of several dozen outraged fowl. Blackbirds caught in the webbing. Jays landed in the basket. The gondola settled into the branches and stuck there like a boat on a sandbar as a shooting party raced across the nearest clearing, shouting and waving.

"Tell them not to be shooting, m'lord!" Hardy ducked below the rim of the basket.

Instead Danvers waved to those in the field and tossed out a rope. "Grab hold of the rope!" he yelled. They obeyed. "Now pull!"

A few strong tugs disentangled them from the branches, and the balloon, the aeronauts, and a basket full of red and gold leaves and blackbird feathers settled to the ground to be engulfed by the shooting party and curious laborers from nearby fields.

A tall, sturdy, graying man in well-cut tweeds and carrying a long-barreled Manton over his arm strode through the crowd. "I say, Charles, is that you? I should have known. Dashed foolish way to make an entrance. You could have been killed. What do you mean scaring us all like that?"

"Scaring *you?* I was under the impression we were the ones being fired upon." Danvers grasped the squire's outstretched hand. "Hello, Boileau. Didn't consider your guests might go in for game birds of this size." He nodded toward the balloon, which now lay on the ground like a deflated elephant, gas rushing out of the valve that Hardy had tied open.

"Rum way to travel." Sir John Boileau shook his silvery head and gave a grimace that made his mustache pull down on one side. The squire's smooth, oval face was topped by a tweed cap that shaded his sharp blue eyes. He pushed the cap back to rub his balding forehead in a perplexed manner.

"On the contrary. It's extremely convenient and offers the most exceptional view of the countryside—when one isn't obliged to be dodging bullets, that is."

"Why'd you choose the trees to land in?" Boileau looked at the open fields just beyond.

"Best to land in trees when the balloon's hard to control—cushions the impact. A few scraping branches and thrashing birds are small problems."

"And if it's not a problem to be shot from the sky like a blessed clay pigeon and clawed by birds and branches, I'd like to be knowing what it is." Hardy grumbled in the background, bailing out leaves and feathers with scratched hands.

Danvers leaped over the side of the gondola. The strap under his instep kept his ivory silk trousers taut and wrinkle-free so that he landed his usual, perfectly-tailored self, while his short-legged servant puffed and clambered over the basket behind him.

Sir John suddenly remembered his role as host. "Well, welcome to Ketteringham." With a wave of his arm he indicated some of the nearer observers. "You remember my son Jack, of course, the young scalawag all this brouhaha is in honor of."

Danvers greeted the heir, whose coming of age was being marked with a full schedule of countywide festivities. Although he bore the blond, blue-eyed coloring and aristocratic features Danvers remembered in Lady Boileau, it was apparent that when the twenty-one-year-old heir was filled out he would carry his father's sturdy, commanding presence. A son to be proud of indeed.

"And Frank—don't believe you've met my second son." Eighteen-year-old, freckled-faced Frank bowed to acknowledge his introduction. Danvers barely had time to note the odd combination of mischievous twinkle in the eyes and thoughtful wrinkle in the brow before the attention of the group swept past the sandy-haired lad.

As they were surrounded by close to twenty family members, guests, and servants, the introductions could have gone on interminably.

Danvers was relieved when Boileau abandoned the effort with another sweep of his arm. "But I daresay you'll meet them all soon enough. High time we were getting back to the Hall."

The squire appointed three servants, including Ringer, the game warden—a black-haired, giant of a man accompanied by his son, an incongruously tow-headed miniature of himself—to assist Hardy in stripping the net off the balloon and rolling the several hundred pounds of lute-string silk into a more or less manageable bundle. Then, crunching leaves underfoot, Sir John led his guests through the park to Ketteringham Hall where Lady Catherine was overseeing the laying of tea on the terrace.

The shooting party just reached the edge of the wide, green lawn in front of the Hall when the bells from Ketteringham Church began pealing in celebration, as they had every hour since breakfast. At the conclusion, the band from nearby Hethersett Village struck up a festive air.

His ears still ringing as if the carillon were inside his own head, Danvers barely managed to resist the urge to clap his hands over his ears at the enthusiastic *um-pah-*

pah of the band. He was more than happy to follow a footman to his room.

Danvers's luggage had been sent ahead by mail coach but had not arrived yet, so he brushed his wiry black hair and sideburns with the pair of silver brushes supplied in the room. His tall, thin build was relieved of the impression of gauntness by his broad shoulders. But even the richness of his brown eyes couldn't quite offset the sharpness of his long nose or the hollowness of his high-boned cheeks. It had not always been so. Before last autumn he had been accounted passably handsome.

He gave a final check to see that his cravat of printed India silk was still lying in impeccable folds before joining the company for tea. It would take more than a rough balloon descent to dislodge Danvers's precise toilette, except for his unruly thick hair, which forever insisted on defying the severe pomadings he dealt it.

The frail, beautiful Lady Catherine in a wide-skirted gown of violet taffeta, locks of her pale hair escaping its spider-lace cap, greeted her latest-arrived guest on the terrace.

Danvers was quickly engulfed by the ladies of the party wanting to know more of his daring arrival. Anna Marie and Caroline, the eldest Boileau daughters, were sincere in their alarm for his safety. But they had little chance to express it, for Lady Antonia Hoover, the layers of her ivory lace tea gown spread wide over rustling crinolines, swept all from her path as she entered on the arm of a man with sleek brown hair whose nip-waisted, bright-blue tailcoat accented the width of his padded shoulders. A miniature, golden-haired dog nestled in her other arm.

"Nige was just telling me what a naughty boy he was in the field today." She smiled saucily at Danvers, tilting her head so that one cluster of amber-red ringlets brushed her fashionably pale cheek beneath the brim of her lace-trimmed straw bonnet.

As the daughter of the third Baron of Breene, the twenty-two-year-old Lady Antonia was accustomed to be-

17

ing the belle of every ball—even when there was no ball in progress. Danvers had known her all of his life, and yet he barely knew her. To the world she was always fashionably coy and flirtatious, and yet he had at times glimpsed flashes of a caring, intelligent person. With her copper curls and fragile features she appeared as delicate as the roses and lace she was so fond of, and yet he suspected a strength underneath.

Nigel Langston cleared his throat. "Following a bird in my sights. Didn't see you till it was too late. Dashed bad shooting, what?" He offered a half-hearted handshake that seemed perfectly to suit his ambiguous appearance. The high forehead tapered to faded blue eyes, the thin cheeks weighted with full lips. Beneath the padding his shoulders were narrow for one so tall, evidencing a build that would run to paunch in middle age.

"On the contrary, it was exceptionally good shooting—or luck. Results could have been much worse." Danvers passed the incident off gracefully, especially as he didn't want to distress the ladies present.

Now that he knew the misplaced round had been fired by Langston, he wondered . . . Yet that was ridiculous. The fact that he had never liked Nigel and that they had been rivals for Charlotte's hand could have no bearing now. Charlotte was dead. The thought erased his smile. The lovely Charlotte with whom all his hopes for happiness had died.

Danvers shook himself and focused on the pair before him. Nigel had never seemed serious in his rivalry, anyway. After all, he was a distant cousin of Charlotte's. And if he had been serious he had little chance for success, for the orphaned Charlotte's guardian—her uncle Edward—made no secret of his dislike of Langston. But that was all long in the past, and Nigel continued to collect women the way some men collected Meissen snuffboxes or Napoleonic memorabilia. Currently he had apparently found consolation in Lady Antonia's charms.

Danvers forced a smile back to his lips. "I will admit, though, for a moment there I thought we were having a repeat of the Montgolfieres' experiences last century. The Frog peasants attacked their balloons with such violence Louis XVI had to issue a proclamation saying that balloons were harmless."

Danvers told the story lightly, but Langston failed to accept it in that vein. "I hope, Danvers, that you are calling me neither a Frog nor a peasant." He gave a jerk of a bow and turned on his heel. The fact that Antonia chose to remain with Lord Danvers did nothing to soothe Langston's ruffled feathers, but Danvers found it pleasant.

"Balloonists took to carrying champagne to placate the peasants—a tradition that still persists." Danvers finished the story to his diminished audience.

Members of the shooting party by now had had sufficient time to change from their tweeds and gaiters into more formal afternoon attire, and to the continuing strains of the Hethersett band the entire company refreshed themselves with cups of tea, finger sandwiches, and macaroons. When Sir John, now resplendent in black frock coat and blue silk waistcoat over a ruffled shirt, observed that all had been served he cleared his throat for attention and signaled the footman standing at the side door to bring out the birthday presents.

With easy grace the young heir stepped forward and began the ritual of unwrapping. These were gifts from family and close friends. Those from tenants would be presented later in the week at the ball given for the county. As tradition required, Jack began with the packages from his youngest sisters—a shaving mug from Mary and a book of verse from Theresa. The prayer book from Andrews, the vicar of Ketteringham, was met with a smile, apparently for its predictability. But the miniature balloon Danvers had commissioned fashioned out of pewter made a hit with all the company.

"I say. Thank you, sir." For a moment Jack's enthusiasm was almost boyish, but he quickly covered it with the man-of-the-world air he normally wore.

Lady Catherine's gift was an elegant table clock for which he thanked her very prettily and then turned to the final package, that from his father.

A few quick rips of paper revealed a Purdey's best double-barreled rifle. Jack ran his hand over the satiny wood of the half-length stock, then lifted it from its case to sight along the gleaming barrel. He lowered the gun, thanked his father, and made a brief, formal speech to the company.

It was all perfectly proper, but Danvers was puzzled by the look that passed between the squire and his son. It seemed to be of warning on the father's side and challenge on the son's. That made so little sense in the situation, however, that Danvers assured himself he must be mistaken.

Now the band, which had taken the speech-making as an opportunity for their own refreshment, resumed playing with renewed vigor, and the guests had their cups refilled or strolled along the terrace, as suited them best.

Danvers, who as yet had seen no sign of the arrival of Hardy or his balloon, decided he should go and check on the proceedings of the crew in the park. He had descended only the first step of the terrace, however, when he heard his name called and turned back.

"Lord Danvers, may I hope you recall our meeting, even though it was several years ago?"

The clerical collar beneath the severely cut black coat was Charles's clue to the identity of the tall, hollow-cheeked man with a fringe of beard and gray, thatched-roof eyebrows that gave a scowl to his face.

"Ah, Andrews, is it not? Boileau's vicar?"

The man bristled alarmingly, and the eyebrows shot even farther forward. "You have the name correct, sir. I am William Waynte Andrews. I have, however, the honor to be vicar of Ketteringham, *not* Sir John's vicar."

Danvers backtracked as gracefully as he could. "I beg your pardon. I intended no disrespect. I merely meant to refer to the parish in which Sir John and his family reside, not to imply ownership."

"Quite right. No offense taken. But one can't be too careful in such matters. After all, my service is to God and His creatures, not to the squire."

Danvers nodded, more to hide his smile at the implication that Sir John was not one of God's creatures than to imply agreement.

"I have taken my leave of Lady Catherine and go now to call on a parishioner. Do I perceive we are headed in the same direction?" Andrews pointed to the northeast.

Danvers agreed and fell into step beside the vicar. The hourly peal of church bells made conversation impossible for several minutes.

When the bells ceased ringing, the quiet was startling. Danvers spoke to break the silence. "Calling on parishioners, you said. Hope no one's ill?"

"No, no. Going to call on Rush at Potash Farm. He's been missing services of late. Never used to miss. Remarkably pious. I do hate to see a falling away of the faithful, but the enemy constantly stalks like a roaring lion. We can't afford to be slack in our vigilance. Actually not of my parish. Potash is just over the boundary. The squire doesn't approve of those out of the parish worshiping at Ketteringham, but I won't refuse a pew to anyone who wants to hear the Word of God."

It seemed that no matter how innocuous Danvers tried to be in his comments, he kept hitting hornets' nests. He certainly had this time, and the vicar was not one to let an opportunity of airing his opinions pass.

Andrews shook his head. "A most melancholy affair, this coming of age. I had hoped the ringing of the church bells might remind them of their duty to God, but I fear the effect has been lost on those of light minds."

Danvers's eyebrows rose. He had long known Sir John Boileau as an honest and devout man—far more devout than himself, certainly. "You cannot mean the squire and his family."

What Danvers had intended to quell a conversation he considered most improper, the vicar took as a spur. "Indeed, not the entire family. Lady Catherine and the older daughters are as sincere in their piety and as devoted to charitable work as one could wish. But Sir John will not heed my repeated warnings against dancing and card parties. I fear for his soul." Andrews jabbed a finger toward the sky as if in his pulpit. "And the soul of young Jack—drinking bouts, gaming debts, bad company at Oxford . . ."

Danvers had heard more than enough. It could well be true—it was typical enough—but he would not have his host and the guest of honor maligned. "I must take my leave of you here, Andrews. Enjoy your walk—it is a beautiful day."

Before the vicar could any more than raise his hat in farewell Danvers turned and was striding across the field. But in less than fifty yards his pace slowed. He swore under his breath. In his hurry to escape that starched-up parson he had turned without calculation and was now ankle-deep in the mud of the plowed turnip field between Stanfield Hall and its neighboring farm. Brown stains covered his black patent boots and the instep straps of his silk trousers.

He started to return to the road. Then he noticed that just twenty yards ahead of him a thick path of straw had been freshly put down across the field. He wallowed forward and gained the path, heaving a great sigh of gratitude for the careful farmer who had laid it. Now he observed that straw also covered the ditch bank at the top of the field.

Happy for secure footing, in spite of the fact that he had undoubtedly ruined a new pair of boots, Danvers paused to survey the countryside. To his right he could see the crenellated towers and glinting leaded windowpanes of Stanfield Hall. To his left, smoke curled from the chimney of Potash farmhouse. And somewhere in the woods behind him, he supposed, was his balloon. Unable to locate with any sense of certainty the clump of oaks that had served as his landing pad, he turned, chose the nearest footpath, and strode into the woods.

At first he contentedly hummed the overture to *Tannhauser,* only slightly off-key, accompanied by a chorus of birdsong overhead and the crunch of leaves underfoot. He had been right to come to the Boileau celebration. The friends who had urged him all summer to get out more, to seek more society—no matter how little appeal it held for him—had been right. It was time to rebuild his life, to find a new meaning to replace the one he had lost.

It was several minutes before Danvers became uneasy over the lack of other human voices. If he was in the right part of the park, he should be able to hear Hardy directing the servants in loading the balloon on the cart. If the task had been completed, he should have met them when he walked along the road with Andrews. He moved on more quickly, his ears attuned for the sound of voices or the clanking of horse and cart.

When at last he heard what he sought, he started forward in alarm. The anger in the harsh voices that reached him must mean there had been a disaster to his possessions. A few strides closer to the altercation, however, he realized his alarm had been ill-founded. That was certainly not Hardy's lilting voice.

"Dash it all, Boileau! I need my money. Two weeks ago, you promised—and the rate will double, remember."

"You're being confounded unfair, Jermy. I need more time!"

Danvers stopped. The embarrassment of intruding on such a scene would be unthinkable for both himself and the speakers.

The heavier voice of the two growled a reply.

Then the voice Danvers now recognized as that of

Jack Boileau shouted: "No! Don't you dare go to my father. I'll see you burn first!"

Again the reply was indecipherable.

A heavy snapping of twigs underfoot told Danvers the adversaries had begun walking. Having no desire to meet one of them on the path, he turned and walked back the way he had come. As he reached the edge of the wood and headed toward the road, a figure emerged from a path to his right and crossed to Stanfield Hall with agitated strides. This must be the man Jack had called "Jermy."

Danvers noted young Boileau's creditor with some interest. He judged him to be in his early thirties, well-dressed, if slightly old-fashioned, not overly tall, although the current vogue of tall hats made that difficult to judge.

The man was nearly to the Hall when a young girl emerged from the house and ran to him with curls bobbing and blue ruffled skirts flying above her pantaloons. Danvers watched the scene with a small smile—she was just such a child as he might have hoped to have had himself, had things turned out differently.

"Papa! Grandpapa is home, and Mama is looking everywhere for you."

The man's apparent anger evaporated as he took his daughter's hand and went into the house with her.

Danvers turned away with a quiet sense of something lost and walked back to Ketteringham, berating himself for his fool's errand. He had ruined his boots, was a party to two conversations he didn't want to hear, and had learned nothing about his balloon.

As he approached Ketteringham gate from the south, however, from the north came the sight for which he had been searching the better part of two hours: a lumbering farm cart with an enormous mound of red and yellow silk on its flat bed and Hardy and the other servants looking painfully jostled in the basket. To his surprise, Jack was with them, perched atop the roll of netting, the breeze ruffling his blond hair, his pleasant young face smiling as if he hadn't a care in the world.

Jack was the first to see Danvers. He waved and jumped off the cart. "I daresay you'll be glad to see all's returned safely."

Danvers was amazed at the youth's jaunty air. After the scene in the park, he would have expected the boy to show some sign of agitation.

"Do you think I might cadge a ride in the balloon with you sometime? By Jove, think I'd rather fancy being an aeronaut myself."

"I'd be delighted for your company—as soon as it's repaired, of course."

"Shame you were fired on. Can't think what Langston was doing."

"Don't blame him. Perfectly understandable—he was swinging fast, following the bird in his sight. We flew in right behind—undoubtedly gave him as bad a fright as it did us." Danvers shifted the subject slightly. "You should have some excellent sport in the field now."

Jack's eyes gleamed at the reference to his prized Purdey. "Can't wait to fire it. Won't be any game left for the poachers when I get through."

"Trouble with poachers hereabout is there?" Danvers looked at the burly gamekeeper directing the transport of his balloon.

Jack followed his gaze. "Same as everywhere, I expect. All the farms are on alert, but Ringer'll sort them out if anyone can."

Just as they turned in at the gate, Danvers noticed a servant girl standing there, apparently waiting for someone. A dark-haired man with a poorly kept beard, about Jack's height but broader and twice his age, approached the maid and asked something. She looked puzzled, then turned toward Danvers and Jack.

"Excuse me, Mr. Boileau, sir, but Mr. Rush here's

inquiring after Mr. Jermy. Do you know if he's at Stanfield Hall?"

Jack muttered a reply even Danvers couldn't catch, so he replied to the question. "If that's the man with a pretty blonde daughter, I saw him there about half an hour ago."

"That'd be young Mr. Jermy Jermy," Rush said in a gravelly voice. "Did yer see Mr. Jermy, senior, the lawyer?"

"Didn't see him, but the child said something about Grandpapa being home."

"That's 'im. Much obliged." Rush replaced his hat and stomped off through the park.

"Strange fellow." Danvers turned toward Ketteringham. "Does he make free of your park?"

Jack shrugged. "Rush would win any contest you care to run for the most disliked man in the neighborhood, but he's harmless enough. Father allows him use of the park since he farms so near."

"Oh, I remember. Andrews mentioned him as tenant of Potash."

"At the moment he is, but Jermy sued him at the spring assizes for an unpaid mortgage, so I don't suppose he'll be tenant much longer. Can't say it'll be any loss to the county."

"Except that you'll have to find another least-liked resident."

At that moment Andrews's church bells began their peal, and Jack grinned impishly. "That might not be so hard to do—I can think of at least one candidate."

There was just enough time to dress for dinner, and Danvers was thankful Hardy was back to do his proper job as valet. Although the servant's late arrival meant that Danvers had to wait while his suit was pressed and repairs made to the unacceptable job the footman had done unpacking Lord Danvers's newly arrived valises.

The evening required my lord's stiffest white collar with white satin neckcloth knotted in front; a silk, roll-collared vest; and a closely cut black tailcoat, as well as Hardy's most careful brushing and macassaring of Danvers's wiry hair. The long face, framed by black locks, was now too thin and craggy to be handsome, but observers seemed to find it worth looking at. Its dark, deep-set eyes readily mirrored kindness, intelligence, skepticism, or anger, and the long lines beside the mouth always reflected the viscount's humor—whether good or ill.

Danvers was the last houseguest to make his way to the banqueting hall across the courtyard to join the other guests—a list that included such elevated personages as Bishop Stanley of Norwich, attending in honor of the heir's coming of age. But as Charles emerged from the west wing corridor and started along the gallery leading to the main staircase, he discovered he was not the last person to leave the house. Angry voices rose from Sir John's library, whose heavy oak door stood ajar.

". . . a note to you? Blast him. I warned him not to!" In spite of his twenty-one years, Jack's voice sounded in danger of cracking.

"And I warned you about running up more debts. I have nine children to support—five of them girls who will need dowrys! I paid your gaming debts and drinking bills at Oxford. I thought I was done with it!"

His host's voice echoing behind him, Danvers sped down the stairs to the marble entrance hall as quickly as he could without making a clatter of footsteps.

"The man is dashed impertinent. I told him I'd pay!"

"I'll not have my son and heir being a spendthrift gamester . . ."

With a sigh of relief, Danvers slipped out the side door and crossed the lawn.

Dinner tonight was to be held in the Gothick Hall, which Sir John had built shortly after buying Ketteringham ten years before. It was a noble imitation of a medieval hall in which the squire gave entertainments for the county and banquets rivaling those of old England. Blazoned across the ceiling in full color was the Boileau arms, the pelican in her piety, and the length of the great room was set with tables in a U-shape, glowing in candlelight and gleaming with silver and crystal, quite unlike any refinement that would have been found in the more romantic days of Sir John's gothic vision.

The footman, in powdered wig and pale blue-and-gold, eighteenth-century livery, announced My Lord the Viscount Danvers to the company milling around the hall being served champagne in tall, thin glasses by a fleet of similarly liveried footmen hired especially for the occasion.

Lady Antonia immediately broke away from her group near the door as if she had been standing there awaiting just that announcement. Her unadorned, low neckline and bare shoulders above the row upon row of lace-trimmed flounces of a jade green silk gown appealingly suggested the female form emerging from seafoam. For a moment she smiled quietly, and the candlelight played on her elegant features—the high-arching brows and long lashes framing golden-brown eyes, the slim nose, and the well-defined mouth that could look severe if it weren't so frequently smiling.

Danvers returned her sparkling smile with his slow one, accepted a drink from the footman, and allowed himself to be drawn into the circle.

"Glad to see you around again, Danvers. Time you put off the black crepe." A young man with blond hair and astonishingly beautiful features, wearing three gold watch chains over his ruffled and tucked shirtfront, raised a glass to him.

"Tommy Frane! Didn't know you were here—didn't even know you knew Boileau."

"Met him in London last season, then was invited along here after I was at Aylsham for the shooting." Aylsham—Nigel Langston's countryseat a few miles to the north. "Have an idea I'm here to be vetted by the charming Miss Caroline Boileau. I can think of worse fates." He eyed Sir John's second daughter across the room, looking sweet and demure in a pale blue dress and wearing a cluster of satin flowers in her hair. Then he turned back to Danvers. "You're an old family friend, what?"

"Sir John and my father served in the Rifle Brigade in the Netherlands."

"At Waterloo, were they?"

"My father was. Sir John—or John Peter as Father still calls him—was on leave in England. He posted night and day to get back in time for the great battle but arrived twenty-four hours too late. Father still tells the story—imagine Sir John does too."

"By Jove, pity to miss the excitement."

"Lucky for my father—Boileau searched the battle-field and found him wounded—would have died if Boileau hadn't brought him in." Danvers took a sip of wine and brought the conversation back to the present. "I'm the official representative of the family for the coming-of-age."

"Good show, this. What do you think of Boileau's latest enthusiasm?" Tommy swept the Gothick Hall with his arm and quoted:

> "I built a lordly pleasure-house
> O soul, make merry and carouse
> For all is well, I said."

Danvers frowned. "What's that, Frane?"

Tommy looked smug. "Tennyson. You think you're the only one allowed to go around quoting? Forever boring on with your great chunks of sonnets."

Danvers laughed. "You mistake the matter, Frane. I'm not objecting to Tennyson—just to the fact that you misquoted him."

Tommy looked puzzled. "Can't have. I got it up special. *Palace of Art.*"

Antonia took his arm. "Don't worry, Tommy. Carry won't notice. Heavy work being invited as a beau for her, isn't it?"

Tommy's forehead furrowed. "Don't understand it. Most females don't find me bad company." He waved to Caroline across the room. Apparently she didn't see him, for she turned away, giving the viewers the full effect of her pale blond hair brushed smooth over each ear and caught in a beflowered chignon at the nape of the neck. "Duty calls." Tommy cleared his throat. "You're sure she won't notice if I get the quote wrong?"

Antonia gave him a pat of encouragement on the arm and turned to Danvers.

His attention, however, was taken by Sir John and his heir, both looking slightly red above their stiff, white collars and well-tied cravats. Father and son entered the hall with a joviality that Danvers, at least, recognized as forced.

The company was directed to their seats by Sir John's well-trained footmen. As a viscount, Danvers was seated at the head table, the Dowager Duchess of Aethelbert on his right and Lady Antonia on his left.

A distant relative of the Boileaus and Lady Antonia's as well, the dowager duchess was a commanding figure in a high-necked, lavender-gray silk dress. Even seated, she evidenced her tall, rail-slim erectness that never needed the whalebone corsets she wore like armor. Her steel-gray hair was piled high on her head in a fashion from which no wisp would dare to slip its coil, any more than her dresser would dare to suggest that the style was out of fashion. But fashion was too paltry a consideration to apply to one whose high cheekbones and long neck still bore the beauty of youth no matter how parchmentlike the skin over them had become. Her grace raised her eyebrows, but not her lorgnette, at Antonia's lapdog, Tinker, as he scampered across the polished floor and disappeared under his mistress's skirts.

Perhaps in deference to his Norman French ancestry, the squire chose to have meals in the Gothick Hall served *à la francaise*—a menu of standard English dishes was highlighted by some continental dishes and served in ordered sequence.

"I find this far more elegant than the English manner of sitting down to great platters of roast joints, bowls of vegetables, and steamed puddings all at once," Lady Antonia remarked to Danvers as she accepted a ramekin of cheese to accompany the mutton cutlet with soubise sauce she had just been served. "And I must say, Tommy was quite right. You've done very well to come out of mourning. Your friends have missed you most dreadfully."

Her voice held a note of concern, and for just a moment she regarded him with a look of wide-eyed caring. Then she bent to slip a morsel of mutton to the red-gold terrier who stuck his foxy little nose out from under her skirt.

Danvers blinked at her solicitude, then took a bite of his cod with oyster sauce. "I can hardly believe it has been as dreadful as you make it sound. But it is time that I make an effort—as Agatha *will* keep reminding me." He gave a wry smile at the thought of his elder sister and her determination to push him into matrimony come what may.

"And is it such an effort to rejoin society?" Now Lady Antonia dropped her attitude of stylishly arch banter, allowing Danvers one of those rare glimpses of the woman beneath the society coquette. "You must still miss Charlotte dreadfully. I daresay we all do. She was so lovely."

"Thank you. Yes, I miss her. We were very well suited." The conventional phrase conveyed no more than the fact that he and his fiancée had come from the same social class. But the tightness of his lips and a whitening of the knuckles of his clenched hand betrayed the depth of feeling he still held for her.

He and Charlotte had known one another from childhood, and the fact that they would marry was always understood. Even with his eyes open he could envision her smooth brown hair looped in long side curls above the soft blue she liked most to wear. *She was such a one—whom to look at was to love.* She loved lace and kittens—which he tolerated in spite of the fact that they made him sneeze. But in quiet moments of conversation she had revealed that, unfashionable as it might be, she could think too.

And pray. Charlotte had been a deeply spiritual woman, and he knew that his own lack of spirituality had distressed her deeply. He hoped her faith in a loving God and a heavenly reward had been justified. It was the only comfort he had. Perhaps if he hadn't mislaid his faith long ago he would have more personal comfort. The philosophers and poets he had filled his thought with had little solace to offer.

"At least you have found some diversion in your aeronautics?" Lady Antonia drew him back to present company.

He smiled. "You have chosen the precise word, Tonia. It is a diversion—a pleasant activity but hardly anything to provide purpose or direction in life."

Antonia chuckled. "Too lightweight a pastime, would you say?"

Charles grinned back at her. "Far too flighty. And Agatha *will* keep lecturing me that I need to keep my feet on the ground. 'But I must mix with action.'"

"'Lest I wither by despair.'" Antonia finished his quotation, then laughed. "Oh dear, Tommy has us all doing it."

Danvers smiled as his thoughts drifted to the morning's flight. One needed new experiences. One could not live forever filled with sadness, as gas filled a balloon. The question now was finding how to live again. Aeronautics was not enough, but perhaps it was a beginning.

The footmen cleared away the first course and brought in steaming tureens of turtle soup. Antonia turned to the distinguished gentleman on her left, a member of Lord Russell's cabinet. Danvers was left with his thoughts.

Ballooning had seemed a perfect answer for his desire to escape himself after Charlotte's death. At first the soaring thrills offered a sensation of relief, and one did achieve a certain perspective—looking down and seeing everything so small made one's troubles appear small in relation to the vastness of the heavens. But, of course, in the end one was always obliged to return to earth and go on with the daily routine, even if one's fondest dreams lay cold in the grave—and one had been responsible for putting them there.

The dowager duchess concluded her conversation with Bishop Stanley and turned to her left. "Well, Danvers." She looked him up and down through her lorgnette while the intricate beading shimmered on her lavender gown. "I used to dance with your father at Almack's. Thirty-some years ago that was, after he recovered from that Waterloo affair. And a very fine dancer he was too. Of course Almack's isn't at all what it used to be. Very plebeian now. Must make Sally Jersey turn in her grave."

Danvers smiled at his outspoken partner. The dowager duchess now spent little time on her estate in Kent, which her son, the young duke, and his family occupied. Rumor had it that she disapproved of her daughter-in-law's Scottish ancestry. The young duchess probably shed no tears over her mother-in-law's plans to remain at Ketteringham until the London season.

The duchess accepted a dollop of red currant jelly sauce on her venison. "Lady Catherine told me this is Francatelli's recipe."

Danvers looked at a loss.

"Francatelli—the Queen's chief cook." She sampled a bite. "Excellent. But far too rich for Lady Catherine's digestion. I shall warn her against it. Her constitution is much too delicate." Then a new thought struck her grace. "Aren't you the care-for-nothing that arrived in a balloon today?"

"I hope I may claim to be an aeronaut without accepting the description of my character, Your Grace."

She snorted. "French invention, aren't they? Napoleon used them for his army. No good can come of it." Then she allowed a glimmer of a smile to escape. "Might be fun, though. Now, tell me about Norville's family. I haven't seen him since Prinney died and the world lost all notion of fashion. We didn't have all these ugly mills and dreadful factories spoiling the country then—and this madness for *trains* . . ." She shuddered.

Danvers obediently sketched the bare facts of his family for her. His father, the Earl of Norville, was at Norwood, his Northamptonshire estate, but would no doubt remove to his London residence when Parliament convened. Danvers's eldest sister, Lady Agatha Burroway, had one son and two daughters and lived most of the time in London where Margaret and Eleanor, the younger Danvers sisters, made their home with her. Their brother Frederick William, at Oxford, completed the family.

"I take it your mother is deceased?" Her voice implied that it was rather bad taste on the part of the countess to have allowed that to happen.

Danvers inclined his head. "Since the birth of my sister Eleanor, Your Grace." The countess's love of operatic music, if not her talent, had been inherited by her elder son, and singing favorite arias to Charlotte's accompaniment—no matter how little his notes matched those played on the piano—had been a link to his past. But now all music was gone from his life.

He was rescued from the dowager duchess's further interrogations by Sir John's rising from his place at the table and clearing his throat for attention. "My Lord Bishop, Your Grace, my friends—Lady Catherine and I wish to thank you for honoring us with your presence on the occasion of our son's coming of age."

The squire paused uncomfortably to clear his throat.

"Our son, John Elliott Boileau"—the look that passed between father and son was not one to make the situation easier—"has been raised in the best of English traditions and educated in the finest English schools, with careful attention given to his moral and religious discipline." The awkward pause was filled with a murmur of "Hear, hear" and "Rightly so" from the guests.

At this point the speaker was expected to launch into a speech extolling the virtues of the heir, but Danvers, who had been privy to their recent quarrel, knew that at this moment the father could think of little laudatory to say about his extravagant son.

Then a happy thought apparently struck the speaker. "The night I arrived to take my place at Ketteringham, I said a prayer that I might be a father to the fatherless in the parish, a husband to the widow, a peacemaker, and a teacher to the poor. This I have endeavored to do. It is likewise my prayer that my son and heir shall apply himself to follow the same path, and himself become the father of the parish." With obvious relief, Sir John raised his glass of champagne. "Ladies and gentlemen—John Elliott Boileau, better known to you all as simply 'Jack.'"

The guests raised their glasses and toasted. "Jack Boileau." Those on the right wing of the table, however, were unable to complete the act by drinking the heir's health. The butler had forgotten to recharge their glasses.

Sir John's color rose as he perceived this final straw to the fiasco.

Jack, though, was perfectly at ease as he stood and thanked his father, the bishop, and all the friends who had gathered to help him mark this occasion. "I understand something of the responsibility that is before me, and, keeping my father's example always in mind, I shall try to be as good a squire as he—God send that it be many years from now." He paused to make certain that the harried Huntley had indeed refilled all the glasses this time, then in ringing tones proposed the Queen's health.

"Handsome boy," Antonia whispered to Danvers. "I can't make out whether he's truly conceited or that suave exterior is a cover-up for insecurity."

"God save the Queen." Danvers joined the toast, turning to Antonia as she raised her glass. Then he continued. "Odd you should say that. I was just asking myself whether Jack was extremely intelligent or merely sly. I don't believe I know him well enough to decide."

Either way, though, it seemed impossible this callow youth could be only five years younger than himself—but then, a lot could happen in five years.

A tiny, scrabbling sound at Antonia's feet announced Tinker's impatience. She slipped him another tidbit, then looked again at the guest of honor. "I wonder what my Sarah will make of Jack. I have a pretty good idea what he'll think of her."

Danvers was lost. "Your Sarah?"

"Oh, haven't I mentioned that my cousin Sarah Mellors is coming up from London tomorrow? She's an absolute darling, but I fear she may prove something of a trial. This will be her first come-out. Our mothers are sisters, and I saw a great deal of Sarah when she was an infant —before my mother died."

Antonia's voice fell, then she gave herself a small shake and continued with a brisk smile. "Somehow I seem to have promised Aunt Betty I'd be something of a shepherdess for her lamb's exit from the schoolroom." Tonia pointed at Danvers as a happy thought seemed to strike her. "You can help me guard her, Charles. She shall have a considerable inheritance from her grandmother when she marries, so we can't be too careful."

Danvers was about to inquire whether Lady Antonia didn't consider enlisting him as guard to be throwing the child to the wolves, but Tonia didn't pause for his acquiescence in her scheme.

"I'm not sure how my aunt wangled the invitation to

Ketteringham for Sarah—I think Aunt Betty and Lady Catherine patronize the same charities or something."

The dowager duchess, who had caught just the end of the conversation, made a noise that in a lesser personage could only have been described as a snort. "And would that be The Asylum for Poor, Friendless, Deserted Girls; The Society for the Relief of Poor Widows and Children of Clergymen; The Society for Bettering the Conditions and Increasing the Comforts of the Poor; or The Forlorn Female's Fund of Mercy, I wonder?"

Antonia muttered, "I don't know, Your Grace."

But obviously the question was merely rhetorical. "It's no wonder Lady Catherine is worn to a frailty. Now, if more people would support sensible works, we could accomplish far more."

"And which would those be?" Danvers asked with a twinkle in his eye.

"Why, the ones for which I am patroness, of course —The Society for the Suppression of Vice, and the Society for Preventing Crimes by Prosecuting Swindlers, Sharpers, and Cheats. Now, the Society for Promoting the External Observance of the Lord's Day . . ."

Danvers was only spared taking a subscription to the dowager duchess's favored compassions by Lady Catherine's rising to lead the ladies from the room, allowing the gentlemen to enjoy their port and cigars undisturbed.

After dinner the men joined the ladies in the garden terrace and pleasure grounds, which were illuminated with paper lanterns and colored lamps.

"May I have the honor, Miss Boileau?" Danvers made a small bow to the eldest Boileau daughter.

Anna Marie smiled and handed him her cashmere mantelet, which he draped over her shoulders. "It is I who am honored, Lord Danvers. Please call me Ama. Everyone does."

"If you'll call me Charles." He offered his arm.

Ama was almost tall enough for Danvers to look her directly in the eye. The coiled loops of her dark brown hair peeked beneath the brim of her bonnet, and the skirts of her moss-green dress rustled as they joined the other guests in strolling through the garden. They paused with special admiration before the group of lights that spelled out Jack's initials and the date: JEB 20 Oct 1848.

Bishop Stanley joined them and raised his tall hat to Ama. "I have happy news, my dear. I received word yesterday that Owen's ship reached New Guinea."

In the flickering light of the paper lanterns Ama blushed prettily. "Oh, I am so glad. Thank you for telling me, Bishop."

After a few more remarks the bishop moved on to greet another guest. The formerly untalkative Ama turned back to Danvers. "That is such good news! Bishop Stanley's son Owen is commanding a Royal Navy expedition to survey the waters of New Guinea and Australia. We are much concerned for his safety. It is so very far away, and he is gone for such a long time—" She stopped suddenly, either from fear of her voice breaking or from fear of appearing unmaidenly in her enthusiasm for the bishop's heroic son. But either way Danvers was certain her interest was more than merely scientific.

A great explosion and burst of light from the far side of the lake interrupted them. Ama took Charles's hand and pulled him to the end of the garden. "The fireworks are beginning! Papa hired the pyrotechnist from Vauxhall Gardens to direct the display."

A skyrocket burst into a glittering green and gold canopy over their heads to accompanying oohs and ahs from the ladies, followed by fountains of red fire shot from Roman candles. Silver and blue pinwheels spun on posts at the water's edge.

The spectacle continued, holding its viewers spellbound with dazzling effects—all the viewers, apparently, but Danvers. Perhaps it was the shooting into the sky that

38

suggested it, but he began thinking about his balloon and wishing he had taken a closer look at the damage. Jack had expressed a desire for a ride, and if the repairs weren't too extensive, perhaps he could fulfill the heir's wish in a few days.

Tommy Frane with Carry on his arm strolled over to join them.

> "While day sank
> The light aerial gallery, golden railed
> Burnt like a fringe of fire."

He gestured toward the display.

"Still at it are you, Frane? Stout fellow." Danvers smiled.

There was a burst of green and gold overhead, then a dozen little fire balloons, set off from a boat, floated over the lake, sprinkling the night with silver stars.

Tommy opened his mouth to quote again, but Danvers was quicker, and, with a brief excuse, he bowed to the ladies and left them to Tommy's care. There would be lanterns in the stable. He would just take a look at the hole in the balloon bag so he could order repair supplies tomorrow.

The stables and servants' quarters were deserted. No doubt everyone on the estate was gathered around the lake to watch the pyrotechnics. A lantern hung by the stable door, and he had no trouble locating the balloon—indeed, it almost entirely filled Sir John's second tack room. The hole torn by the lead shot was ragged, but not large. It should not be difficult to repair if a shop in Norwich could be found to supply the elastic gum with which the silk must be impregnated to make it gas tight.

He doused the lamp and started to hang it on its hook when he heard footsteps from the other side of the stable. Something about the stealthy manner of the tread made him draw back into the doorway just as Jack walked by. His new Purdey reflected a pale gleam from the moon.

Strange that the boy would leave his birthday celebration while the fireworks were still in progress. But he had been thrilled with the gift and was undoubtedly anxious to try it out. Danvers recalled Jack's earlier remark about running the poachers competition. He must be going night hunting to try his hand at poaching conditions.

Danvers returned to the terrace in time for the final exhibit, a wide, silver waterfall of sparks that cascaded right into the lake. Then all strolled back to the house where trays of tea and hot chocolate were set out.

If Sir John noticed the guest of honor's absence, he did not comment upon it. "Care for a drop of port, Danvers?"

Danvers accepted, and Boileau led the way to the library. After the bustle of the evening's festivities the quiet of that wainscotted room was a welcome relief. A fire crackled on the hearth, and its golden glow was reflected in the patina of the rich paneling and the gold-embossed, leather-bound volumes filling the shelves. Danvers settled in a deep chair upholstered in moroccan leather and savored the scented bouquet of Sir John's fine old port.

But he never got to taste it.

The library door opened with a crash and a distracted, mud-caked servant girl rushed in ahead of the butler, who was trying to restrain her. "Blood! They's blood everywhere—it all splattered—"

Danvers caught her swooning figure just inches from the floor.

2

Like a grim portent of doom Vicar Andrews stepped over the prostrate maid. The black tails of his frock coat flapped behind him, and his gray fringe of beard looked like frost on his chin.

"For man that is born of woman hath but a little time to live, and then the judgment. In the midst of life we are in death. Of whom may we seek for succor, but of thee, O Lord, who for our sins are justly displeased."

The prostrate maid began a soft moaning. Danvers struggled to drag her to the sofa in spite of the fact that Andrews, hands clasped across his breast, was standing squarely in front of it.

"Yet, O Lord God most holy, O Lord most mighty, O holy and most merciful Savior, deliver us not into the bitter pains of eternal death."

"Enough of that!" Boileau shouted at the vicar. "What is going on?"

Andrews jerked to attend to what he had come for. "There's been a horrid murder. I've come for you, Sir John."

"Where?"

"Stanfield Hall. I heard the alarm bell ringing. Not sure whether it's Jermy junior or senior or both of them. Apparently some of the servants wounded too. Your

41

laundry maid here—" he gestured to the limp form Danvers and the butler had placed on the sofa "—was out walking with a servant from Stanfield. Apparently they were in the lane when it happened and ran to look. He fetched me. I thought that as a magistrate of the county you should be summoned too."

Danvers now recognized the maid as the one he'd seen waiting at the gate hours before.

"Quite right. Huntley—" The squire turned to his butler. "Order the gig to be at the front door in five minutes. You may tell Lady Catherine I've gone out, but don't alarm her. And get the housekeeper to see to Lizzie here."

"I'll come too." Danvers sent a footman to fetch his hat and cloak from Hardy.

Lights blazed from every window at Stanfield Hall. Like jerky puppets, figures rushed to and fro in the yellow squares. The fact that the blinds had not been closed in a house visited by death betokened the chaos that must be inside. The Norwich police had arrived ahead of Boileau's party, and lanterns flashed across the grounds as officers searched for evidence.

Danvers and Boileau approached a group on the front porch. A man's body sprawled just as it had fallen. A deep red stain looked obscenely out of place on the victim's white, starched shirtfront.

Skoulding, the police surgeon, knelt beside the lifeless figure. "It's Mr. Isaac Jermy, all right. Clean through the heart. Shot at close range. Even in this light you can see the powder burns on his clothes." He ran his finger across the shirt, leaving a smear like chimney soot. "Nothing we can do." The surgeon shook his head and stood up. "Cover him."

A constable moved to obey.

"The others are back here."

"You mean there's more?" Danvers felt numb. The whole thing had a nightmarish sense of unreality.

A young, very blond sergeant, whose badge bore the name *Pont,* led them around the house to a side door where they were met by a dithering butler.

"Well, Watson, what's all this?" Boileau's shock expressed itself as anger.

"I heard a shot." Watson ran a trembling hand through his mousey brown hair. "I—I came out of the pantry. An armed man passed right in front of me—not more than three feet. Mr. Jermy Jermy opened the door." He pointed shakily to a swinging door at the end of the passage. "I—I saw the murderer point a gun—or pistol—I—I'm not sure—" The butler's voice caught. He pushed his wire-rimmed glasses up on his thin nose.

"Yes, yes, man, get on with it!"

"He fired. Mr. Jermy fell down backwards—into the staircase hall. I—er—I went back into the pantry. There were more shots and screams. The screaming kept up. I—I—" He gestured helplessly.

A constable opened the door. Moans and sobs came from the hall as ghostly echoes of the earlier screams—more horrible in their intensity of pain than the earlier shrieks could have been.

Boileau stepped through the door the constable still held. He almost fell over the body of Jermy junior, lying on the mat just as the butler described him. His bullet-torn, powder-stained, bloodied shirt was a duplicate of his father's that they had encountered on the outside porch. The police surgeon knelt to his examination. A constable stood by to take notes. Another policeman stooped to pick up a brass-tipped ramrod lying beside the floorboard.

Danvers, Boileau, Andrews, and Sergeant Pont continued following the path of the murderer to the source of the sobs of pain and dismay. A maidservant was huddled at the foot of the stairs, her skirt soaked with red. Blood was on the wall behind her, and a scarlet trail led up the stairs. Two maids attempting to give comfort were howling louder than the injured girl.

43

"Stop that, you two!" Boileau looked as if he might slap them. They were instantly quiet. "Watson! Get these females out of here. Doctor, leave that gory corpse and come here where you can do some good!"

"No, sir. My mistress. She's dreadful hurt. They took her upstairs." The maid pointed weakly.

Skoulding, the doctor, looked uncertain. Blood still oozed through the rip in the maid's skirt, but the mistress would have priority. His dilemma was solved by the arrival of the Jermy family physician. "Nichols, glad to see you, man. I'll do here. You go to Mrs. Jermy upstairs."

Sergeant Pont stayed to question Eliza, the injured maid. The others accompanied Dr. Nichols upstairs. Mrs. Jermy's room was easy to locate by the trail of blood and the cries coming from the bedroom.

Again Boileau cleared the room. "You bellowing females get back to the servants' hall."

The younger two scurried out, but the older one held her ground. "I'm Maria Blanchflower, Miss Sophia's nurse. I can assist Dr. Nichols." Her snapping black eyes and sturdy form looked anything but the delicate white blossom her name implied.

"Fetch me a basin of water then, woman. I've got to get the bullet out of this elbow." The doctor had already assembled the instruments from his bag on a bedside table and was tearing the shredded sleeve away from the wound.

"My husband," the injured lady gasped. "I heard a shot and went in—he's—he's—isn't he?"

Sir John lost his gruff manner and moved to hold her uninjured right hand. "Yes, Mrs. Jermy. I'm sorry, but he is."

"We were drinking tea in the drawing room—about to play picquet—he heard a noise outside—oh . . ." Whether the sobs that followed were for her husband or because of the intensified pain caused by the doctor's probing made no difference. Nothing could be worse. Then with a sharp cry of alarm she voiced a new fear. "Sophia! Where's Sophia?"

Danvers remembered the golden-haired child he had seen race across the lawn—was that really only a few hours ago? Glad for something to do, some action he could take in the midst of this overwhelming destruction, he stepped forward. "Your daughter, Mrs. Jermy? I'll find her and bring you word. Don't worry." His encouragement rang hollowly. There was every reason to worry.

At the foot of the staircase Dr. Skoulding was shaking his head over Eliza's wounds. "The hip. Nasty place to be wounded. But—do my best."

Danvers noted the powder marks on the wall made by the discharge of the weapon. "Can you tell whether it was a rifle or pistol? The butler didn't seem sure."

Skoulding shook his head. "No way to tell. Not a shotgun, that's certain." He handed Danvers a lump of lead. "Found this under her. May be another one inside." He signaled the constable. "Help me take her to the dining room table. I need to operate. It's a mercy she swooned. Hope she stays out."

Danvers handed the misshapen bullet to Sergeant Pont, who was overseeing the laying out of the bodies in the drawing room, and went back along the passage. Near the butler's pantry he noticed a paper on the floor and picked it up. It was heavy, like an endpaper torn from a book. The handwriting was crude, either that of an uneducated person or someone wanting to appear so:

> There are seven of us, three of us outside and four of us inside the hall, all armed as you see us two—if any of you servants offer to leave the premises or to follow us, you will be shot dead. Therefore, all of you keep in the servants hall, and you nor any one else will take any harm, for we are only come to take possession of the Stanfield Hall property.
>
> —Thomas Jermy, the owner

Danvers blinked and read it through again. What an extraordinary document. Who was Thomas Jermy? And why would he sign so blatant a confession?

He found Watson in his butler's pantry being questioned by a constable who identified himself as Stephen Amiss. Danvers gave him the paper.

"Oh, yes. I'd forgotten, but now I recall seeing him drop that," Watson said. He scanned the writing. "That wasn't Thomas Jermy. Stake my life on it. It was Rush. I'm as sure as if I'd seen his face." He handed the paper back with hands that were still shaking.

"How can you be so sure if you didn't see him?"

"I saw enough. He was in the habit of calling here. Always used that side door. Never rang the bell—just walked in like he was the master. Broad-shouldered, not over tall—he wore a disguise—a mop of long, thick black hair—but I could tell."

Constable Amiss was scribbling fast in his notebook, so Danvers asked the next question too. "Who is Thomas Jermy?"

"Cousin or something of Mr. Isaac Jermy. I saw him once. He must be upwards of seventy. The gunman was a much younger man."

"But if there were several of them as it says here, he could have been one you didn't see."

Watson nodded at Danvers's suggestion. "I suppose. There was some dispute over the property a few years back. That was before my time. I don't know—I . . ."

"Steady man." Danvers put a hand on the butler's shoulder. "Plenty of time to worry about that later. Do you know where Miss Jermy is?"

Impossible as it seemed, Watson's face turned whiter yet. "No. I haven't seen her! Isn't she in the nursery or the schoolroom? Miss Blanchflower, her nurse—"

"She is attending Mrs. Jermy. No one knows where the child is."

The butler dropped his head into his hands. "It was

46

a quiet evening, peaceful, just like any other. I'd just taken in the tea tray after dinner—they were a fine family, never hurt anyone. How could his happen?"

Wondering the same thing, Danvers walked outside to the porch, undoubtedly following the same path Isaac Jermy had taken a short time earlier, going out on an autumn evening after dinner to enjoy his pipe. Could he have perhaps seen some of the fireworks at Ketteringham?

Danvers looked into the darkness, then realized that the house faced the opposite way. A shame Jermy hadn't been invited to the dinner—might have saved his life. He was undoubtedly planning to attend the county ball scheduled for tomorrow night.

It was as if there was a sense of mockery over the whole occurrence—mockery of all their world stood for. Solidity. Respectability. Progress. And, above all, goodness. When the young Victoria took the throne she said, "I will be good." She married her prince—Albert the Good. And the whole fabric of society was built on the principle of being good. From all appearances the Jermys had been good, solid, respectable. But death and destruction mocked the security of their goodness. If you couldn't rely on goodness, what could you rely on?

With a shake of his head, Danvers stepped off the porch and crossed the lawn to a pair of policemen searching the grounds with lanterns. "Found anything?"

"Muddy footprints going off that way. Big feet." The taller policeman pointed east toward the turnip field Danvers had crossed earlier in the day.

"Have you seen anything of Miss Sophia Jermy? She seems to be missing."

"No, we haven't. But we're finished here. I'll help you look." He signaled his partner to return to the house.

"Thank you, Constable . . .?"

"Morter, sir." The officer's red hair and red cheeks glowed in the lantern light. "Constable John Morter, Norwich Police." He answered with obvious pride in his position. "Don't think the stables have been searched yet." He led around to the back of the hall, holding his lantern high.

The first door they opened produced results. Danvers's initial thought was that the scuffling came from a small animal, but the muffled cry accompanying it was undoubtedly that of a young girl.

"Miss Jermy?" Danvers took care to speak in a voice that wouldn't frighten her more yet. "Your mother is asking for you."

"Oh!" With an exclamation that was half sob and half shout, a small figure shot toward them from the darkest corner of the stable. She was followed by the broad figure of the cook in white mobcap and apron.

"I thought we'd all be murdered!" Sophia flung herself into Danver's arms.

"Lord bless the poor lamb." Cook patted the child's trembling shoulders. "The dear thing ran straight to me. 'Read! We shall all be murdered!' she cried. I hid her right here in the stables straightaway, as I thought best, sir."

"Well done, Read. It's quite safe to go back now." Danvers brushed the child's forehead, wondering what nightmares she would have for the rest of her life. "Safe," he'd said. He thought of the corpses of her father and grandfather laid out in the drawing room, of the terrible wounds of her mother and Eliza. Of the blood-splattered hall and staircase. How could he call the place safe?

"It's cold in here. Read, can you make us some cocoa in the kitchen? Constable Morter here will take a message to your mother that you're unharmed, Sophia. You can see her later." He hoped it would be much later, when all the gore had been cleaned away. Danvers doubted it would ever be cleaned away from his own mind.

Fortunately, a door led directly from the stables to the back kitchen so there was no need to invent a circuitous route in order to avoid taking the child through grisly scenes.

Sophia took three enormous gulps of Martha Read's hot chocolate before she set her mug down and looked straight at Danvers. The time had come. "Is Mama all right? There were so many shots."

"Your mother is alive, but she was shot in the arm. Dr. Nichols is with her in her room. Eliza was shot in the leg. Another doctor is with her." He paused for a breath.

The blue eyes in front of him were wide, unblinking, prepared to hear the rest. "Papa?"

"Your father and grandfather are dead. They died very quickly. I hope it helps you to know they could have hardly felt anything."

Tears spilled from the blue eyes. "They are in heaven?"

"Yes." It was the best comfort he could give her.

"My little brother is in heaven—he had a fever . . ." The last word came out in a sob. Martha Read gathered the trembling child in her arms and began rocking her back and forth.

They sat for several minutes. The only sounds in the room were the crackling of the fire and Sophia's muffled sobs.

Then the door from the servants' hall opened and Andrews came in. "Ah, you found her, Danvers. Good work. Would you like to see your mother, Miss Sophia? She's asking for you."

"Is everything all . . . cleared away?" Danvers asked quietly.

"We'll use the back stairs," Andrews said, then held out a hand to Sophia.

With a final sniff she slid off Martha Read's lap and took the vicar's hand.

"You're a brave girl, Sophia," Danvers said. "You must support your mother now."

Constable Morter came in as they left. "Didn't want to question you in front of the child," he said to Martha, taking out his notebook but eyeing the cocoa.

She got him a cup and refilled Danvers's before beginning her story. "I and Eliza Chastney was in the servants' hall. We heard shots outside, then a minute later, a shot inside the house. Chastney left, then I heard two more. I heard the screams of a female and rushed to the servants' hall door."

The constable held up a hand for a pause in the narrative to catch up on his note-taking. Then she continued. "Miss Sophia came running into the servants' hall, yelling we'd all be murdered. I saw a man coming along the passage. He had some firearm in his right hand—I cannot say whether a gun or pistol, but it was larger than a usual-sized pistol. The man had a cloak on, which appeared to have a cape to it. He was a man the height and carriage of that Rush from Potash Farm."

Morter's head jerked up. "Why do you say that?"

"I don't rightly know. I've repeatedly seen Rush at the Hall. As soon as I saw the man in the passage, my impression was that it was Rush. I and Miss Sophia ran out of the servants' hall into the stable—you know the rest."

"Thank you, Read. That is a most precise account."

"What did the doctor say?" Danvers asked the officer.

"He'll try to save Mrs. Jermy's arm. I met Skoulding on my way in here. He doesn't think Eliza Chastney will ever walk or stand again." He shook his head. "It's a rare mess it is."

Danvers agreed, but he wouldn't have expressed it so mildly. That such a horror could come seemingly out of nowhere to shatter the lives of respectable Englishmen—in their own home—was unthinkable. As unthinkable and senseless as his taking Charlotte for a picnic on the day of a sudden, drenching rain that produced the pneumonia that caused her death.

It had begun as a day of golden sunshine, and Charlotte, thinking they were merely going to the lake at the end of the park, had instructed her maid to bring only her lightest shawl. But Danvers took a notion into his head to visit the ruined abbey in a far corner of Northamptonshire and then ignored the gathering clouds to walk the extensive grounds. When the thunderstorm struck, they were thoroughly soaked and had many miles to drive before finding a poor inn for shelter. If only . . . but it was no good thinking that. It happened. She was gone. And he would have to come to terms with the fact.

And come to terms with himself—with the guilt—and the fear that another action of his might produce such disastrous results. That was the hardest part to go on with—the fear of taking responsibility for the life of another.

3

There you are, Danvers." A haggard Sir John entered the Stanfield kitchen. "Constable said he thought you were still here. Police are getting ready to go to Potash. Think I'll go along—not really necessary for a magistrate to be there, but might be a good idea. Why don't you go back with Andrews and get some sleep? You look beat."

"Potash? Why are you going there?"

"To arrest Rush. Servants identified him."

"Just like that? Without any more evidence than the size of a cloaked figure? Besides, I thought there was a gang."

Boileau shrugged. "Might have been a conspirator or two. But whatever, you can be sure Rush was in on it. Everyone knows he quarreled violently with Jermy—quarreled with everybody for that matter. Add to it he knew the place well."

Danvers shook his head, more to clear it of drowsiness than to express his doubts over the flimsiness of the evidence.

"Go on back and get some sleep, man," Boileau said.

"Not on your life! I'm interested in this. Doubt I could sleep now anyway."

He was putting on his cape when a policeman he hadn't seen before came in.

"Constable Osborn, just come from Norwich, sir." He presented himself to the squire.

"Everything in hand at the station, Constable?"

"Yes, sir. Superintendent Yarrington sent out telegraphic messages along every railway in the kingdom with a description of Rush."

"Before intelligence reached Norwich as to who was suspected?" Danvers asked.

"Yes, sir. You have to get up mighty early to beat Superintendent Yarrington—he's a real knowing one, he is."

"Well, it's gratifying to know our police are so efficient." Danvers let it drop.

Boileau chose to drive his gig to Potash. It was almost a mile going around by the road but preferable at night to crossing the muddy turnip field on a straw track. When they arrived, the police had Potash Farm surrounded. The tall, pale gray house, amid a few nearly leafless trees stood desolate in the dim, predawn light.

Danvers shivered and drew his cloak tighter around him, wishing he'd chosen a heavier coat. He tried to recall the man he'd glimpsed by Ketteringham gate. The impression had been one of a solid, rustic farmer. Not a man of great intelligence or charm, certainly, but hardly one you would pick out as a brutal murderer. And yet one heard of acts of violence being done by far less likely people. It was a sobering thought that a seemingly normal person could carry around the seeds of such evil.

A faint light glowed in an upstairs room. The police edged forward. When the light appeared in the kitchen, young Sergeant Pont stepped forward and knocked on the door. It was unbolted by Rush. Pont immediately warned him that anything he might say could be used in evidence against him and snapped handcuffs on his wrists.

"What do you think you're doing? As God is my witness, I'm a respectable man." The lids sagged heavily over his dark eyes. His broad features scowled.

"The two Mr. Jermys have been shot. You are suspected of doing it, James Bromfield Rush." In the pale light the sergeant appeared to be half the size of the stocky farmer.

"Good grief! I hope they don't think it was me. That's a most serious charge. What time did the murder take place?"

The prisoner's question was ignored as Pont took him upstairs to dress. A few minutes later a woman wearing a dark dress and plain white cap entered, followed by a servant boy carrying an armload of firewood. The woman stopped at the sight of the police.

Red-haired, round-faced Constable Morter stepped forward. "You are Emily Sandford, Mr. Rush's housekeeper?"

"Yes. What has happened? Why are all these police in my kitchen?"

"There has been a tragedy at Stanfield Hall, ma'am. Did Mr. Rush go out last night?"

Emily paled slightly and took a gulp of air, but she stood straight. "Yes, sir. He went out for about a quarter of an hour after the evening meal."

A haphazardly dressed Rush came back into the kitchen with the sergeant, and Emily took a step toward him. "What has happened, James? What—are you handcuffed?" She reached out as if to touch the cold steel, then drew back.

"I am accused of murdering Jermy and his son, but that fellow Clarke has done this—it is he that has caused me to be suspected. But you and Savory—" he pointed at the servant boy— "can clear me, for Savory washed my boots at half-past five, and you know I did not go out again until after tea, to look for poachers. Have you been questioned?" His words came out in jerky phrases as if he were unaccustomed to speaking so rapidly.

"Yes, that stout man asked me if you went out last evening. I said you went out for about a quarter of an hour."

Rush frowned. "I was not more than ten minutes, and you know I had my slippers on."

"I don't know if you had or not. I didn't see you put your boots on." Emily turned woodenly to set the coffee on to boil and began cooking porridge. All her movements seemed detached from her thoughts.

Rush sat at the table to await his breakfast. Except for the handcuffs and the presence of officials, it could have been any other day. The servant Savory scuttled out to pump a bucket of water.

"I suppose it should be no surprise that I am suspected because I have lived on such bad terms with Jermy, but latterly the old man and I have been more friendly— the young one was my greatest enemy."

He looked at the constable holding his cloak. "Might I have my cloak to put on? I am cold." The cloak was given to him, as well as a mug of coffee from Emily. He drank it awkwardly with the handcuffs clanking against it. "Someone mentioned that the affair happened not long after eight o'clock. I might have been there about then had I not been told young Jermy was at home. I had no desire to meet him as we didn't get on."

Constable Amiss entered, carrying a shot belt and a powder flask. "Found these in a drawer in the bedroom, Sergeant. There's another shot belt, powder flask, and a dark lantern in his closet too."

"Well, go fetch them, man. Eat your porridge, Rush. There's a four-wheeler from the Norwich Bridewell waiting for you." The sound of the police wagon on the gravel lane sounded clear in the room. "Please don't entertain any ideas of leaving the county, Miss Sandford. I shall send for you to take your statement tomorrow."

A few minutes later the police took away the sullen prisoner, leaving Emily, apparently in shock, staring at her coffee. "I'll send the vicar to you, shall I, Miss Sandford?" Sir John asked.

She shrugged.

Danvers felt he should say something. "Will you be all right?"

Again she shrugged.

The chorus of birdsong and a golden sunrise seemed the ultimate incongruity as the men drove back to Ketteringham. Danvers sat quietly, under the cover of sleepiness. The truth was, he was reluctant to discuss the events of the night with Sir John. The squire's presence as magistrate had made him a quasi party to the proceedings, and any criticism might be taken personally.

But the haste concerned Danvers. He remembered a boy when he was at Eton who was universally disliked. No matter what went wrong, Munford was blamed for it. Admittedly, he usually was the perpetrator of any misdemeanor that occurred. But because of his unpopularity, he also took the brunt for some pranks he did not pull, but that others conveniently blamed on him.

Was it possible that this was happening now, on a far more serious scale? Rush was notorious for being disliked. Indeed, in his brief time in the man's presence, Danvers could detect nothing likable in him. But was that sufficient reason to arrest him for murder? Weren't there perhaps half a dozen likely possibilities the police had ignored in pouncing on the most obvious suspect? Surely, as a lawyer Jermy senior would have disgruntled clients— perhaps some with cause to be more than displeased with him. What of the family dispute over the ownership of the Stanfield estate? Danvers would like to know more about that. What about the talk he'd heard of poachers? They would be roaming around at night armed—certainly plenty of means and opportunity, if perhaps weak motives for murder. And at last Danvers admitted to himself the thought he had held at bay throughout the long night: Jack had quarreled with Jermy and then left his own party to go out with a gun. Danvers did not want to examine the idea, but he must. The witnesses' confusion over the type of weapon—could a gun with a half-length stock, such as the Purdey, have been the cause of such uncertainty?

The idea was too terrible to entertain, but the very fact that it was so appalling demanded that it not be ignored. Danvers felt a tingle of the intellectual excitement that had often kept him long hours in the Bodleian, tracing the root of an obscure Latin verb during his days at Oriel. He could never have been accused of being a scholar, but he had a restless mental energy that would not leave him at peace when a puzzle presented itself.

He thought of a line he himself had often quoted from his favorite philosopher, John Stuart Mill—"The fatal tendency of mankind to leave off thinking about a thing when it is no longer doubtful is the cause of half their errors." He would talk to Jack—find out what the boy had done last night.

Jack's room was in the west wing not far from Danvers's own, so he could stop there without causing comment. Just as he raised his hand to knock, the door opened, and Dalling, Jack's tall, bald manservant, came out bearing his master's clothes to be cleaned. The sight of the muddy boots and blood-splattered jacket made Danvers's stomach lurch. "Young Boileau didn't have an accident, did he?"

"No, sir. He's at breakfast hale and hearty." The servant, who wore a look of perennial concern, seemed to realize that the condition of the clothes he carried required some explanation. He lowered his voice. "Went shooting last night. Not the most gentmanly hour to be about, if you'll forgive my saying so, but boys will be boys."

"Quite so. Well, get on with your work, man."

Dalling departed, leaving the door ajar behind him.

Danvers stepped inside. The Purdey was on a table by the window, its accessory case open beside it. Danvers

57

picked up the gun and ran his finger around the inside of the barrel. It came out covered with powder. The boy must have been out late indeed—or have returned in a state of agitation—to leave his gun uncleaned. Black powder was highly corrosive, and such a fine instrument as a Purdey should not be left like this.

He set the gun down and glanced at the case. The standard mold, flask, nipple key, turnscrew, and patch-cutter were all present, as well as some additional refinements added by the London gunsmith.

Danvers closed the case and hurried to his room. He needed to think.

The earlier sunrise was now dimmed by heavy, gray clouds. He lit a candle, but he could not make himself sit in the chair beside it. Instead he paced back and forth, making an oval track around the fine maroon and azure Persian rug. It was really a question of loyalty—did he owe the greater allegiance to the man who had saved his father's life or to the abstract idea of justice?

It was unlikely the police would search for other suspects or even spend much time on the conspiracy theory for which there seemed to be ample evidence. They had made their arrest, and such efficient police work would look good in the *Norfolk Mercury.* Superintendent Yarrington, who had telegraphed Rush's description to every corner of the kingdom before he even knew of the servants' statements, would want no doubt cast on his case.

If the police had prejudged the situation, however, Danvers had not. Could he allow a possibly innocent man to sit in gaol when he had information that might force the police to look elsewhere for suspects? But on the other hand, could he, on such purely circumstantial evidence, so affront his host and friend of many years and cast suspicions on the young man who would someday administer authority in this county? Suspicions that might linger no matter what was later proved?

But ultimately could he take the responsibility of *not* interfering? If Jack were capable of such brutality, might he not do it again? And then the victims would be on Danvers's conscience. Jack was to become in time the lord of the manor—that's what this whole coming-of-age celebration was about. What sort of squire would he make if he were guilty of murder? No, it was obvious Danvers couldn't let his knowledge lie buried—if indeed it proved to be knowledge and not mere unfounded suspicion as he prayed it was.

He quit pacing and sank into the green plush, wing-backed chair his room offered. He sat long, staring at the candle without really seeing it. Or was he deceiving himself in couching the question in high-flown terms of loyalty and justice? Was the reluctance he felt really his own shrinking from taking responsibility—responsibility for the life of another? He had been responsible for Charlotte, and so simple a thing as taking her for a picnic had produced tragedy. What might be the outcome of such a serious involvement as investigating a murder?

Raindrops splattered his window. He hit the arm of the chair with his fist. The truth was, it was folly to think he could escape responsibility. If he buried what he knew about Jack, he could then be responsible for the execution of Rush. His conscience would never accept the sop that it was the work of the police and lawyers and he could wash his hands of it all. It hadn't worked for Pilate, and it wouldn't work for him—no matter how un-Christlike a figure Rush might be.

4

The candle at his elbow guttered and drowned in its own wax. The fact that such a slight sizzling sound could waken Danvers evidenced how lightly he had been dozing. He walked to his window and lifted the lace panel. The rain had stopped, but the sky hung low and gray.

He needed someone to talk to. Betraying his thoughts to a member of the family was unthinkable, and none of the other guests evidenced the depth of insight Charles felt he needed. He thought briefly of Antonia. If she were in one of her thoughtful moods she could be a good listener, but if not . . .

He looked out his window and saw the square Norman tower of Ketteringham Church, not more than a thousand feet from the hall. Andrews had struck him as being intelligent and concerned, in spite of his long-faced legalism. Besides, giving counsel on questions of conscience was a vicar's job.

The formerly crisp autumn leaves were soggy under Danvers's feet as he trod the tree-lined walk to the church. He wondered whether perhaps Andrews would be asleep, as he himself would like to be after the night's adventure. But the questions would not let him rest, and it was far better to face them awake than to sleep and chance seeing blood-splattered Stanfield Hall in his dreams—perhaps dreams in which the murderer would be unmasked and bear the image of Jack Boileau.

Danvers entered the churchyard through the south wall, which was also the wall of the squire's garden. He removed his tall black hat and stepped into the little stone church he had been told went back to the Domesday Book. There were no aisles, and its low, enclosed pews would accommodate fewer than 200 people. But the first thing to catch the eye of one who entered was a large, scroll-like monument to Sir John Boileau's father, giving a long account of the ancient family of which Sir John was so proud.

A flicker of movement made Danvers turn to his left. The curling red tendrils escaping their lace cap identified the wearer of the dove-gray morning dress.

"Tonia, what brings you here?" He saw instantly that the lady was, indeed, in one of her thoughtful moods.

"I heard about that terrible murder. I couldn't think of anything but praying." Her prayer book trembled in her fingers as she spoke. There was no doubt of her sincerity now.

Danvers covered her cold hand with his. "I came looking for Andrews. He isn't—"

Antonia pointed with her free hand, and Danvers saw the black, ascetic figure kneeling at the altar. Danvers waited until an uplift of the beaky features told him the prayers were concluded.

With increased desire that his actions should bring no disgrace to the Boileau family, Danvers approached the vicar. "Andrews, I feared my chances of finding you here were slim after you worked all night."

"Ah, but our Lord admonishes us to work while we might, for the night is coming when man shall work no more." Andrews opened a pew and offered Charles and Antonia a seat. "The truth is, sleep wouldn't come after such a ghastly night. I thought my time better used here praying for the soul of Rush."

"Do you believe him guilty?" Danvers went to the heart of his doubts.

"We are all guilty before God until the blood of Christ has covered our sins." For once the vicar spoke quietly, not as if from his pulpit.

Still, Danvers shifted uncomfortably. "I daresay. But I meant guilty of the immediate charge."

Andrews shook his head. "Ours is not to judge. But Rush is a strange man."

Danvers held his breath, hoping the vicar would go on.

He did. "Four years ago Rush's father died from the accidental firing of a gun in his own kitchen. I called at the house immediately, but Rush refused my efforts at consolation. Soon after that, however, he became a regular attendant at services at the church. He always sat in that pew." Andrews pointed to one behind them on the left. "Many times I observed him weeping like a child when he received the Sacrament."

Danvers's high forehead furrowed in his effort to integrate this image with the rather boorish picture he had formed of Rush.

"The attendance of Rush and his family at divine service were a source of comfort to me that year. James Rush's wife was alive then and his son still living at home. They were a model of piety. I was especially impressed with the devotion of Mrs. Rush."

"And were they accepted in the parish?" Antonia asked.

"Ah, there you have hit upon a sore spot, indeed. It was widely gossiped in the cottages that the death of Mr. Rush, senior, had not been accidental. The villagers thought of our Rush as a kind of ogre." Andrews put a thin hand to his chin and fingered his bristly beard.

"Not accidental? They thought the senior Rush committed suicide?"

Andrews sighed. "They believed he was shot by his

son. Rush stated he had left his father alone in the kitchen examining his gun after a day's sport. The coroner's jury returned a verdict of not guilty, but you'd never convince the villagers."

As you would never convince them of Jack's innocence if once doubts were raised.

"I prayed fervently that there would be a sign of the workings of grace in Rush, but . . ." The vicar shook his head. "About that time I dreamed a strange dream that has been vividly renewed on my mind this morning. I dreamed Rush was at the vicarage when the house was surrounded by a crowd of armed men wanting to murder him. In my vision I knelt down and prayed for Rush's preservation, ordered the shutters to be closed, and then took him upstairs to hide him from the mob, first in a chest, then behind the battlements above the dining-room window." He paused. "I awoke to find myself clutching a sweat-drenched pillow."

Recounting the experience had produced beads of sweat on Andrews's forehead. He pulled a handkerchief from his breast pocket and wiped his face.

"And did you find those marks of grace in Rush for which you prayed?" Danvers asked.

"Alas. On November of that year Mrs. Rush died, and something seemed to go wrong with her husband's piety. His church attendance became irregular, and there was renewed gossip that relations between Rush and his son's young governess were not what they should be. I saw that he needed a housekeeper and exerted myself to find a pious woman. I was able to secure a most sedate woman of excellent character from the Readers Society."

"And was her influence beneficial?"

"I fear not. Rush changed governesses—you met Emily Sandford at Potash. He brought her to church, but I sensed that she was a young woman entirely indifferent to divine things. A month later, the housekeeper left. She told me she had found that Mr. Rush was not, after all, er—" the vicar paused and looked at Antonia "—er—respectable. The gossip of the village had been justified, at least in that case."

These were not answers to the questions Danvers had come to ask, but they provided much fodder for thought. Here, indeed, was the characterization of a man who might be capable of murder—perhaps had even murdered his own father, if gossip could be credited. But here also was ample evidence that Rush had indeed been prejudged on the basis of prior acts rather than on the facts of this case.

He thought again of Emily's statement that Rush had been gone from home no more than fifteen minutes on the night of the murder. Whatever the degree of her respectability or lack thereof, her testimony had been clear.

Danvers took his leave of Andrews and escorted Antonia back to the hall. Rain had begun softly to fall, but she seemed to be in no hurry. "You don't believe Rush guilty then?"

He sighed. "I only wish I knew what I believe."

Antonia stopped and looked at him long through the gently falling mist. "Then you are right to keep asking questions. 'Truth gains more even by the errors of one who, with due study and preparation, thinks for himself than by the true opinions of those who only hold them because they do not bestir themselves to think.'"

Danvers blinked in surprise. "That's Mill. Do you read him?"

"Father does—and quotes him at length when Aunt Emma isn't around to disappove. I hope I got it right."

"Very right, indeed. Very right."

They were silent the rest of the way into Ketteringham Hall.

Danvers was taking his leave of his companion when she looked down at her empty hands. "Oh, my prayer book. I left it in the pew."

"Allow me, Tonia." He looked back toward the path. "The fresh air stimulates my thinking, and I have much to think about." He turned before she could thank him.

He wanted with everything in him to believe Rush guilty and Jack entirely innocent, but he needed to know more before his conscience would let the case rest. And the questions appealed to him as a puzzle too. He had always had a kind of insight that saw relationships between words and situations that had helped him excel in logic at Oxford. The same skill applied to numbers and had been useful in mathematics. Perhaps his ability could be put to work understanding people if he put his mind to it.

Until now he had preferred to accept people as they presented themselves to him rather than bothering to look deeper. Closeness to people was not always a comfortable thing. But now he felt ready for a new challenge. The image of Antonia appeared briefly in his mind, but that was not what he had meant.

Surely if he knew more, understood the people better, he would find other lines of questioning that would lead away from Jack. He kicked a pile of sodden leaves, then swore under his breath as a rock buried in the leaves scratched his highly-polished shoes.

He could only hope that leading away from Jack would mean leading toward the truth. Andrews would say truth was the highest value—but was that where the vicar had gone wrong in his sanctimonious legalism? Was truth the highest value or was love? How often did people use love of truth, though, as merely an excuse to delve into affairs that were no business of theirs? Where did one draw the line? It would be as wrong to turn one's back on truth and accept a lie for the sake of love, as to abandon all love in a slavish following after truth.

He quickened his pace along the yew-lined path as the rain increased. This philosophizing was getting him nowhere. He must learn the truth for himself. Then he could decide in love what to do with it. He must learn the facts first.

The police would be swift and thorough in gathering evidence to support their preconceived case against Rush.

And Danvers shrank from the idea that there might be more evidence against Jack—anything concrete that could be more damning than the purely circumstantial information he possessed. What he needed was another suspect to concentrate on. He must find either the guilty party or Rush's conspirator—he didn't care which, just as long as it wasn't Jack.

He thought again of what he had witnessed last night and recalled the note dropped by the gunman. It had said something about being there to take possession of the property. And Watson said there had been a violent quarrel in the Jermy family some years back. Stanfield Hall was a valuable estate. Surely that was an excellent motive for murder. And when he thought about it, no substantial motive had been established against Rush.

That was what he would work on—either prove an undeniable motive on the part of a third party or find one for Rush.

As he crossed the entry of Ketteringham Hall, Danvers saw that Boileau's library door stood open and that the squire was at his desk. It seemed none of the participants in the night's events were making up their lost sleep.

Danvers stepped into the dark wood-paneled, book-lined room, then started. "Forgive me, Lady Catherine, I didn't realize you were in here with your husband." He bowed.

The lady was in a brown merino dress that blended perfectly with the morocco chair where she sat in a corner. "Come in, Charles. We'd be glad of your advice on a matter of some delicacy." She smiled and indicated he should take a chair near hers.

Danvers hoped the matter of delicacy was not the one with which he was wrestling, but Lady Catherine's next words put that fear to rest. "As you know, the whole county has been invited to a ball tonight for Jack's coming of age. And Tonia's niece—the daughter of a friend of mine—will soon be arriving from London. But we can't help questioning the propriety of continuing our celebrations in the face of this shocking tragedy in the neighborhood." As she spoke she nervously fingered the silk fringe of the cut velvet cloth covering the table beside her.

Danvers nodded, uncertain as to his own feelings on the matter. Then a rustle of silk at the door made them all turn.

"What's this nonsense I hear of canceling this evening's festivities?" The Dowager Duchess of Aethelbert swept into the room, the mauve silk over her crinolines swishing as if she were already at the ball.

Danvers and Sir John stood.

"Do you think it would be proper to continue, Your Grace?"

"You aren't in any way related to these Jermys, are you?"

Sir John agreed that they were not.

"And do you propose to go into black gloves for them?"

"We shall attend the funeral, of course," Lady Catherine said. "But prolonged mourning is not required."

"Well, there you have it then." The duchess sat in the chair vacated by Danvers. "I have no patience with the current vogue for maudlin show of emotion over people one hardly knew. It cheapens one's real feelings for those about whom one truly cares. We must do all we can for Mrs. Jermy and her daughter, of course, but disappointing your guests and tenants will do them no good."

"Thank you, Your Grace. Your views are most refreshing. I believe I shall be guided by them." Lady Catherine rose. "But do you think perhaps just a hint to the ladies that no bright colors should be worn would be in order?"

"I shall wear lavender." The dowager duchess's statement came as no surprise, as she seldom wore anything else. "And I am sure you and your daughters will set the proper tone. A warning to the servants against gossip would be most in order—not that I expect it will do any good."

The ladies left the room, talking of arrangements for the evening. Danvers closed the door after them and resumed his seat.

"You wanted to talk to me of something other than black crepe, I suspect," Boileau said. "Would you care for a drink?"

"It's rather early, but under the circumstances a small port wouldn't be amiss."

Boileau poured them each a drink, then sat at his massive, heavily carved desk.

"I wondered about the rumors I've heard of a quarrel in the Jermy family over Stanfield Hall," Danvers began.

Boileau took a slow sip of his dark red drink. "That was ten years ago—thirty-eight—the year we were just settling into Ketteringham. I was still much in London, so I'm uncertain of all the details. There had been a dispute over Isaac Jermy's inheritance of Stanfield. Two cousins— Thomas Jermy and John Larner—claimed rights to it. Seems the property had come to Jermy through an entailment on a nephew-in-law in the past—a very tangled tale. At any rate, when Isaac Jermy advertised some of his father's furniture for sale, Larner protested and attempted to take possession of the Hall. Oddly enough, Rush, who had been a close friend of Jermy's father—the father of Isaac Jermy, that is—was acting as bailiff and threw Larner out."

"Rush was friendly with Jermy senior's father?" This was the first account Danvers had heard of Rush's being friendly with anyone.

"Rush was his tenant and apparently on intimate terms with his landlord, acting as his agent and, as I understand, holding his entire confidence. All before my time, of course, so this is only hearsay."

And not the kind of hearsay Danvers hoped for. An intimate friendship with Jermy's father hardly sounded like

68

a motive for murdering Jermy and his son. Danvers dropped his forehead into his hand.

Boileau continued. "Larner circulated a handbill against Jermy, stating he had no right to the property and warning against anyone trying to prevent his taking lawful possession of the Hall. About a month later, Larner appeared at Stanfield Hall with a large party of men and demanded admittance from the housekeeper, who, by the way, was a relative of Rush. She refused, and they carried her out. When old Mr. Jermy arrived from Wymondham with two police constables he found his furniture piled in the yard, being drenched with a heavy rain. As a commissioner of the peace for the county of Norfolk, Mr. Jermy read the Riot Act in front of the house and warned the people that if they remained an hour after the Act was read, they would be guilty of felony. The Fourth Dragoon Guards were called out from the Norwich barracks, and the rioters found it the most prudent part to give up further resistance."

"Were the rioters punished?"

"They were tried at the Lent Assizes. Larner was let off with three months."

Danvers rubbed his forehead. A relation of Rush's had tried to defend the property against Larner—didn't it sound as though this dispossessed cousin who had served a jail sentence for trying to lay claim to the property might have a strong motive for violence? "And Rush?"

"Isaac Jermy redrew the lease his father had granted Rush but at an advanced rate."

"For Potash?"

Boileau shook his head. "There's another tangled tale—perhaps the whole crux of the matter. Rush leased two other farms on the Stanfield estate. When Potash came for sale, Jermy empowered Rush, who had often acted as his father's agent, to buy it for him. But Rush purchased it for himself. When he found he lacked the money to complete the transaction, he induced Jermy to advance it to him upon mortgage."

69

"So Rush was Jermy's tenant on no less than three farms and heavily indebted to him?" Danvers shook his head. This would require a great deal of thinking out.

Boileau nodded. "Indeed, I believe it would be fair to say he was hopelessly indebted."

Danvers's chance to explore this glimmer of hope was interrupted by Huntley, the butler.

"There's someone to see you, Sir John." The butler's overly stiff posture showed what he thought of the person demanding to see the squire. "A policeman, sir."

"Well, show him in, Huntley."

"Yes, sir." The butler exited, then returned shortly. "Inspector Futter."

The officer's rumpled clothes and sunken, dark-rimmed eyes showed he also had lost a night of sleep. "I'd like permission to interview your household, Sir John."

"What? Surely you don't believe any of my people are involved? I thought you had your man."

"Yes, sir. That is, no, sir. Er—we do have Mr. Rush in custody, sir. But we'll need evidence for court. I'm sure you understand, being a magistrate yourself. We just want to know what any of your people might have seen. Servants do get around, like."

"Yes, yes. Of course. Huntley will show you to the servants' hall. I hope you won't need to take too much of their time. They have a ball to prepare for."

Futter's eyebrows rose, as if he were surprised that the ball should be going forward, but he merely thanked Sir John for his cooperation and left with Huntley.

"I hope to heaven those fellows don't think up some excuse to come snooping around here. Cooperating with them as a magistrate is one thing, but it's dashed bad form to have the police in the house. Questioning servants only encourages snooping at keyholes. The whole business is blasted impertinent. Police are no better than tradesmen—not as good, if the truth were known—and they expect one to turn the house over to them. But still, they have a job to do. Although what they've got to investigate, now that they have Rush, I don't know." He strode to the door. "Excuse me, Danvers, I have to go inform Lady Catherine of these fellows in the house. Don't want them bothering her—very delicate, you know. If they bring on one of her attacks it'll spoil the whole celebration."

The squire left Danvers alone, plying himself with new arguments. If he told the police of Jack's fight with Jermy just hours before the murder and Jack's disappearance from home with his new Purdey at the time of the murder, Ketteringham Hall would indeed be swarming with policemen, and the effect on Lady Catherine's health could be devastating. It seemed the responsibility for yet another life was in his hands. Where would it end?

Back in his room Danvers hoped to take his mind off his dilemma by turning to philosophy. He picked up the copy of *Westminster Review* he had brought with him and turned to the article by John Stuart Mill he had begun reading before he left home. It offered a precise summary of the utilitarian philosophy that had replaced his earlier adherence to Christianity.

"I regard utility as the ultimate appeal on all ethical questions; but it must be utility in the largest sense, grounded on the permanent interests of man as a progressive being."

Danvers ran his long fingers through his wiry hair, making it more disordered than usual. He had always taken the progress of man as a given. One had only to look at the material progress around himself or observe a map of the world, which showed the steady march of the British Empire. Of course man was becoming steadily better and better in this age of progress. And yet . . .

His hand moved to cover his eyes, but nothing could blot the blood and horror of Stanfield Hall from his mind. Was this an act committed by a human being who was progressing toward the highest good? Or was there an evil in man's being that even the Industrial Revolution and the progress of British civilization couldn't overcome?

Hardy bustled in, cheeks shining, tails of his bottle-green coat flapping, to poke up the fire. The poker clanged on the grate, and the fresh coals clunked into place.

"Hardy, must you make such an infernal racket?"

"Sorry I am to be disturbing you, m'lord. There's troubles enough in this world without our adding to them." His words were obsequious, but his voice seemed to relish articulating the woes of the world. "I'll just bring you a wee bit of tea and some cold meat, shall I?"

"No. Make it a lot of tea. And meat and cheese and bread—" Hardy was half out the door when Danvers called after him, "And don't forget the pickle."

His room warmed and his stomach filled, Danvers was finally able to rest. A few hours later, in spite of the continued determination of his dark, thick hair to escape its well-macassared grooming, Hardy approved the viscount's appearance in a black tailcoat, white jacquard silk vest, and white satin cravat. The refreshed Danvers could almost look forward to a festive evening and felt the dowager duchess had been wise in advising that they continue the celebration.

Besides, Danvers had not seen Jack all day, and the ball should provide a welcome opportunity to observe him in the light of all the questions that filled Charles's mind.

Danvers was just crossing the courtyard to the Gothick Hall when Antonia joined him on the arm of Nigel Langston. They were followed by a vision of porcelain skin, black curls, and shell pink ruffles that could only be the awaited Sarah Mellors.

"Charles, where have you been keeping yourself all afternoon?" Lady Antonia had put aside her introspective mood of the morning. She looked her ravishing self in a blue, shot-taffeta gown, scalloped flounces caught up in back with bows and flowers. She fluttered her fan in a gesture that had nothing to do with a need for fresh air on this crisp evening, but served rather to draw Danvers's attention from the young Sarah to the stunning effect a pale blue flower wreath had on Antonia's luxuriant auburn hair. "You disappeared so thoroughly I thought you'd been arrested for that ghastly murder."

Danvers offered his arm, ignoring Nigel's frown. "Please, let's not talk about murder tonight." Then he smiled as Nigel's dark looks continued to be directed at him. "I wouldn't want to give Langston any ideas."

Antonia refused to take either arm offered to her. "Now, Nige, none of that famous temper of yours tonight. If you behave yourself I might allow you a dance with Sarah."

The girl, not quite certain how to take her aunt's banter, dimpled prettily, accenting her heart-shaped face and up-turned nose. Danvers had seldom seen a more charming child, completely unspoiled, yet blessedly free of the giggles one expected in a schoolroom miss. He turned and bowed to Sarah, then extended the arm just refused by Antonia. "Miss Mellors, would you do me the honor—the very great honor—of dancing your first dance with me?"

Sarah dropped a graceful curtsey that made her black curls and pink ribbons bounce. "Thank you, Lord Danvers. I shall endeavor not to step on your shoes."

Danvers laughed as he swirled her onto the dance floor. "My man, Hardy, will thank you for that. He scolds me mercilessly when I scuff my footwear."

The truth was, Sarah danced as gracefully as she seemed to do everything else. And Danvers was grateful. He had not danced since Charlotte's death—for many months had not thought he would ever dance again. Sarah's simple naturalness was just what he needed for his own return to society. Just as the music and steps of the dance marked Sarah's leaving the schoolroom behind and entering the wider social world, so they marked his own metaphorical putting off of black crepe and looking ahead to a new life.

When the music ended they were at the top of the hall where Jack had just ended his dance with his sister Ama, and handed her to her next partner. Danvers introduced Jack to his newly arrived guest and recommended her as a dancing partner.

But even in that instant it was clear that no endorsement was necessary. Jack's eyes grew wide, and his tongue tangled as his cheeks reddened.

Danver's had never before seen the lad nonplussed. "I believe it's customary to offer the lady your arm," he prodded.

Jack obeyed.

The musicians struck up a country dance. Danvers now had the opportunity to undertake the observation he had hoped the evening would provide. If he was to make progress on the puzzle he hoped to untangle, he needed time to watch and think. Inexplicably, his relief was shattered as a pang of loneliness caught at his breast. Ridiculous in a room full of people.

Then Tonia whirled by him in Nigel's arms. She looked back at him over her shoulder as her set of dancers circled to the right. He wasn't sure whether her smile made him feel better or worse. He forced his mind back to the questions he had set for it.

He walked around the room until he could observe Jack dancing with Sarah. The wide sleeves of her pale peachy-pink dress emphasized her tiny waist, and her full skirt swung like a bell over her crinolines. Danvers smiled at the picture.

Jack was a graceful youth and seemed perfectly comfortable as the center of attention, whirling his guest around the floor and accepting congratulations from friends. Was it possible the boy could be such a good actor? Or his conscience so hardened that he could commit an act of infamy and it leave no visible mark on him? Or was his liveliness a cover-up for dark things inside? Was he *too* animated?

Disgusted with his own suspicions, Danvers turned away. The love of an intellectual puzzle, which had often led to bursts of scholarship in his undergraduate days, had never carried over to curiosity about the activities of his fellow humans—an interest that he could only characterize as vulgar gossip. But now asking such questions seemed inescapable.

The tune ended, and Tommy Frane and Caroline Boileau ended their set just in front of Danvers. He couldn't help admiring how her soft lemon-yellow ribbed silk dress set off her delicate blonde coloring. "You look very lovely tonight, Carry."

"Oh, thank you, Charles. You don't think my dress too bright, do you—in the circumstances? I'd far prefer not to dance at all, but Papa insists."

He assured her she looked precisely right and requested the next dance—a waltz, which the musicians were just beginning.

"I do hope we've done the right thing to hold the ball. Mr. Andrews will be terribly upset. He's sure to denounce Papa from the pulpit Sunday."

"For continuing the celebration?"

"Yes, he'll say it's unseemly. If any of the musicians get drunk, I fear we'll never hear the end of it. And I do believe he may be right—encouraging sinful levity . . ."

The music swept them around the room. Danvers noted that Nigel had collected his promised dance with Sarah.

The evening passed pleasantly, and Danvers was amused but hardly surprised when Lady Antonia just happened to be in his path, with her back innocently turned to him, before the supper dance.

He had no objection to taking the hint and asking her to dance, then escorting her in to supper. It was held in the dining room of Ketteringham, since the Gothick Hall had been given over entirely to the dancing. Just ahead of them Jack led a smiling Sarah through the door. "Your protégée seems to have found her sea legs with remarkable speed."

Antonia sighed. "Was life ever so simple and carefree as it seems to be for those two?"

Sir John greeted their entrance as he surveyed the scene with satisfaction. "It is truly said that the nation which knows how to dine has learned the leading lesson of progress. Here you see both the will and skill to reduce to order and surround with graces the more material conditions of human existence."

"You were quite right to continue the celebration, Sir John." Antonia gave him her dazzling smile. "It's important at such times as this that we remember the good in life as well as the evil."

The squire looked even more pleased with himself, having found moral justification for his pleasure.

Danvers helped Antonia to a seat, and for a time they turned their attention to the offered delicacies. Then Danvers put his fork down. "Your reply to Sir John was very clever."

Antonia surprised him by sighing rather than returning the bright smile he expected for his compliment. "I suppose so, but one gets weary of being forever clever. I must be grateful it was taken as a witticism. To be taken as a philosopher would ruin one socially—as Aunt Emma never fails to remind me."

Danvers leaned forward. "Is that what you think seriously, then—about good and evil in the world?"

"Oh, I know we are told constantly that there is more good in the world—or at least in England. Father is forever fond of quoting Mr. Mill and his utilitarian friends about greater good for greater numbers and all the good our industrial progress is achieving, but I don't know—when something happens like it did at Stanfield Hall, one doesn't feel we've achieved such a laudable degree of goodness." Suddenly Antonia stopped and fluttered her fan. "Oh, dear me, whatever must you think of me, Charles, boring you like that?"

Her bright laughter and fluttered eyelashes brought the standard reply from him. "You could never be boring, Tonia."

The truth was that that was the least boring he had ever found her. He would like more time to explore the nature of good and evil in society, but a footman set a new dish in front of them, and their attention shifted to other matters.

Antonia was halfway through her mold of macaroni, garnished to resemble embossed Wedgwood, when she smiled at Danvers and said, "When you return to London you must give my best love to Lady Agatha."

Danvers nodded and pushed aside his jelly-filled puff pastry. "I'll do that. My sister will be delighted to hear that I've seen you."

"No more than I am." Her hand just brushed his, resting on the edge of the table. It was not an unpleasant sensation. There could be worse candidates for the job Lady Antonia seemed to be applying for—especially as he seemed to be seeing her in a new light. He stifled the thought that he was being unfaithful to Charlotte. After all, one must go on—the family line must go on—no matter what one's personal feelings.

In spite of the fact that he chided Agatha about being unmotherly in her desire to see him wed and producing heirs, her own son Alfred Emory was in line to inherit after their brother Frederick. If Danvers failed in his duty to God, country, and family and died without having produced a son of his own, Alfred Emory might someday become the Eleventh Earl of Norville.

The truth was, that was the most powerful argument in Agatha's arsenal. And although unspoken by her, Charles couldn't help wondering if she secretly shared his conviction that the Honorable Alfred Emory was a bit of a nincompoop. Perhaps enough of a nincompoop to make marrying Lady Antonia worthwhile for the sake of preventing Alfred from inheriting the title.

And there was something else he could never admit to Agatha—or anyone else—but he would like to take a wife not only to fulfill his duty to the family but also because he was genuinely fond of children. Perhaps much of the ache he felt for Charlotte was for the daughter he would never know—blonde, with her mother's quiet merriment. With a smile less forced than formerly, Danvers turned to Antonia.

5

Two days later, Hardy's thick, sandy eyebrows rose to his receding hairline when Danvers directed him to put away his tweeds and hang out his somber black morning coat and gray trousers. "And are ye not joining the shoot today?"

Charles frowned. The only thing he wanted to do even less than look for a murderer was to go shooting—now that he had stayed in his room long enough to avoid family prayers. He would like above all things to sail away in his balloon—allow himself to escape the necessity of making a decision. But ballooning hadn't allowed him to escape his loss and guilt before, so there was no reason to think it would work now.

He sighed. "No, Hardy, no shooting. Make some excuse for me. I must see about another matter."

"If you'll excuse me, m'lord, it's noticing I've been that you've something weighing heavy on your mind. Is it of help I might be with such woes?"

Ironically, Hardy's lugubrious tone lightened Danvers's spirit. He smiled for the first time that morning. "Yes, Hardy, I should be very glad of your company. I can't convince myself that the police have the right man in this murder case. I'd like to do a spot of investigating of my own. Ask

Sir John for the use of his gig, and you may drive me to Potash—after you change out of your sporting clothes."

A chill mist hung close to the ground holding in the acrid smell of burning leaves as the horse plodded along the road to Potash. In just the few days since they had come to Ketteringham, most of the leaves had fallen, leaving bare, twisted branches where before there had been boughs of red and gold foliage. Danvers observed the skeletal limbs for several moments before beginning a plaintive tenor aria.

"When lofty trees I see barren of leaves,
Which erst from heat did canopy the herd,
And summer's green all girded up in sheaves . . ."

Hardy hastily took his fingers out of his ears as his master switched to a speaking voice. "Blast, I've forgotten the next lines, Hardy—something about 'nothing 'gainst time's scythe can make defense.'"

"If you say so, I'm sure, m'lord. It's a world of sadness, that's the truth."

Danvers laughed. "Never could convince you of the perfect beauty of the sonnet in song, could I, Hardy? Too much Irish blood in you to admire the disciplined expression of emotion."

"I'm sure you're right, m'lord." His round mouth turned down at the corners.

Danvers laughed again and drove the rest of the way struggling for the forgotten Shakespearean lines—something about beauty dying as fast as others grow . . .

"And what is it that's going on here? More trouble, that's for certain." Hardy brought Danvers's attention to the scene before them as they turned into the lane to Potash. The Norwich police four-wheeler and two smaller carriages were parked in the drive.

"Well now, I was hoping you could entertain Emily Sandford with some of your blarney and talk her into allowing me to go through Rush's papers. If he acted as Jermy's agent, he must have documents about the property dispute over Stanfield Hall. Looks like maybe the police had the same idea."

Young Sergeant Pont met them at the gate. "Morning, my lord. You come from the squire to help us search?"

Here was a handy excuse Danvers hadn't thought of. "Hello, Sergeant. Sir John is busy with his guests this morning, but Hardy and I will be glad to give any assistance we can."

"Fine, fine. We can use you. My men've been slogging around in this muck all morning and haven't found a thing yet."

"And what might it be that you're looking for?" Hardy asked.

"Murder weapon. Constable Amiss seized a shot belt and a powder flask when he arrested Rush, but no gun to match yet."

A familiar, red-haired constable joined them. "Find anything, Morter?" his sergeant asked.

"Enough broken bottles and rocks to build a garden wall, but no murder weapon. What's this about no searching in the bullpen, sir?"

Pont shrugged. "That's what Rush's son said, and seems he's boss here now. Course we could force it, but the super wants to keep young Rush cooperative if we can. Besides, the fact that he has a bad-tempered bull in there right now is a powerful argument."

"Well, we've got plenty to search without that. But I can take an oath there's nothing in that turnip field but turnips." Morter returned to his work.

"Has the house been searched again?" Danvers asked.

"Not since the night of the murder. You want to take that on? Miss Sandford's in there, but she's pretty subdued. Don't think she'll give you any argument."

"Right. Come on, Hardy. We'll see what we can find." Danvers walked to the front door. "Get her to make you some coffee in the kitchen, Hardy. I want some time alone with Rush's papers."

Through the door they heard the strains of a Beethoven sonata. Danvers hesitated, surprised at the skill of the musician, then he knocked.

The music stopped, and Emily Sandford, in a black dress that was straining at the waistline in spite of the thinness of her face, opened the door and made no objection to Danvers's search or to Hardy's company in the kitchen.

In the corner of the parlor was an oak rolltop desk. On top of the desk, among a clutter of memorabilia, was a letter addressed to Emily Sandford from a Henry Sandford in Melbourne, Australia. Danvers moved it aside and considered the closed desk, then salved his conscience with the assurance that if there should be a gun in there, he would certainly turn it over to Pont.

The top drawer yielded a cluttered assortment of notes written by Rush to himself, accounts of the farm, and letters from his mother. One letter seemed it could be of significance, as Mrs. Rush, Sr., complained to her son that Jermy had given her notice to quit the Felmingham farm she had continued to live on since her husband's death.

But then in the space under the right-hand cubbyholes, Danvers found three documents that seemed to negate any possibility of property disputes being a motive for Rush to commit murder. Sir John had told him Rush was hopelessly in debt to Jermy over the purchase of Potash, but these documents revealed that all had been settled amicably.

The documents were all dated the month before, signed by Isaac Jermy and James B. Rush, and witnessed by Emily Sandford. The first provided that the mortgage should continue for three years longer. Another, that the mortgage should be canceled, on condition of Rush's putting Mr. Jermy into possession of certain papers. And the third secured to him a beneficial lease of Felmingham Farm where his mother lived.

Danvers's shoulders slumped. This was the last thing he had hoped to find—evidence of friendly relations between Rush and Jermy. He reread the first two documents carefully in hopes that he had missed something—some clause unfavorable to Rush or a fault in form that would make the agreements unenforceable. But all seemed in order.

He picked up the last sheet and moved to the window to read it in better light.

Memorandum of an Agreement made this tenth day of October, 1848, by me Isaac Jermy, Esq., Recorder of the city of Norwich . . . to let to James Blomfield Rush, the two farms lately occupied by Mr. John Rush, for the term of twelve years, from Michaelmas, 1848, at the annual rent of three hundred pounds per annum . . . and that a clause in the said lease is to be inserted that my son, Jermy Jermy, is to have the right of shooting over the said farms, that he is to have a sitting-room and a bedroom provided for him, when he requires the same in the shooting season, and to be boarded in the farmhouse and to pay what is reasonable for the same. In witness hereto, I have this day set my hand.

I. Jermy

Witness—Emily Sandford

It was the appealing everydayness of the final clause, more than any of the legal details, that made Danvers's heart sink. He could picture in his mind the aging lawyer, expressing his concern for the comfort of his son after a day's shooting, and Rush offering to provide all that was necessary for him as they discussed the matter in friendly terms, no doubt over a glass of port or a second pipe. This could not be an instrument leading to murder.

Danvers rose as Emily and Hardy came into the room.

"It's telling Miss Sandford here, I was, about your theory that Rush might not be guilty as charged, and she has offered to show you some papers."

"I would be grateful for your help, Miss Sandford. I'm sure you would like to do all you can to clear your employer."

Emily nodded but hung back. "I don't know if I'm doing the right thing. Seems to me you should know . . . but I'm not sure . . . if I'm wrong and it makes things worse—"

"I understand, Miss Sandford, but I'm sure you are anxious to do your duty. And you know the golden rule of human conduct is to do one's duty and to brave the consequences." Danvers felt he was preaching to himself as much as to Emily Sandford.

Emily hesitated for a moment longer, then moved to a closet set in the back wall beyond the piano. "Mr. Rush told me he kept his papers in a secret place under the floor of the closet. He said it was known only to his mother and himself. I've never seen it, but—"

"Thank you, Miss Sandford. I appreciate how difficult this must be for you." Danvers signaled Hardy to take Emily back to the kitchen, and in a few minutes he had the planks pulled out of the closet floor.

There was a large metal box, for which a quick search of the desk produced a key. He drew out the legal-looking papers. The farther he read, the wider his eyes opened. Here was an agreement with the cousin Thomas Jermy of the property dispute fame, dated seven days before the one Rush signed with Isaac Jermy, giving Rush a lease on the three farms for twenty-one years at an annual rent of two hundred thirty pounds—significantly better terms than those agreed to with Isaac Jermy.

The next clause was even more significant. "The aforesaid James Blomfield Rush agrees, as soon as conveniently he can after the signing of this agreement, to put Thomas Jermy into possession of the said estates, and do all he can legally to assist him maintaining possession . . . " At the very least Rush was playing both ends against the middle.

One final document, headed "Notice from Thomas Jermy to Isaac Jermy, Esq." and dated just last month, seemed to imply not only intent of action on the cousin's part, but also completed action:

> Take notice, that I have entered upon and taken peaceable possession of the messages, farmhouses, lands, and hereditament, situate and lying in the county of Norfolk, by reason and on account of the fraudulent and unlawful means in which you and your late father have been holding possession and receiving the rents of the same . . . and I give you notice that I demand of you the money that your father took in exchange for a farm in the parish of Felmingham . . .

Here, indeed, was evidence, signed with Thomas Jermy's mark, to support Danvers's theory that the Jermy cousins had been involved in the murder. Why it should be in Rush's hands was a puzzle, but the implication was clear: Men who had once taken property by force—property they believed to be rightly theirs—would be willing to do it again.

John Larner and Thomas Jermy apparently had ample motive for murder—perhaps a murder set up by Rush, who had made sure the Jermys were at home and directed his servant to lay straw in the muddy field for a quick escape but had no hand in the actual shooting himself. Danvers longed to put a dark cape on the Jermy cousins and demand a positive identification from the Stanfield Hall servants. At the very least he could send Hardy to find where these men were on the night of the murder.

Danvers replaced the documents and told Emily she must show them to the police when they inquired for Rush's papers. Then he thanked her for her cooperation. He hurried Hardy to the gig after a brief pause to inform Pont that he had found no gun in the parlor, but that Emily Sandford would show him the hiding place of some interesting documents.

"Hardy, I shall have to do without your excellent services for a few days. I want you to question a couple of Rush's friends for me."

Hardy shook his head. "Anything you say, m'lord. But trouble's sure to follow."

Danvers hesitated. Was he demanding unfair service? "Do I ask too much, Hardy? Shall I request Sergeant Pont to go?"

Hardy allowed the twinkle to show in his eyes as he raised one eyebrow. "No, m'lord. Truth be told, I'd rather suffer and grumble."

Danvers clapped him on the back. "Spoken like a true son of the Emerald Isle. I promise you I'll listen to all the grumbling you want to do if you get this information."

He gave Hardy the direction of the cousins as stated on the agreement: Thomas Jermy in Upper Tooting, Surrey, and John Larner, No. 9 James Street, London. "Just be sure they were home the night of the murder. And if not—where they were."

"As you say, sir. You can be counting on me."

"And Hardy—"

"Yes, m'lord?"

"Hurry back. I shall miss your services abominably."

Hardy turned the gig to exit through the gate in the stone wall around the farmhouse, but the way was blocked by the entrance of another vehicle.

Danvers raised a hand in greeting to Andrews, who drew up alongside them. "I came in hope of offering spiritual consolation to Miss Sandford, but I see the police are here."

"Only in the field, I believe," Danvers said. "We have just left Miss Sandford alone inside."

"Ah, well, perhaps a few well-placed words might not go amiss then. Such times as these often open even the hardest heart to spiritual matters."

Danvers muttered something noncommittal and started to signal Hardy to drive on when Andrews seemed struck with an idea. "I say, Rush has refused the spiritual counsel of Chaplain Brown and requested I call on him at the prison. I wonder if you'd care to accompany me, Lord Danvers? After all, our Lord admonishes us all to visit the sick, the widows, and the imprisoned."

Danvers didn't need scriptural exhortation. He would welcome an opportunity to speak to Rush. "I'd be glad to, Andrews. I'll just wait here while you call on Miss Sandford."

"Fine. Fine. Excellent." Andrews tied up his horse and strode briskly to the house, exuding the righteousness he had come to impart.

"And if you're wanting to know, I'd say that young woman is needing some counsel," Hardy said.

Danvers cocked one dark eyebrow. "I didn't know you had become zealous for souls, Hardy."

"As I'm seeing it, her soul's her own affair, but Miss Sandford has more immediate concerns."

Danvers looked puzzled.

"And weren't you noticing, m'lord? She's er—enceinte."

"What? Do you mean to say the woman's with child?"

"That's what I'm telling you. She didn't make any bones about it—told me herself. It's Rush's. He promised to marry her, but he hasn't done it."

Danvers shook his head. "The more I get to know of this man the more I think he should swing whether or not he murdered Jermy."

In a few minutes Andrews returned. From his affronted air, Danvers assumed the young woman had not been duly repentant. Danvers joined the vicar in his carriage and sent Hardy on his way, with renewed instructions that he come back as soon as possible.

The gaol, built in the gray stone keep of ancient Norwich Castle, stood like a grim fortress on a hill on the outskirts of town. Danvers shivered as the warden led them through the dark hall to Rush's cell. Outside, a pale sun

87

had begun to penetrate the morning's mist, but Danvers doubted if any warmth ever penetrated these walls.

The heavy iron door grated on its hinges as it was drawn open for them, then shut with a clank that echoed on the stone walls as Danvers and Andrews were locked in with the prisoner.

Rush was standing near the door gazing expressionlessly at them, but when Andrews took his hand he began to tremble. "My poor friend, how little could I have expected to see you here." The vicar's voice lost the disapproving edge it often carried and instead seemed to hold true compassion.

Rush did not answer. He began weeping. Prisoner and vicar sat together on the cot. Danvers sat on a small stool by the table where Rush took his meals.

"Oh sir, I am quite innocent, and it would break my heart if you did not think so." Rush sobbed.

"I would not be uncharitable," Andrews replied, "but I cannot ignore the evidence against you, any more than can the police. The important matter now is that your heart be right before God. Have you repented?"

Rush stiffened. "Repented? I have nothing to repent of. I know only the greatest peace and confidence. They will tell you, I have attended chapel every day since they brought me here. And I derive the greatest comfort from my reading." He pointed to a large family Bible on the floor beside his cot. "I asked for you to come to me not because I want to repent but because I have requested the Holy Sacrament be administered to me, and I have been refused."

His tears forgotten, the prisoner pushed to his feet and began pacing the cell. "I was told that it is not the practice to administer Communion to a prisoner before his trial, lest it should be received for an unworthy purpose. I cannot believe that any should be so wicked as to act thus."

"I can assure you, my friend, that I have known many so wicked and hard-hearted as to make that very request in the face of undoubted evidence of their guilt."

Rush seemed confused by Andrews's answer. He sat on the cot without answering.

Andrews opened the Bible he carried and began reading. But Danvers didn't follow the vicar's words. He was trying to make sense of what he had seen. If Rush was honest in his affirmation of peace, then he must be innocent. Or was he—as Andrews said others had—using a show of religion to induce the world to believe that so happy and unperturbed a state of mind must be incompatible with guilt? Or was it possible that here was the worst of all criminals—one whose heart was so hardened that he had no sense of guilt even after committing a horrible crime? Andrews's reading came to an end before Danvers reached a conclusion.

"Let us pray with our unhappy friend before we leave him." Andrews stood. "Is there anything in particular you should like us to pray for, Mr. Rush?"

"Yes, pray that I may continue in the same state of mind in which I now am." It was spoken with great force, but whether of conviction or belligerence, Danvers was uncertain.

"And will you not confess?"

"Confess? I have nothing to confess. You may talk as long as you please, but you cannot destroy my peace of mind or make me feel unhappy."

Andrews, obviously uncomfortable in the face of Rush's declaration, led in a brief, stiff prayer, then banged on the door for the turnkey to let them out.

Andrews was out of the cell and had started down the hall behind the warder when Rush grabbed Danvers by the elbow. "Will you take a letter for me to my legal advisers?"

Danvers hesitated, unsure of proper prison procedure.

"Listen, my lord, they need to know what happened! On the Friday before the murder, a lawyer fellow by the name of Joe—I think his last name's Clarke—told me in the village that he wished to go down to Potash and speak to me because Jermy's cousins had made up their minds to take possession of Stanfield Hall as they had done a few years ago. They wanted all the help they could muster.

"I told them that I thought as I had always done and advised them not to come to the house, for if they were seen at Potash I would be suspected because of the unfriendly terms upon which Mr. Jermy and I had lived for the last eighteen months.

"Joe said they did not expect to be seen and wished me to come out and speak with them on the road. I said that if they would come into the garden in the front of the house I would speak to them—going out on an excuse to see if there were any poachers stirring about."

Rush spoke with increasing speed, apparently trying to get his story told before the turnkey returned. "They came and stood in the garden that night. Joe asked again what I thought of the undertaking. I told him I thought it a very dangerous thing, particularly if attempted with violence and without plenty of help.

"Even then I did not think they would succeed. Joe said they had made up their minds to see what could be done. He asked if they might have use of my men as were not working on the farm. I refused, not wanting my son to be drawn in."

To Danvers's relief, the warder returned for him, but Rush rasped a hurried conclusion under his breath, "I had a sort of presentiment that all would not turn out well." He thrust the letter at Danvers, who took it with the determination to deliver it to the magistrate.

Danvers thought fresh air had never smelled sweeter as they emerged from the gaol. When they neared Ketteringham Park, he asked Andrews to stop. He would walk the rest of the way. He could hear the guns of the shooting party in the distance and thought it must be about time that tea would be taken out from the Hall to the sportsmen. A cup of strong, hot tea was just what he needed to wash the taste of the gaol cell out of his mouth.

If only Rush weren't such a perfect villain—a man who seemed to have no redeeming qualities, a man one *wanted* to be guilty. Danvers shook his head as he thought of Rush's apparent character traits: remorseless, pitiless, lecherous, cunning, obstinate, hypocritical . . .

The clacking sound of beaters just ahead of him told Danvers he was near the shooting party. Sir John preferred the new method of hiring servants to scare up the game rather than the more common practice of rough shooting, which required walking over the field with dogs oneself.

A dog gave tongue. A flock of pheasants rose from the hedgerow. A volley of shot followed, and Danvers stepped from the woods into the clearing behind the row of shooters in time to see several birds fall.

The sportsmen handed their rifles to the servants behind them to be reloaded. The most efficient in the field used two weapons so that one could be reloaded while the other was being shot.

Danvers watched as a partridge flew across the horizon. From his end of the row, Nigel shot quickly, but the bird flew on. Tommy Frane's shot was so close it appeared to ruffle the brown feathers. But it was Jack who felled the prize.

"Good shooting," Danvers said.

"It's the Purdey. She's a beauty, isn't she? Would you care to try it?"

"Thank you, I would." Danvers stepped into line as Jack handed the gun to Dalling.

The servant tipped in a measure of black powder from the flask, laid a small patch of greased cloth with the ball on it over the end of the barrel, and started to tamp it down with the ramrod.

But something caught Danvers's eye. He grasped Dalling's wrist and took the rod from his hand. The wooden ramrod bore numerous scratches and was darkened at one end from repeated pushing down on lead shot. Now Danvers knew what had been missing from the survey he had made of Jack's accessory case the morning after the murder.

"Surely this isn't the rod that came with your gun?"

Jack looked uncomfortable. "It isn't. I took this from the gunroom. I seem to have lost the original." He glanced over his shoulder. "Be a good fellow and don't mention it to the pater. He'll think it terribly careless of me. It is, of course."

Lord Danvers's hand froze on the gun Dalling held toward him. The scene was as clear in his mind as if he again stood in the passage of Stanfield Hall and watched the constable pick up the ramrod from where the murderer had dropped it when reloading in haste after firing on the younger Jermy.

"Shall I load for you, my lord?" Dalling's voice called him back to the present.

"No, I've lost my taste for the sport." Danvers thrust the weapon from him and strode back to Ketteringham Hall.

6

The next morning Danvers awoke with a sour taste in his mouth and the sense of a weight bearing down on his head. In Hardy's absence a maid brought his morning tea and made up his fire. But when she drew the heavy velvet curtains from the windows the scene only added to his gloom. It *would* be raining—it always rained at funerals. At least it might wash Isaac Jermy's blood off the Stanfield porch—even if it couldn't wash it out of Danvers's memory.

Danvers shook himself and got up to dress. He was becoming alarmingly morbid. He hadn't even known the people. If he hadn't been an unwilling witness to what must surely prove to be only circumstantial evidence against his friend, he wouldn't be involved at all. Why couldn't he find the detachment he sought—the detachment he thought he had been making such excellent progress toward since Charlotte's death?

The mourners' somber clothing and black umbrellas, the gray stone church, and the dismal sky were all of a piece. The congregation stood in the dripping churchyard awaiting the arrival of the crepe-hung hearses pulled by black-plumed horses. When they pulled up at the lychgate, the bearers in their black-draped top hats shouldered the coffins and followed in solemn procession behind Andrews and his curate. Behind the coffins followed young Sophia Henrietta Jermy, carrying herself with amazing dignity for one of such tender years, although Danvers noted how tightly she clung to Mary Read's hand.

"I am the resurrection and the life, saith the Lord," Andrews intoned as they walked toward the church.

Danvers recognized many of the Stanfield servants and was comforted when Sir John pointed out several relatives of Mrs. Jermy's. Since he had serious reasons to distrust the Jermy cousins, he was relieved to see that Mrs. Jermy and Sophia would apparently have adequate support from the mother's side of the family. Their lives would not be easy now.

But the one he had most hoped to observe in the congregation was absent. The Ketteringham party followed those from Stanfield in the cortege, and Danvers took his place beside Sir John in the Boileau pew. Jack was not there.

Danvers fought for other explanations, but the devil-born doubt that Jack could not face the final consequences of his handiwork was so strong it allowed for no others.

"I know that my Redeemer liveth, and that He shall stand at the latter day . . ."

Danvers reminded himself that he was supposed to take comfort from the priest's words. But he found them as chilling as the stone walls of the church.

After what seemed to be an interminable reading of Psalms and lessons, the congregation proceeded, in spite of even heavier rain, to the churchyard, where two gaping holes were prepared to receive the physical remains of Isaac Jermy and his son. The piles of mud around the graves reminded Danvers of the sodden turnip field their murderer had slogged through.

"Man that is born of a woman hath but a short time to live, and is full of misery." Andrews read. "He cometh up, and is cut down, like a flower . . ." The Jermys were cut down all right, but not like flowers. They were not even given the sporting chance of animals at a hunt.

Suddenly a hot rage burned away Danvers's depression. He would see the murderer punished, no matter who it was. There was no more room for philosophical soul-searching over whether he owed the higher loyalty to friendship or to abstract justice. He was resolved that the criminal should be punished—he took a deep breath—even if it was Jack.

That determination was strengthened later at Stanfield Hall, where the mourners gathered to take a glass of sherry with the family of the deceased. Lady Antonia told him the latest report on the other victims of the shooting. Pretty, young Mrs. Jermy would lose her arm. And the maid who had struggled to save her mistress would be crippled—a death sentence to one required to labor for her bread. Somehow this outcome of the shooting seemed more horrible than the death of the two men.

If the police held the right man, then that was fine, but if there had been a conspirator, or if the crime was the work of another entirely, Danvers was determined to discover the truth.

Even if the police were entirely right, truth demanded that their conclusion rest on solid facts, not on mere prejudice. What had Mill said about that? Danvers could almost quote it—something along the idea that if truth abode in the mind but lived there as a prejudice—a belief independent of and proof against argument—that was not the way truth ought to be held by a rational being. That was not knowing the truth . . . ah, he had the last line, "Truth, thus held, is but one superstition the more, accidentally clinging to the words which enunicate a truth."

He would find the truth for its own sake—and for his own as well, for somehow it was as if in avenging Mrs. Jermy's loss, he would be doing his own penance for Charlotte's needless death. He looked around the room, dismal with its shuttered windows and black-draped portraits.

"Do you know the Jermy cousins who disputed ownership of the estate?" Danvers asked Antonia. "I wonder if they are here?"

"I don't know, but I'm sure Sir John—" Her reply was cut short by Nigel who presented her with a glass of sherry so abruptly he nearly sloshed its contents on her black silk gown.

"Dismal affair. Need something stronger, but this is all they have." It was obvious from Nigel's breath that he had already taken stronger fortification. "Beastly dismal," he repeated in a louder voice. "Don't see what good it all does. Dead is dead. Why not leave it at that?"

"I think it's time you left it, at any rate, Langston. How about stepping outside for some fresh air with me?" Danvers gripped his arm just below the black crepe armband.

"Of course, out on the porch. Hope I'll get eliminated like Jermy? Then you'll have a clear path to Antonia. You didn't get Charlotte's money, so you'll console yourself with Antonia's."

"You're drunk." Danvers shoved Langston through the crowd. But he was relieved of having to deal further with the situation when they were met at the door by Nigel's man, Hickling. "Take care of your master. I'm sure you've had experience of him in this state before." Danvers rubbed his hands as if to clean them.

"Oh, he'll take care of me all right, won't you, Hickling? The perfect servant, always knows exactly what to do."

Danvers was shocked by the malice in Nigel Langston's watery blue eyes. Hickling's scrawny neck protruded above its stiff collar, presenting a sharply vulturine image. But Langston's glance indicated a loathing of something far deeper than his man's predatory look.

Back in the drawing room, Danvers sought out Sir John to continue his inquiry after the Jermy cousins.

"Don't think Larner's here," the squire said. "But there's Thomas Jermy now, signing the guest book on the sideboard."

Thomas Jermy, whose signature had been on the paper dropped at the scene of the murder.

Danvers swung around, expecting to find a burly man of murderous countenance. "What? That frail old man leaning on a cane?" That couldn't be right. He must be seventy—probably nearer eighty.

"Shows proper family feeling to have come all the way up from Surrey for the funeral, what? Especially since he once disputed Isaac Jermy's inheritance of the property. But I daresay that's over many years since."

Danvers had to think Sir John must be right. It was still possible Thomas Jermy could have agreed to the murder in spirit, but there was no possibility this feeble old man could have been mistaken for the bull-like Rush, no matter how many capes he wore.

Danvers moved through the other guests to the sideboard and, under the guise of signing his own name, glanced at Jermy's signature. The quill stopped in midair. Thomas Jermy had made his mark—a wobbly X.

Of course. Danvers berated himself for not realizing it sooner. The documents Emily Sandford showed him also bore only a mark for Thomas Jermy. The man was illiterate. There was no way he could have written or signed the paper dropped the night of the murder. And if that document was forged, what of the validity of the others Danvers had examined? How much weight could be given to any of them? Surely they were in the custody of the police by now. He would suggest to Sir John that they be examined by a handwriting expert.

Danvers groaned at the necessity of crossing a suspect off his list. That left Larner. Perhaps Hardy would return from London with news that the man had no alibi.

As soon as the party arrived back at Ketteringham, however, Danvers had to check a different alibi. He sought out Jack in his room. The sight of the young man polishing his Purdey put an end to any reticence Danvers felt about questioning him.

"So this is the way you spend your afternoon when the neighborhood is in mourning!"

"Terribly bad form, wasn't it? You needn't upbraid me for it—my father is sure to see to that. Doing one's duty is one of his favorite themes. Especially to one's neighbor—that's in the Bible somewhere, isn't it?" Then Jack hit his forehead. "Oh, no! You don't suppose Andrews will be after me too? I don't have any excuse, you know. I hate funerals. They depress me. I wasn't really needed, anyway—nothing one can do but look solemn and drink a glass of sherry afterwards—hate sherry too."

Danvers hoped it wasn't just wishful thinking to tell himself that a guilty person would have had a better excuse. And then, with a glint in his eyes, Jack bettered his explanation. "Besides, Miss Mellors had no reason to go to the funeral, and it would have been shockingly rude for the whole family to desert her."

The funeral seemed to have produced a more dampening effect upon the Ketteringham party than the murder itself had. The shooting was canceled the next morning—heavy rain being given as the reason.

With relief at not having to invent an excuse for missing the shoot, Danvers settled himself in the library, his feet on a red plush hassock before the blazing fire one of Boileau's well-trained housemaids had laid. He was instantly absorbed in his favorite magazine, *Westminster Review,* and the article by his favorite writer, John Stuart Mill.

"The beliefs which we have most warrant for have no safeguard to rest on but a standing invitation to the whole world to prove them unfounded." This was perhaps "the best that the existing state of human reason admits of certainty."

Danvers sighed and tossed the magazine aside. Was that really the best mankind could do—choose a position and invite debate? Was there no surer way to find truth? Would he find that to be as valid in his search for legal truth as Mill did for philosophical and spiritual truth? Was there no certainty? If that were the case, why did he try? What was the use of any of it?

He more sensed Antonia's presence than actually heard her enter. He looked up and nodded slightly.

"Does that mean I may intrude on your thoughts?" Her voice had a mellow modulation, well-suited to the room.

He forced a half smile and indicated the chair across from his. Today her dress was of a soft, sprigged muslin, so she settled in her chair without a rustle of skirts. "The murder still troubling you, is it?" It was a simple question, but she asked it with a note of deep concern, as a mother might ask a beloved child about a headache.

"In a way." Her obvious caring made it easy for him to express his thoughts concerning the hopelessness of searching for truth, whether about a murder or a personal system of belief.

She was quiet for a time before she spoke. "But surely, that is why we have the Bible as a standard for all."

For a moment her simple words flooded him with the warmth and comfort he had known as a devout youth. The possibility of assurance leaped before him as the flames on the hearth. Then they dimmed. If reliance on such assurance meant legalism like Andrews's, he would live with doubt, thank you.

That evening, torpor continued to hang over the assemblage. The response at Lady Catherine's musical entertainment that evening was indifferent, in spite of the more than competent performances given by the Boileau daughters of several Schumann *lieder* and the "Moonlight Sonata" by Lady Antonia.

The lassitude was not improved by poor Sarah's performance. In spite of Jack's assiduous attendance at turning the pages for her and her bright approach to the Clementi sonatina, it seemed her fingers simply would not obey the notes' direction. Everyone clapped politely for her brave ending, but tears glistened in her bright eyes as she cast a single look of depressed appeal in the direction of the yawning Nigel, then turned from the room, leaving Jack staring at the empty doorway.

Danvers probably had the most pleasant evening of anyone. After the concert he sought out Mary and Theresa in the nursery and amused them with spillikins until their governess reprimanded him for keeping the youngest Boileaus up past their bedtime.

Dalling, Jack's man, who was valeting Danvers in Hardy's absence, reported that even in the servants' hall the evening had been dismal. "No gossip at all. Attempted to pass the time with cards, but Hickling was the only one with any taste for it. Handy with the pasteboards, he is."

Danvers nodded. He could picture Nigel's man, sitting slightly stooped over his hand of cards, scrawny wrists jutting out of his white cuffs, and, as always, the beaky visage above the long, thin neck looking like a buzzard.

The next day Sir John invited Danvers to accompany him to Wymondham where the coroner and several magistrates would be examining Emily Sandford. On the ride over, Danvers brought up the subject of having a handwriting analysis of Rush's papers. Sir John put limited faith in the accuracy of such a scrutiny, but he agreed it should be done.

Outside the gaol the sidewalk was crowded with patterers hawking their broadsheets proclaiming bizarre revelations in the murder case. "Read the latest 'orrible divulgements in the butchery of Norwich lawyer and 'is family.'"

Sir John stopped the approach of an aggressive salesman with an icy stare, and they went through the iron door. The Wymondham gaol, although newer than the Norwich Castle where Danvers visited Rush with Andrews, was no warmer. Emily Sandford sat at the end of a long table, huddled under a black shawl that was insufficient both for keeping her warm and for hiding her pregnancy.

The magistrates were not unkind in their manner but were exacting in their determination to get at the truth. "You were alone in the house with Mr. Rush on the night in question?"

Emily's voice was soft, but her answer clear. "Yes. Mr. Rush had given a family ticket for the concert in Norwich to James and his wife—that's Mr. Rush's son—they live in the house too."

"Was that unusual—for him to buy concert tickets for his son and daughter-in-law?"

"I had not known of it before. I asked him why, and he said he would give them a treat, as James had been doing rather better work of late. Mr. Rush and myself were to go to the concert by ourselves—it was my birthday, and I was especially keen to hear the music."

"But you didn't go?" The questions passed round the table from magistrate to magistrate.

Emily shook her head, looking at the table. "I was in all day, preparing for it. We were to leave about six, as James being from home—already gone to Norwich, that is—Mr. Rush had to look after the men until six. I aired his clean shirt and brushed his best pants and had his hot water all ready for shaving. Then I laid tea things about five and went up to prepare for the concert, which I partly did, then ran down to get the tea. Mr. Rush returned, and saw I was all ready excepting my silk dress, which I told him I should put on at Norwich so as not to soil it on the carriage ride—the roads being so muddy. He made no remark but sat down to tea.

"I saw there was something the matter with him, as he continued to fix his eyes on me in a very strange manner. I asked if he was unwell. 'That's right,' he said, 'I'm not well. We can't go to the concert.' Then when he saw how much disappointed I was, he said he would still go, though it was rather late. I, of course, on seeing he was unwell, did not press going, though I did feel much disappointed. We had a long conversation about the concert and planned going to the morning concert the following day."

Danvers reflected on the result of that decision. Perhaps the Jermys' lives, and now Rush's, had hung on the decision of whether or not to go to a concert. The crucial question was, Would the murder have occurred anyway, had Rush gone to Norwich?

"Go on, Miss Sandford," Sir John prompted.

"Mr. Rush was silent at tea. He just sat looking at me in that strange way of his. I asked why he looked at me so. I observed tears rolling down his cheeks. His answer was, 'Come and kiss me.' While I was standing by his side, he said it was a great shame to be so disappointed, for he knew I contemplated going very much. We talked a great deal, when all at once he said, 'I shall just go out again tonight where I did last.'"

"Go out? I thought he was ill?" a gray-haired magistrate asked.

"I remonstrated with him for doing so, but he said he should only have two or three more times to go out, when he should, he hoped, succeed. He asked me how many evenings he had gone out of late. 'Five or six times,' I replied. He called to my recollection an anecdote in the history of Scotland—which he knows I am much interested in—where one of the chiefs sat looking, after being frequently conquered, at a spider springing from the wall. It had made six attempts without succeeding and prepared again to try for it, when the Scottish chieftain remarked that if the insect should succeed this time, he would rally his men.

"So Mr. Rush said he believed it to be the seventh time with him also. As the spider did succeed that last time, and also the chieftain, so, in like manner, he thought he should succeed, and that he should not be long gone."

"And what sense did you make of this extraordinary tale, Miss Sandford?"

"Why, poachers, Your Honor. We had been much troubled by them, and I knew he had gone out many times to try to catch them. He said the night was just right for the rascals and that he had seen a fresh stake driven in the ground that day."

Sir John muttered at this. "Poachers—a constant trial. Even the best efforts of my gamekeeper've failed to conquer the wily rascals."

Emily continued. "Then Mr. Rush said he thought a little gin in his tea would relieve the pain he felt. I asked if I should get the brandy, the cholera being about. I told him that would be better than gin.

"But he replied he would rather have gin and rose to get it out of his closet. He poured some in his cup and offered me some. He then put the bottle to his mouth and drank some. This very much surprised me, knowing him to be a most abstemious man. Jokingly I said, 'Why, you must be mad to drink raw spirits in that way.' He replied that, as he had to go out, it would help to keep the cold out."

"And then Rush went out?"

"About a quarter of an hour later, I think. I was upstairs reading the Scottish history Mr. Rush had brought home from London, and I heard him go."

"And how long was he gone?"

It seemed all in the room leaned forward at this question. Here was the crux of the matter. Had Rush merely taken a quarter hour's turn around his fields to search for poachers, or had he been gone half an hour or more—

long enough to walk the straw-strewn field to Stanfield Hall and perform a brutal murder?

"I read only one chapter. Fifteen or twenty minutes, I suppose." Emily looked straight ahead without blinking.

The rest of the questions seemed anticlimactic and uncomfortably personal, but Danvers followed closely, trying to determine whether the witness was lying. So much hung on her testimony. He must be sure.

"And what did you do when he came in, Miss Sandford?"

"He opened the passage door and said, 'Where are you?' I replied, 'Here in your room.' He said, 'Just step into your own a moment.' I did so, and was there some time—I should think nearly twenty minutes—when he opened his and said, 'Are you not coming in?' I went in and found him already in bed. He appeared very strange—what I thought rather tipsy.

"I said, 'This comes of your taking that gin.' He said, 'Ah! I was a great fool for drinking it. I'll take care I don't touch gin anymore. But make haste into bed.' I answered, 'No, I will make you a strong cup of tea, then you will be better.' When I returned with the tea he was asleep."

She paused, and Danvers wondered if it was possible that one with blood-stained hands could drift off so easily. He himself had found it impossible to sleep after observing the murderer's handiwork.

"It was nearly two in the morning when he awoke to drink the tea. I then got into bed. After some time he jumped up. I asked what was the matter. He said he was afraid he had lost something he had in his pockets and got out to look for it. I asked what it was. He said, 'My keys.' He found the keys under my side of the bed, and then went to his closet—what for I do not know—but he came out soon and said it was all right, he had not lost anything, and got into bed again.

"We rose rather early in the morning as he was going to Felmingham before we went to the concert in Norwich. He was still very unwell . . ." Emily's voice trailed off, and for the first time she gave way to emotion.

The magistrates had no more questions.

"What do you make of it?" Danvers asked Boileau as they drove back to Ketteringham.

"The gel's lying. Has to be."

Danvers looked sharply at his friend. Did the vehemence with which Sir John spoke the last three words betray desperation on his part? Was his involvement in this investigation more than mere duty? Did he, too, carry his own load of suspicion? Certainly he knew better than Danvers of Jack's indebtedness to Jermy and the violence of his reaction to Jermy's having taken the matter to the squire. Was his own continued silence fair to Boileau if each suffered his doubts in silence?

But it was another apparent lie Sir John was concentrating on. "We'll break her story. It's only a matter of time—the man was out longer than she says. Has to have been." Boileau whipped his horses into a brisk trot which required he give all his attention to driving.

The company was already gathering in the drawing room before going in to dinner when Danvers and Boileau arrived, so Charles hurried to his room to do the best he could without Hardy's assistance to make himself presentable for Lady Catherine's dinner table. Thank goodness for pre-tied cravats that hooked in the back.

He shrugged himself into a black tailcoat and arrived in the drawing room in time to escort Ama in to dinner. In the past days he had paid scant attention to his duty to his host's family, and the eldest Boileau daughter was pleasant company in spite of her forlorn look whenever the name of Captain Owen Stanley happened to come into the conversation.

They were just about to cross the hall when a disturbance near the doorway made them turn. Hickling had entered the drawing room to deliver a message to his master.

Nigel Langston's eyes narrowed, and the lines around his mouth hardened. "Tell him to go to Jericho," he ground between his teeth. "And you go with him!"

The gawky servant bowed. "As you say, sir." He departed with a smirk.

Lady Antonia, in amber satin and ivory lace that highlighted her amber ringlets, laughed and took Nigel's arm. "What impertinence! Whyever do you put up with the fellow? I should have given him the sack long ago."

"Excellent advice." Nigel smiled at Antonia, but his eyes were still hard.

"What was that all about, I wonder?" Danvers asked Anna Marie.

Her dark blue skirts whispered against the inlaid wood of the hall floor. "No doubt a bill collector. But imagine the fellow's having the audacity to present himself at the dinner hour. I can't think what he could hope to gain by it."

"Bill collector? Dunning Langston?"

Ama fluttered an ivory fan and waited for Danvers to pull out her chair. "Surely you knew—it's no secret. They line up regularly at Aylston Manor. Papa thinks that's why Nigel prefers to stay here, though his estate is so close. Rumor was he came into some money last spring, but he must have run right through it, because his property is in shocking repair."

"I wonder if he gambles?" Danvers said half aloud, but there was no reply as the footmen were handing round the first course.

Danvers was delighted to find the Dowager Duchess of Aethelbert seated on his right. After the strains of the day, nothing could have been more refreshing than listening to her incisive comments on the company. "Mark my words, Lady Antonia will be receiving an offer from that Nigel Langston. But she'll be a fool if she accepts."

"Then I shouldn't worry, Your Grace. Lady Antonia

Hoover is many things, but she is not a fool." Their few quiet conversations the past days had assured him of that beyond any doubt.

"Yes, I think you're right. But it's Caroline I worry about. Too somber and introspective by half. If her family were Catholic I shouldn't wonder if she became a nun. Too given to doing good works with that long-faced vicar. Enough to ruin any girl. I wonder that Sir John permits it."

She raised her lorgnette to scrutinize Sarah, who was in her usual good humor as she entered the room almost at a skip on Jack's arm. "Now there's a lively one. Will lead some man a merry chase if she gets her way. Don't like the way she looks at Langston, though. Antonia will keep a sharp eye on her if she takes my advice."

Another course was laid, and the evening wore on, but it wasn't until hours later when the tea tray was brought into the drawing room before bedtime that Danvers learned just how prescient the duchess had been. Antonia entered the room, her eyes sparkling, her face flushed, and took a chair near him.

Danvers rose at once to secure her a cup of tea. "Is anything amiss, Antonia? You look extremely agitated."

Antonia, who had been cradling her terrier lap dog in her arms, held him out to Danvers. "Here, hold Tinker while I compose myself."

"Not even for you, Tonia. The little monsters make me sneeze."

"Charles! Not an animal fancier? And here I thought you the perfect man. Oh, well." She set Tinker at her feet and accepted the tea. "But listen, Charles, I must tell someone, or I shall burst. Nigel Langston just asked for my hand in marriage!"

"What?"

"Yes. In the conservatory, on bended knee, in the most solemn tones imaginable. At one point he even put his hand over his heart. It was all I could do to keep from bursting out laughing."

"What reply did you give?"

"What reply could I give? I refused him, of course. He begged me not to be too hasty, apologized because the desperation of his love had driven him to rush matters. Desperation, my eye. If he is desperate for anything it's for my money. Certainly not for love of me." She almost choked on a giggle. "Not the most flattering proposal I've ever received but quite the most amusing. Perhaps Aunt Emma was right to think that I still need a chaperone."

Danvers smiled at his vague memories of the socially conscious aunt who had reared the baron's daughter.

She took a sip of her tea, then set the cup down. "Would you see me to my room, Charles? I don't want to encounter Nigel alone again tonight."

Danvers offered his arm, and they ascended the staircase together. Tinker padded behind. Outside her door Antonia paused. "Because I laugh at Nigel, you mustn't think I would be so heartless to all proposals, Charles."

He took her hand and just brushed her fingertips with his lips. "Sleep well, Antonia." He strode to his room without a backward glance.

In his room a pleasant surprise met him.

"Hardy!" He shook his servant's hand warmly and clapped him on the shoulder. "How I've missed you! If I ever send you off like that again, be a good fellow and refuse to go."

"Miss me, did ye? And I suppose ye're thinking I was having a pleasure trip with soft carriage rides and fancy meals. Why I can tell you, that inn in Horsham is the most iniquitous—"

Danvers held up a hand. "None of your moaning, Hardy, or I shall send you out again."

Hardy eyed a fleck of lint on his master's lapel. "Indeed, sir. And I'm seeing it's been a trial for you too."

"But tell me what you learned, man. No, wait—let me tell you first—Thomas Jermy is a feeble valetudinarian who can't so much as write his name—a complete failure as a suspect. I hope you fared better with Larner, or we shall be in a fix."

"Its relieved I am you gained information on Thomas Jermy, m'lord, as his place was shut up tight, and I could be learning nothing of him. Larner I did meet. He is neither feeble nor illiterate. But there's no doubting he was in London on the night of the murder."

Danvers slammed a fist into his left hand, then ran his fingers through his hair in the careless manner that, as always, drew pained looks from his manservant. "You're quite sure? He couldn't have been inventing a story?"

"It's hours sooner I'd have been back, sir. But I took time to talk to every one of the fellows he claims to have played cards with that night. They are all agreeing within an hour or so of the time and ten pounds or so of the pot. The housekeeper can even testify to the number of ham sandwiches they consumed. The least doubting there's not."

"Dash it. Sir John questioned Emily Sandford again today. Her alibi for Rush seems unshakable too. Everyone has an alibi except the one person above all that I want to prove innocent."

7

The next morning Hardy brought Danvers his tea at an unusually early hour, then turned to the wardrobe and began pulling out tweed jackets and a selection of worsted waistcoats.

"Whatever are you fussing around about, Hardy?" Danvers never liked a commotion, and before morning tea it was intolerable. "And what's the idea of disturbing me so early? It's barely daybreak out there." A gray light illumined the vast quantities of solid furniture, heavy fabrics, and crowded ornaments in the room, depressing him further.

"It's the shooting this morning, sir. And you not telling me which suit you prefer." Hardy's voice carried an offended ring.

"Oh, blast. I forgot all about it." The fact of the matter was, that business at Stanfield Hall had rather put Danvers off the use of guns for any purpose, even sport.

But it would be rude to refuse his host yet again. And it would postpone the moment when he had to face Jack and accuse him of suspected murder. In spite of everything, he had come to like the boy. "Oh, the Harris tweed, I suppose, with the green waistcoat—whatever you think best."

Hardy approved and began brushing Lord Danvers's double-breasted waistcoat. "And you'll be using the Mantons in the field today?"

"Yes, yes. Just see to it—do whatever needs to be done. And keep those beastly spaniels away from me. If any of Boileau's dogs take a fancy to lick the polish off my boots, I won't be responsible!"

But Danvers's irritation began to fade an hour later as he strode through the park in company with Boileau and the other guests. The crisp air, the bark of the dogs, the rat-a-tat-tat of the beaters all served to raise his spirits. They walked to the western edge of the park, an area that had not been shot over in recent weeks, and took their positions facing an open field. Hardy handed Danvers a loaded Manton.

"Thank you, Hardy. Now see you stay well back when the shooting starts. I'd hate to find a hole in that new cap of yours."

Hardy threw both arms over his head and retreated. Danvers took his place in the line of sportsmen.

The efforts of the game warden and his beaters met with immediate success. They raised a covey of grouse on their first pass-through. Danvers bagged a bird as it took wing. One of Sir John's spaniels raced into the field to retrieve it. Hardy took the empty gun and handed a loaded one to Danvers.

In spite of his earlier reluctance to join the party, the morning passed quickly. The exhilaration of the sport took over as the pile of game in the wagon mounted.

At noon the shooting stopped, and the ladies from Ketteringham Hall walked out to join the men at luncheon. The servants had set out long, linen-covered tables at the edge of the woods.

Danvers, noticing Antonia's care to avoid Nigel, offered her a seat next to himself. Nigel, however, took no notice of Antonia as he paid extravagant attention to Caroline and Ama and went out of his way to see that Hickling

111

and the other servants, who took their meal sitting on grass and stumps further into the woods, had plenty of ale.

"Seems our friend is making amends for his churlish behavior last night," Danvers said.

"I think I liked him better the other way." Antonia watched as Nigel whispered something in Sarah's ear that obviously embarrassed her. "Sarah, dear, I fear you're sitting in a draft. Come, you'll be much more comfortable at this table." Antonia's smile and words were satin smooth, but her voice held a ring of steel that would brook no argument.

In spite of her blushes, Sarah seemed reluctant to leave the attentions of the suave older man.

Jack sprang to his feet, offering Sarah his chair. She accepted with a quick backward glance at Nigel. The luncheon continued, punctuated with Sarah's bright responses to Jack's attentions.

The shooting resumed after lunch. A few of the ladies, including Antonia and Ama, stayed to watch. But Sarah expressed her opinion to Jack that she loved to walk in the woods and watch the cuckoos and wood pigeons and listen to the pheasants calling in the undergrowth. She could in no way stand to watch a shoot. So she returned to the Hall with Lady Catherine and Carry.

The sportsmen changed their position in the line. Nigel moved to Danvers's end, and Jack stood between them. Danvers frowned over whether Nigel had moved to that part of the field in order to be close to Antonia, but at any rate he was pleased to have Jack close to hand so he could observe him. Dalling was still using the battered ramrod, which meant the original had not been recovered. Was that because it was on a shelf at the Norwich police station marked "Exhibit A"?

At first the shooting was a bit sporadic as the beaters were slow to raise any quarry. Then they flushed a large covey of quail, and excitement surged. The servants barely had time to recharge the guns when a flock of pheasants flew across from the other direction.

112

Danvers turned to grab a fresh gun and out of the corner of his eye saw Nigel's ramrod shoot through the air like an arrow. In his haste to fire, Nigel had grabbed the gun from Hickling without giving the servant time to pull the rod out.

Hickling darted forward to retrieve the rod. At the same moment the last pheasant veered sharply and seemed to head back toward the hunters at treetop level.

Nigel grabbed his second rifle. Two shots rang out. No one noticed the pheasant plummet as a cry of pain tore the air.

Everyone ran forward to where Nigel was already kneeling over his servant, making futile attempts to staunch the red flow from Hickling's buzzard-shaped head. "The blasted fowl swooped, and I swung fast. Why couldn't the man have stayed back as I instructed him?"

Danvers pulled out his handkerchief and started to offer assistance when a pair of slim, strong hands gripped his arm and spun him around. He held up a hand to block the newcomer's view. "No, Tonia, don't look." But he was too late.

She had seen. The look of horror in Antonia's eyes made her almost unrecognizable. She shook all over.

Danvers put his arm around her for support.

"I—I heard—he—" she began, but her words were choked by the hysterical sobs and laughs that came out at the same time.

At that moment Sir John left the group around Hickling to instruct his servants, and Antonia was presented once more with a clear vision of the man with his face blown half off.

Nigel looked at her. "Antonia . . ."

She swooned.

Danvers caught her. "Brandy, Tommy?" he shouted.

Tommy Frane drew a small flask from his jacket pocket.

Danvers forced a little down Antonia's throat.

She came around with a series of violent, racking hiccoughs. Tinker set up a salvo of short, sharp yaps to add to the confusion. Ama and a maid hurried to them. "We'll take her back to the Hall."

"Get a blanket," Danvers ordered. "She needs to be kept warm."

Antonia seemed barely able to walk.

"I'd better go with you." Danvers's voice was not pleasant. Of all the stupid times for a case of fashionable hysterics. Certainly it was a horrible sight, unfit for ladies' eyes—not fit for men's eyes, either—but to have to be playing nursemaid to a lady's vapors when he could be giving assistance to the real victim infuriated him. At least it was as well he had learned this about her—a female with delicate nerves was not his ideal for the post of Lady Danvers.

It was fortunate, however, that Danvers accompanied the ladies, because Antonia fainted again after a few moments of walking, and he was required to carry her to the Hall, as Tinker panted at his heels. The one cart they had in the field would be needed for the corpse.

Danvers placed Antonia on her bed without ceremony and left her to the care of her maid and Ama.

When Jack returned an hour later, Danvers was sitting in the heir's room waiting for him.

The grisly scene in the field had intensified his memory of the slaughter at Stanfield, and Danvers was determined to get to the truth once and for all.

The door burst open, and Jack came in, muddy and blood-spattered, just as Danvers had seen his clothes on the morning after the murder.

"Ghastly affair—" Jack began.

But Danvers cut him off, his words biting in their anger. "Yes, indeed. Almost as ghastly as that at Stanfield Hall. Except here one man died in an accident. At Stanfield two were purposely massacred and two women crippled for life."

114

Jack flung himself into a chair, his legs sprawled in front of him. "Unbelievable, isn't it? This was always such a quiet neighborhood—"

Danvers hit the arm of his chair. "Blast it, Jack! I heard you quarrel with Jermy. I saw you sneak off with your rifle that night. The police haven't found the murder weapon yet, but they have found a ramrod!"

"I know, ruddy impossible—" Jack halted and jerked upright. "My word! What are you saying? You don't think—you can't—are you accusing *me* of murdering Jermy?"

The accusation made, Danvers's anger drained from him, and he spoke quietly. "God knows I don't want to. But what *can* I think?"

"But Rush—"

"Rush is a nasty character, handy for the police, but their evidence is shaky, and he has an alibi. Jack, if your temper overcame you, or if you joined forces with Rush for some God-only-knows reason, I'll do everything I can to stand by you. I owe it to your family. But I've got to know the truth."

The moments Jack waited before answering were the longest of Danvers's life.

"The truth is, before God, I was so angry with Jermy after I learned he'd gone to my father over that debt I *did* want to attack him—but with my bare fists, not a gun."

Danvers was quiet, waiting.

"I went poaching—the night of my birthday and several nights since. Poaching needs a great deal more skill than this gentlemen's game where beaters scare birds up in front of you and a servant hands you a loaded gun. Someone else does everything but pull the trigger—what kind of sport is that? You can ask Dalling. He knows all about my outings—and disapproves vehemently. Or better yet, ask Buckby."

"Buckby?"

"The best poacher in seven counties. Old Buckby has taught me more than these gentlemen shooters will

115

ever know—how to freeze a hare with a lantern, how to shoot a whole treeful of sleeping grouse from the bottom up without scaring the others off, how to lay a snare—"

"All right, all right—" Danvers held up a hand to stop Jack before he spoiled it all by protesting too much. Danvers knew he wanted to prove Jack innocent even more than the police wanted to prove Rush guilty. And he really had no doubt of the truth of all Jack had said. He was certain the boy had been poaching with his disreputable friend—even on the critical night—although in a dark woods it would take only a few minutes' contrived separation while Buckby watched by one snare and Jack another . . .

Still, Danvers reasoned, far better to play along as if he believed wholeheartedly—as if believing a thing could make it so. Whatever would Mill say to that?

He ran his hand through his hair before leveling another look at Jack. "But if you weren't the second man with Rush, who was?"

"Was there a second man? I thought the police said Rush did it all."

"Oh, the police are so busy gloating in their self-satisfaction you wouldn't change their minds if Rush could prove he'd been dining with the Queen that night. All I know is the witnesses report that the two killings were very close in time and that the killer or killers used two different entrances."

Jack thought for a moment. "Which Rush could have done to make it look like two murderers—or how about those cousins of Jermy's?"

Danvers shook his head. "Not a chance. I've checked thoroughly."

"Well, if you're looking for a trigger-happy suspect, you couldn't do better than Langston."

"Nigel?"

"Why not? He shot at you. And I could swear that shooting in the field today wasn't any accident."

116

"What?"

"Hickling was way below that pheasant. Langston lowered his gun."

Danvers was speechless. Was this a blind? Jack accusing the nearest person handy to avert suspicion from himself? Or did he have a valid point Danvers had failed to see? "I'll admit he had the weapon and the opportunity—in both cases. But what possible reason could he have for either killing?"

"I suppose you know Jermy was his solicitor?"

Here was something Danvers hadn't considered. But it was reasonable—Nigel's estate was nearby—it was perfectly natural that Isaac Jermy should be his counselor.

Jack continued, "And if he did do Jermy in, and Hickling knew it somehow . . ."

"Yes, I suppose it makes sense." Danvers considered for a moment. "I can't imagine what his motive might be, but maybe I can think of an excuse to get a warrant from your father to search Jermy's papers. If there's any grounds for your suggestion, something should show up there. Langston was heavily in debt, but I don't see how killing his solicitor could help."

"Maybe Nigel didn't like the way Jermy took care of his affairs—blasting the whole family to kingdom come is a bit extreme for a poorly drafted contract, I admit, but Langston always did have a nasty temper."

Danvers was about to reprove Jack for his levity, but the heir continued, "Come to think of it, Nigel came into some money this past year, yet he never has two pence to pay his debts with. Maybe there was some kind of hanky panky going on, and Jermy found out and tried a spot of blackmail."

It was plausible. But then, Nigel had a lot on his mind—bill collectors dunning him, Antonia having just refused his proposal. It was also entirely plausible that a moment of carelessness, which could happen to anyone, had

117

produced tragic results in the sporting field, and there was nothing more to it.

All the speculating on accidents caused Danvers to recall the story of the accidental shooting of Rush's father and the rumors that that death had in truth been murder. Had Rush murdered his father and, because he went unpunished, believed he could get away with murdering Jermy? But why? There didn't seem to be a motive for either killing.

Or had Nigel believed himself safe from discovery of having committed Jermy's murder and so staged an "accident" to cover his tracks? Either way it seemed it would be a case of "Be sure your sins will find you out." That would please Andrews. He could get a whole month of sermons from it.

8

Ironically, it was the unusual arrival of the estimable vicar that quashed Danvers's plans for examining Jermy's files the next day.

Charles had just found Sir John in the library and was about to approach him on the matter of inspecting the papers at Stanfield when an exuberant blast of trumpets and pounding of drums sent them to the window. Up the long drive toward the Hall marched upwards of twenty children, all wearing party hats, carrying banners, and waving flags, accompanied by Andrews and led by the Hethersett band.

"Oh, saints help us!" Sir John said it as a hearty prayer. "The children's games! I forgot. Go find Jack. We've got to meet them outside and think of something."

Sir John and his heir met the procession at the iron gate that opened onto the front of Ketteringham Hall.

Andrews held up his hand for the band to cease and cleared his throat. "This is a fine day for the Sunday school children of Ketteringham Parish and a fine opportunity for them to experience the precept that even as there have been ample opportunities in our parish of late to weep with those who weep and mourn with those who mourn, as Saint Paul admonishes us, it is also meet that we should rejoice with those who rejoice."

Jack, whose birthday they had come to celebrate, received a rousing cheer from his future tenants, and the squire proposed that his son should lead the procession in a rather lengthy march around the grounds. In the background frantic hammering sounded from the gardener and gamekeeper, who had been summoned by Huntley to erect goalposts and assemble equipment for the frolic that had been scheduled weeks before but forgotten in the recent hectic events.

As Danvers surveyed the situation he heard first huffing and then grumbling behind him. He turned to see green coattails flapping on either side of a huge bundle of sticks that extended to the bearer's eyes. "What have you there, Hardy?"

His sudden question brought disaster. Hardy faltered. The top stick began to roll. The others followed in a topsy cascade while Hardy, continuing his forward progress, stepped on the first of the fallen bundle. His feet flew from under him.

Struggling to keep from laughing, Danvers extricated his servant from the tangle. "What's this in aid of, Hardy?"

"Stick race, someone said, but I can see no sense in it. Whole business sure to come to no good." Hardy brushed his coat and trousers vigorously as if he would brush away the wound his dignity had received.

"Well, never mind about that right now," Danvers said. "I've another matter for you to attend to." Hardy didn't seem the least disappointed to leave the sticks as Danvers continued. "Have you noticed whether Norwich has gaslight?"

"I'm thinking it has, sir." Hardy squared his shoulders.

"Then take the balloon over on the cart and hook it up to the city main. We'll help out on the entertainment here."

Hardy's eyes sparkled at the idea. "Ah, just so, m'lord. And that's better than any silly stick race." He kicked at the offending sticks, so agitated that he didn't even notice the scrape it produced on his brown leather boots.

Jack's improvised march came to an end with a final blast from the intrepid lead trumpeter of the Hethersett band. Sir John stepped forward with Lady Catherine, Ama, and Carry.

With the grace demanded of their position, the ladies directed the lively group of children in two hours' worth of old English games including climbing a soapy mast for a shoulder of mutton, a sack race, and finally a footrace in which the Boileau family coachman and footman ran along with the children. The footman would have easily won, but he held back so that Pip, the gamekeeper's tow-headed boy could claim the prize. The ten-year-old accepted his ribbon with gravity, then expressed his delight by turning a series of handsprings.

The final field event was a blindfold wheelbarrow race. The greatest surprise came from Lord Danvers, whose polished perfection did not mark him as one likely to volunteer for children's games. "Come along now, Jack. I can beat you across this lawn any day—even if I were blindfolded and you not!"

That was not a challenge the guest of honor was likely to dismiss, although no gentleman would accept so unfair an advantage as to forgo the blindfold. Each chose a child for his barrow, then because the little blonde girl Danvers selected was so light, he added her brother to it.

With black scarves tied firmly over their eyes, the contestants set off in a drunken path to the bottom of the garden. Cheers and shrieks of laughter rang in Danvers's ears as he struggled to keep his barrow on a steady course—no mean feat when his two lively passengers were bouncing up and down in response to the crowd's excitement.

"We're winnin'! We're winnin'!"

"We got 'em, m'lord—just about—"

It was their near success that upset them. The brother and sister were so excited over their victory that they jumped up too soon, overturning the wheelbarrow, tripping Lord Danvers, and landing them all in a muddle of squirming arms and legs, while Jack and his sandy-haired urchin sped to victory.

Danvers pulled off the blindfold and sat laughing in the sun-warmed grass as his passengers crawled out from under him.

"Jolly good try, m'lord," the boy encouraged their fallen charioteer.

"I do 'ope you don't feel none too bad," the little girl added gravely. "You made a very stout try!"

Danvers laughed again and patted them on their heads. But the main event had now shifted to the top of the lawn.

The band struck up a fanfare and Sir John, from the front steps of the Hall, announced at Danvers's suggestion the greatest event of all. "If I might direct your attention to the field beyond that copse of trees . . ."

He pointed, and a great *"Oooh"* arose from the crowd as through the leafless branches they saw a red and yellow balloon tugging at its moorings.

"Lord Danvers has offered to take those as wish it up in his balloon." The cheering for the balloon far exceeded that earlier for the heir.

The band played, and the children, in obedience to Andrews's order, queued up in orderly procession.

"Are the repairs secure, Hardy?" Danvers asked when the parade reached them.

"Oh, it's good as new she is, m'lord. Right and tight." Then he couldn't resist adding, "Until something else goes amiss, that is."

The basket accommodated five children at a time, plus Hardy. Hardy's presence was purely precautionary to see that no one fiddled with the valve or leaned too far over the edge, as the balloon was never let off its tether.

A boatload soared upward the length of the two-hundred-foot rope to the admiring squeals and giggles of those on the ground. Then the strong arms of several servants hauled it down after a few minutes for the next load. Mild as the adventure might seem to a seasoned aeronaut, it was clear that this was the adventure of a lifetime to the children.

A few of the younger girls hung back for a while, but in the end all chose to go. On the last load were four girls who had waited to build up their courage. Danvers helped them into the basket, then looked around. Pip, the gamekeeper's son, who had gone up in an early load, hadn't taken his eyes off the operation the entire time since. "Fancy being a balloonist, do you?" Danvers asked.

The boy nodded his shock of sun-bleached hair, speechless with wonder.

"Well, come up again then and keep Hardy company. He'll show you how to work the valves."

With a whoop, Pip scrambled aboard, and Danvers let out the tether from the ground. The band struck up a new number, and the children holding flags waved them. Danvers had just started to pull in the balloon a few minutes later when a newcomer joined the group.

"The very idea, Lord Danvers. Giving out balloon rides and not inviting me. I should have expected better manners of Norville's son."

Danvers bowed to the Dowager Duchess of Aethelbert. "Forgive me, Your Grace. I had no notion you aspired to aeronautics. Is it too late to hope you would honor me by taking a ride now?"

"What do you think I walked all the way out here for? But none of this being led on a rope like a child at a pony show. I want a real flight."

Danvers hauled on the rope, his eyes sparkling at the duchess in her lavender afternoon gown. "Would you report my ill manners to my father if I told you I find much to regret in the fact that it would be indecent of me to propose marriage to you?"

If they had been in a ballroom, Danvers was sure he would have felt the sharp reprimand of her fan across his knuckles, but the duchess's still-youthful laughter told him his sentiment had pleased her.

Sir John lifted the girls from the basket, and he and Danvers helped the Duchess in. The band was marching the children off when Hardy reached to boost Pip out.

"Oh, let him stay," the duchess said. "Anyone can see he'd prefer this to eating sweets in the Hall. Right, lad?"

Pip clapped his rather grubby hands, and his blue eyes shone. "Oh, yes! Thank you ever so much, my lady."

Ringer, who was nearby, reached in to box his son's ears. "Where's your manners, boy? Say 'Your Grace' to a duchess. And take care you don't tread on her skirts. It's most kind of you to take notice of him, Your Grace." He tugged his forelock.

Danvers told Hardy to drive the carriage after them and instructed Ringer to follow with the farm cart to bring the balloon back. Then the two servants untied the tether to set the golden ball free.

It was hard to say whether the dowager duchess or the gamekeeper's son found greater delight in the adventure, and the enterprise brought much-needed balm for Danvers as well—partly because Pip's questions kept him far too busy to engage in any of the soul-searching that had become so uncomfortable of late.

"And what does the yellow cord do?"

Danvers touched the lightweight rope hanging from the inside of the balloon. "If you pull it, it opens a valve at the top and lets the gas out. Then we go down."

"And you cut those bags off to go up?"

"That's right. It's really very simple. Think you could fly one?"

124

"Sure I could. That's what I'm going to be some-day—a barrow-nut."

The passengers were quiet after that, observing the patchwork of fields below. In the corner of one field a gaggle of geese honked, barnyard cackles and crows came from another farm, and the soft moo of cows followed them across a pasture.

"It's perfectly amazing to be able to hear all that so high up," the duchess said.

"Yes." Danvers pointed up at the great sphere above their heads. "It acts as a reflector of sound—you can even hear people yelling at you from the ground."

Just then an angry farmer shouted at them with upraised fist for making his horses run in their paddock.

Danvers grinned. "But then, being able to hear isn't always an advantage."

He brought the balloon down in a field near Wymondham, letting Pip help tug on the cord to open the butterfly valve. Their ground crew arrived only a few minutes after they landed, and Hardy and Ringer, with the assistance of several sturdy farm laborers attracted by the astonishing sight, set to deflating the balloon for the return trip in the cart.

Danvers assisted the duchess into the carriage. "Would you like to drive home with us, Pip?"

It was a close question whether the boy would rather stay with the balloon or with his new friends from the great world. In the end the high-stepping spirit of the carriage horse won the day, and he scrambled up on the driver's seat beside Danvers.

"Well, did ballooning live up to your expectations, Your Grace?" Danvers asked.

"Entirely satisfactory, I think. What do you say, young Pip?"

"It were—" he paused to search for an adequate word "—wonderful!" Then he seemed to sink deep in thought and didn't speak for a long time.

Finally, Danvers felt a tug on his coat sleeve and looked down. Pip was holding a small, brown leather book out to him. "What's that, Pip?"

"I dunno. I found it in the field after the shoot. I thought as 'ow you might like it, since you been so nice to me."

"Well, that's very nice of you, Pip. There was no need for you to give me a gift, but it was very thoughtful. I shall tell your father your manners are excellent."

Danvers slipped the little book in his pocket and enjoyed the glow of Pip's smile all the way back to the Hall.

Ketteringham had never seemed quieter than it did that evening as the family and their few remaining guests gathered in the drawing room after a light supper.

In spite of the fact that the room was fashionably crowded with pictures, needlework, and potted palms, it seemed empty. All would readily admit they found the peace blessed after the tumult of entertaining twenty-some squealing youngsters accompanied by the *um-pah-pah* of the Hethersett band. But it was impossible to overlook the chair vacated by Nigel, who had accompanied Hickling's body back to Aylsham Manor.

And the void left by Antonia—whose physician had taken her to her own home for a complete rest—was one the remaining company tried to cover with forced conversation. When that failed, they took refuge in giving conspicuous attention to their reading and needlework.

Sarah had offered her services as a nurse for Antonia but had been quite bluntly refused on the grounds that her presence would make the patient feel obliged to act as hostess—a strain the doctor did not wish imposed on his patient. So Miss Mellors sat demurely in a corner—her wide, raspberry moire skirt spread over a dark wine velvet chair—while Jack labored to entertain her and his sisters by reading to them from a volume of Wordsworth's poetry.

126

Danvers was aware of one distinct advantage of Nigel's departure—he no longer need concern himself about Langston's advances to Tonia's cousin. Or the more worrying aspect that the child had seemed to welcome his attentions more than those of Jack. Now her head was bent forward prettily as she listened to his reading.

Perhaps his selection of the poet's meditation "At the Grave of Burns" was not a happy choice however:

> "For he is safe, a quiet bed
> Hath early found among the dead . . .
> And surely here it may be said,
> That such are blest."

The lines left the company silent.

Jack switched to "Lines Written in Early Spring," but the closing, "Have I not reason to lament what Man has made of Man?" defeated even Sarah's most determined effort to be good company.

Carry stifled a yawn, laid her embroidery in the workbasket at her feet, and, after kissing her mother, bade the company good night.

"A very wise idea, my dear," Lady Catherine said. "I think perhaps we should all have an early night. I believe I'll just finish this hemstitch and follow your example."

Tommy laconically suggested a set of piquet, but the responses were so half-hearted the idea was abandoned.

Danvers sat in a profusely carved black oak chair that was stiff with respectability. No matter how he shifted, he could not find it comfortable, so he rose and paced the room, ponderous with its proper ornamentation, until he felt compelled to part the red velvet drapes with their weighted fringes to find a breath of air.

"If you'll excuse me, my lady—" Danvers bowed to his hostess "—I believe I'll just take a jaunt around the terrace and turn in myself." He hurried out through the French windows at the end of the room, then moved to the far side of the terrace and leaned against the balustrade, breathing in great gulps of fresh air. The night was chill. He shivered as a breeze stirred the bushes.

Then, with an alert of his senses, he realized the motion to his right was not merely that of the breeze. A dark figure moved swiftly but quietly—as quietly as a female in a fashionably full skirt could move.

Danvers strained his eyes in the gloom, wondering who it could be. A servant girl meeting a lover? That would be a terrible risk to take, for if she were caught she would be dismissed without a character, and future honest employment would be impossible. But the unmistakable swish of silk and the modish silhouette of the deep poke bonnet told Danvers this was no servant girl. The moon peeked out from behind its cloud cover for only an instant. But it was long enough for Danvers to identify the mysterious figure. Caroline Boileau.

Quiet, introspective Carry? The daughter the dowager duchess had characterized as "too holy," slipping out for a rendevouz? Not only did it seem totally out of character for her, but who could she possibly be going to meet in this neighborhood? Had Boileau's plan to match his daughter and Tommy Frane come to nothing because Caroline had given her heart elsewhere?

Who could it be? She was going in the direction of the church. Since Andrews was married, that left only his plump, earnest curate, Parnell. Danvers had seen him only at the funeral, but the thought of the cherubic face with its bespectacled eyes gazing in rapture at Carry—and having that rapture returned in a nighttime tryst—was unthinkably comical. There must be another explanation.

9

The next morning Danvers dutifully adjusted the knot in his black silk cravat and applied a final dose of macassar to his wayward hair before leading Hardy to the morning room. Most of the family, guests, and servants were already assembled. The ladies, in lace caps and subdued morning dresses, sat on sofas and upholstered chairs, flanked by gentlemen on straight-backed wooden seats. The servants made do with stools and benches in the back. Sir John, looking even more the sturdy paterfamilias than usual, his hair and mustache silvery above his black coat, sat at the heavily draped, round oak table. The large family Bible lay open before him.

Everyone in the room sat with clasped hands and lowered eyes, the better to concentrate on the words of the prophet Ezekiel. "When the wicked man turneth away from his wickedness that he hath committed, and doeth that which is lawful and right, he shall save his soul alive . . ."

Danvers lifted his eyes just enough to look at those around him. How he envied the assemblage their unquestioning acceptance of the prevailing standards of right and wrong. What an immense support it would be to find oneself relieved of any necessity to think out these matters for oneself, to be free simply to go forward building one's life, doing one's own work and the nation's on the unshakable foundations of faith.

"I acknowledge my transgressions, and my sin is ever before me." Sir John read from Psalm 51 next, then turned to the prayer book. "Almighty God, the Father of our Lord Jesus Christ, who desireth not the death of a sinner, but rather that he may turn from his wickedness and live . . ."

The daily service concluded with all in the room praying the Lord's Prayer. For an instant Danvers recaptured the joy of assurance such times had brought him in his childhood—although the Earl of Norville had been less assiduous in his duty than Sir John, who as a mere knight was just one step above the middle classes and therefore more beholden to their rigid standards. But then, as quickly as the light flickered, the old confidence faded in the shadow of doubt.

Yet doubts in another direction offered refuge. The pleasure of a new piece for his intellectual puzzle beckoned. Leaving the assemblage behind him, Danvers escaped outdoors.

He strolled the length of the stone-flagged terrace, puzzling over what he had seen the night before. He was no nearer to an adequate solution, however, when Hardy came to him.

"Found this while brushin' your coat, m'lord. I'm not recognizing it as yours, but thinking you might want it, I am." He held out Pip's little brown book.

"Oh, yes. The gamekeeper's lad gave that to me—a thank you for the balloon ride. Said he found it in the park. Don't know what it is. Do you?"

Hardy puffed up like an offended wood pigeon. "I'm sure I did not open it, m'lord."

Danvers smiled. "You'll never make a detective, will you, Hardy? Far too upright. Well, let's have a look. Hmm, appears to be someone's pocket diary—no name in it— just a list of dates with numbers beside them. What do you make of it?"

"And might it be an account book?"

"Could be—no pounds or shillings marked, but these slashes and periods could mean that. Apparently someone dropped it at the shooting yesterday. Suppose we'd better ask around. It could be important."

"Morning, Danvers. Recovered from our invasion by the infantry yet?" Jack, likewise escaping the heavier air indoors, joined them.

"Oh, yes. Lively mob, but I daresay I made out better than your father's shrubbery." Even from the terrace, the lawn showed marks of yesterday's trampling.

Danvers hesitated. What if he held something important? Should he test it on Jack? Might the boy's reaction tell him anything? He held out the slim volume. "Did you lose a diary in the park? Young Pip found this and gave it to me."

Jack took the book and flipped the pages. "What is it? A payment register of some sort?"

"Seems to be. Hardy thought it an account book. Hardy, you ask around in case someone has missed it. Whatever it is, if it was important enough to keep track of, it must be needed."

Jack started to hand it to Hardy, then stopped. "What's this on the edge?" They all looked at the reddish brown stain on the inside of the back cover.

"Looks like blood," Danvers said.

Jack nodded. "That's what I thought. Well, don't suppose that's too surprising if it was found on a shooting field. Still—I wonder—"

"Yes, it would be interesting to know just exactly where Pip found it. Care to walk to the gamekeeper's lodge with me? I'll hang onto this for a bit, Hardy, but you go ahead with your inquiries in the servants' hall."

Jack and Danvers walked across the lawn and into the park where the gamekeeper lived at the edge of his domain.

"Morning, Ringer. Pip around?" Jack asked.

Ringer pulled his heavy, black forelock in respect to the young master. "'E's out back. The lad 'asn't been up to no mischief 'as 'e? I'll tan 'is 'ide good if 'e gives any trouble."

"No, no, quite the contrary. We've come to ask him for some help. No problem his going on a walk with us?" Danvers asked.

Ringer was quick to agree to the plan.

"Fine, tell his mother we'll have him back in time for his midday meal."

They found Pip behind the lodge, sitting in his mother's laundry basket tied with bits of rope and string to an old blanket hanging over a tree branch.

"Ahoy, there!" Danvers waved. "Can you bring her down in this field?"

With great seriousness Pip pulled the valve cord, tossed a piece of tissue over the side to check his descent, and threw out a small branch attached to a cord for a grapnel.

Danvers stepped up and tied another string to a nearby sapling. "She'll be secure now. We want you to show us where you found the book you gave me."

Pip's blue eyes widened in alarm under his corn-shock hair. "I didn't steal it, honest!"

"No, no. We know you didn't. But it might be important to somebody, and if we know where you found it, we might be able to return it to its owner."

That satisfied the child.

He led off at a skip and a run through the park toward the field where the shooting had been earlier in the week. At the edge of the field he slowed his step and looked around uncertainly.

"Here's where the luncheon tables were set, if that helps you any," Danvers pointed out.

"Oh, yeah. And there's the log where I sat with me dad to eat. Mighty good beans and 'am those was!"

Jack smiled. "I'm glad you approve the efforts of our

cook. I'll tell her. Or you can tell her yourself the next time you sneak into the kitchen for a tart."

Pip looked worried, then gave a crooked grin when he saw the heir's smile. "'Ere." He darted forward. "I found it right 'ere after they carried off that poor fellow what got shot. Orful bloody mess 'e were."

Danvers caught the sparkle of excitement in Pip's eye and shook his head at the callousness of children. "Right here, was it?"

"Yep. Right by that big patch of blood on the grass."

"Well done, Pip. You're a bright boy. We promised your mother you'd be back for elevenses, so you'd better scamper."

Pip hesitated, so Danvers added, "Besides, there's a good breeze coming up, just right for your balloon."

Pip was off.

Jack examined the spot Pip had pointed out. "Doesn't help much, does it? Could have been anyone— we all ran up here." Jack considered for a moment.

"Could have been anyone—but it was most likely Langston's or Hickling's. It could have been pulled out of Nigel's pocket when he yanked out his handkerchief, or it could have fallen out of Hickling's coat when he was being lifted onto the cart."

Danvers didn't add that it could as easily have been from Jack's coat pocket. The lad seemed so sincere that continuing to doubt him made Danvers feel like a jaded cynic.

"We were inexcusably awkward—suppose it was the horror of what we were handling," Jack continued with a shudder. "May I see the book again?"

Danvers handed it to him.

"Hmm. Thirteen dates, more or less a month apart. Could be an account with any tradesman."

"The amounts vary, but they're all large—if we're right that those numbers represent payments made or owing. Don't think even a dandy like Langston visits his tailor that often."

133

The jaded cynic in Danvers won. He couldn't help wondering, *And how often did you make payments to Jermy? Is that why you're so certain it's an account book?*

"Not like Nigel to take that much care over trades-men's bills. If you aren't going to pay, why keep track of it?" Jack's mind appeared to be running at a straight target. "Langston's one of those fellows with a highly developed sense of self-preservation—would never keep records of anything to his detriment."

"Unless it was something he *did* plan to pay, and that's what made it worth a separate accounting. A debt of honor, for example." Danvers joined Jack's line of reasoning.

"Gambling debts! Yes, that could be it. Mind if I keep this for a while?" Jack asked. "I might be able to come up with something."

The viscount agreed, and they returned to the Hall where Danvers took his leave of the son to seek out the father. As usual, Sir John was to be found in his library.

"Review Jermy's papers? You've taken quite an interest in this case, haven't you, m' boy? Well, I'm delighted to see you taking an interest in something—get you out of yourself—good for you. I'm going to examine them myself tomorrow. You're welcome to come along. But today I'm going to Wymondham to hear testimony on the handwriting of those papers they found at Potash. Interested?"

Danvers was indeed interested.

On the drive Danvers asked Sir John about the letter Rush had asked him to deliver.

"Oh, I sent it on to Messrs. Tillett & Mendham, as he asked—quite within his rights to write to his solicitor, of course. Tillett showed it to me." He shook his head. "The tangled tale it told of some fellow named Joe apparently acting for Thomas Jermy and Larner was quite incredible. If Rush wants to pin his hopes of defense on a cockamamy story, he'll have to do better than that."

"You don't think there's any truth to it, then?"

"Not a shred of evidence to back it up. There is no Joe Clarke on the county roles. Rush said he was a lawyer, but if he is he's not licensed. I think it's pure invention."

At the Wymondham police station they were met by Inspector Futter, who had brought the documents over from the Norwich gaol for the convenience of the witnesses, who both lived at Wymondham. Another magistrate was there as well as Sir John. They sat around a long table, and the documents were spread before the experts.

A short, bald banker who was introduced as Samuel Bignold drew out a pair of silver-rimmed spectacles, polished them carefully, hooked them behind his ears, and began a meticulous inspection of the signatures on the papers.

Jesse White, a thin, stooped man, was already wearing spectacles, so he took a large magnifying glass out of his briefcase to examine certain details in the writing. No one spoke for some time as both men considered.

At last, Sir John began the questioning by asking Mr. White what his acquaintance was with Rush's handwriting.

"I am an accountant. I have known the prisoner ten or twelve years. He was at one time an auctioneer and valuer at Wymondham. I acted as his clerk for about four years. He made inventories and other papers, and I copied them."

"So you know Rush's hand well?"

"Indeed, I believe I do. These letters"—he indicated several papers addressed by Rush to various lawyers and agents—"are all in the prisoner's handwriting. And"—he picked up the letter purporting to be from Thomas Jermy to Isaac Jermy and stating the cousin's determination to take possession of Stanfield—"this also is by Mr. Rush."

Sir John leaned forward. "You are saying this letter purporting to be by Thomas Jermy is a forgery?"

"I am."

"Would you be willing to swear to that in court?"

"I will swear that that is what I believe."

The other magistrate peered at the forged document and the letters that had been declared genuine. "Can you tell us the reason for your conclusion? They don't look to me like they were written by the same hand."

"Aside from the fact, which I'm sure I needn't remind you of, that Thomas Jermy's signature is only a mark, notice the shape of particular letters. Although there was an obvious attempt to disguise the writing in the letter signed 'Thomas Jermy,' you will note that the curve of the 'J' on Jermy is the same as that found in the earlier letters. Notice also the shape of the small 'a,' its distinctive roundness."

He pointed with the tip of a pencil, and everyone drew closer to observe. "The 'F's' are the same, generally speaking, and notice the flourish on the capital 'P.' It is smaller on the forged document, but still present."

"Amazing. I would never have seen that," the magistrate said.

"Seems quite conclusive." Sir John nodded. "And now, what do you have to tell us, Mr. Bignold?"

The banker removed his spectacles and rubbed his eyes. "I knew the late Mr. Jermy for many years and was acquainted with his handwriting."

"He was a client of your bank?" Sir John asked.

"He was. We have had the honor of serving three generations of Jermys, although now who knows what will become of the poor lass and her mother." He shook his head.

"Melancholy, indeed," Sir John agreed. "But the signatures?"

"Oh, yes, yes. Forgeries, to be sure."

Sir John's colleague hit the table with relish. "Aha! The rascal signed Jermy's name to those deeds and notices giving Rush and his heirs such good terms on the Stanfield farms?"

"This is Mr. Isaac Jermy's signature." The banker placed a document from his own files on the table.

136

"These"—he pointed to the agreements between Rush and Jermy—"are not Mr. Jermy's signature."

Danvers sat silently at his end of the table. At last Rush's motive was clear. The documents, which he had thought showed good feeling between Rush and Jermy, and therefore indicated the prisoner's innocence, were fakes. As such, they could only become valuable by the death of the parties then in possession of Stanfield Hall.

By the death of Mr. Jermy, his son, and his wife, property to the amount of many thousand pounds might have passed into Rush's hands. That, of course, would only have been if the documents had been undisputed. Here, indeed, was motive for murder, and in the prisoner's own handwriting.

Motive, of course, didn't prove murder, but surely with a motive this strong, the rest could be proved. The weapon must be discovered and Rush's alibi broken.

Still, Danvers drew back from accepting the full application of such proof too quickly. Rush was a respectable farmer, a member of the middle class upon which so much of their nation's solidity and prosperity rested—not one of the lower orders who had always been a prey to violence and vices. If middle class respectability were such a thin veneer, what hope was there for the rest of society?

Nothing more could be done on the investigation now. That evening was the final county celebration for Jack's coming of age. The owner of nearby Tacolneston Hall was holding a feast for the cottagers and laborers of the parish to be followed by a giant All Hallow's Eve bonfire.

Six carriages lined up in front of Ketteringham Hall to transport the party to Tacolneston. Danvers was pleased when the dowager duchess offered him a place in her landau. She was the only one in the party who could make up for the loss of Lady Antonia's company. No matter how severely he had judged Tonia's attack of the vapors, he found he did miss her.

The duchess's coachman tucked a heavy fur rug around her legs before shutting the door and springing onto the driver's seat.

"All this celebrating is certain to make young Jack old before his time. I declare I'm quite surfeited with observances."

Danvers had to admit he was hardly in a festive mood either, but he was willing to make the best of it for the sake of Sir John. "Perhaps you'd be more enthusiastic if I offered to transport you there in my balloon, Your Grace? At any rate, you may be at ease. I understand tonight is to be the last event."

"I should hope so. Lady Catherine isn't strong enough to be forever galavanting about like this. I trust that young scalawag Jack is attending his mother. I had thought to invite him to ride with us, but I didn't see him."

Danvers acquiesced to the duchess's opinions but privately thought it much more likely that Jack was attending to Sarah, making good time now that the field was clear of Langston. He had caught a glimpse of her earlier, wide paisley skirt rustling beneath a richly embroidered, short velvet cape, and her dark curls peeking from the ribbon adornment of a deep-brimmed bonnet.

Doing his duty as escort, Danvers kept up a light conversation with the duchess in spite of a niggling sense of foreboding induced by the duchess's pessimism. When they arrived at Tacolneston, however, there was no opportunity for anything but a festival mood. The carriages let the party off at the end of the avenue, and the celebrants walked in procession to the Hall, accompanied by guns firing, church bells ringing, and a band, somewhat smaller than Hethersett's, but no less enthusiastic.

Flags, mottoes, and garlands decorated the grounds, and long tables loaded with plum pudding, roast beef, and vegetables covered the central grass plot in front of the Hall. At one table sat a hundred men, at the other a hundred women—the cottagers of the parish.

"I tell you"—Sir John clapped Danvers on the shoulder—"it makes my heart leap to see the cordiality of these good people. Hope this gives Jack a sense of the position he's to come into. Where is he, anyway? Must be promenading one of his sisters about—or Sarah Mellors. Pretty little thing. Wouldn't mind if something came of that. You come walk with me."

Danvers was happy to accompany the squire up and down the rows. Everywhere the laborers raised their mugs in greeting and cried, "Cheers!"

The band played until the last crumb of plum pudding disappeared, then Sir Sidney Howes, the lord of Tacolneston and an old friend of the Boileau family, led the cheering for the guest of honor. Sir Sidney jumped up on a table and proposed Jack's health three times, each time to the accompaniment of livelier acclaim. "Hip, hip hooray! Hip hooray! Hip hooray!"

Then, before there could be a response, Mr. Corbould, the rector of Tacolneston, proposed Sir John's health with much emotion. "The finest squire, the best landlord, the most dedicated magistrate, the most devoted husband and father, the most faithful Christian, and the truest friend one could ever know—I give you Sir John Boileau!"

The company shouted its response, and Sir John jumped onto the end of the other table. "My good friends, my most worthy friends, I thank you." He was interrupted by cheers and whistles. "And I want you all to know that if you are ever in need of a friend, you may rely on Lady Catherine and myself. You are to come over to us at Ketteringham at any time." He waited for the response to quiet before he finished. "And, I say to you all, good English men and women, God save the Queen!"

The response was the more moving for its quiet intensity as two hundred loyal subjects stood and, with mugs upraised, repeated, "God save the Queen!" All remained standing and sang as the band played "God save our gracious Queen, God bless our noble Queen . . ."

At the end of the song, Mr. Corbould then proposed Lady Catherine's health, and Sir John led her forward to warm applause and spoke for her. "Friends, as Lady Catherine is so overcome by your gracious warmth, she cannot speak herself, she wants me to tell you that she feels a deep interest in you all and thanks you all."

The carriages then drew up, and the gentry rode to the end of the avenue, followed by the cheering crowd on foot, to where a great mountain of firewood waited. When the party was assembled, Sir Sidney's man came forward bearing a flaming torch.

"No, no, not to me," the host protested. "The guest of honor. It is Jack's bonfire. He must light it."

The party was quiet as no one stepped forward.

"I say, Jack, come up! We're waiting." Sir John's voice rang with command, but there was no response.

The crowd murmured and shifted uneasily. "Frank." Sir John nudged his second son. "Take the torch. In this light no one will know. Where is that blasted brother of yours anyway? If he's off in the corner with some country wench, I'll—I'll—"

It was never made explicit what he would do, because Frank, with a look of open delight, grasped the torch from an amazed Sir Sidney. Milking his moment of unaccustomed glory for all its worth, Frank held the torch aloft like an Olympic runner and circled the bonfire three times, touching his torch to each side, then stood back with an air of satisfaction to watch the spreading ring of flame.

Once more the crowd cheered. The band struck up a lively country dance. The farm lads swung their favorite girls around and around to the spirited rhythm.

But the Ketteringham party would not stay for the dance. Sir John stomped back to his carriage, helped Lady

Catherine in, and then checked the members in each coach.

Was this everyone who had driven out with them? They were quite sure Jack had not been with them? Nor ridden on the box with the driver? Had anyone seen Jack the entire evening? At the conclusion of each series of negative answers the squire slammed the door shut and ordered the driver back to Ketteringham.

At the Hall every servant was roused, and a complete search organized of the manor, stables, church, and grounds. The squire ordered Ama to accompany her mother to bed and sit by her, the younger children were to stay in the nursery with their nurse, and it was understood that the dowager duchess would be excused with her maid and Sarah to bear her company. But everyone else was to search for Jack.

Danvers took to the park. If Jack had chosen to go poaching tonight rather than attend his celebration, it was ridiculously bad judgment on his part, and he richly deserved the upbraiding he was sure to receive. The viscount did not choose to entertain darker considerations.

Off to the right of Ringer's lodge, Danvers heard a rustle in the brush. He stopped and covered his lantern. All was silent. It must have been merely the wind or a small animal. He reached to open the lantern when he heard it again—the snap of a twig, as if someone were trying to move undetected on the other side of that hedgerow.

As silently as he could, Danvers moved along the path toward where he knew there was a stile over the barrier. Every few steps he stopped, held his breath, and listened. He fancied he could hear breathing on the other side of the bushes.

Danvers was only a few feet from the opening when he blundered into the low branch of a tree and reacted with a started gasp that surely gave his presence away—if his quarry didn't already know he was there. The sound of running footsteps crashing through the brush told him it was too late for caution. He dropped his lantern and plunged headlong, clearing the stile in one leap and lunging forward into the dark, following the black form he could just make out disappearing into the trees ahead.

Danvers was clearly the younger man and longer in stride. But the leader knew his territory and found trails Danvers could not put his feet to in the dark. Using his ears more than his eyes Danvers darted down yet another invisible trail. Thrashing through snagging branches and over matted leaves, he barely kept up with his prey.

Had not the most startling misfortune befallen the fleeing man, Danvers would have had no chance of catching him. But there came a metallic snap. A clank of iron. The man fell to the ground with a howl of pain.

Danvers was on him in a moment. "Who are you? What do you think you're doing skulking around here at night?"

"*Aeoww*, me leg! It's broke!" the man wailed.

Danvers saw the situation.

"All right, hold still." He grasped the iron jaws of the trap and pulled with all his strength. The metal refused to move.

"The lever. Push the blessed lever!"

Danvers fumbled in the direction the man was jabbing his finger. After a couple of false attempts he found the release. The trap sprang open. The man pulled his foot out and rocked back and forth, cradling it and whimpering.

"What is this? I've heard Sir John repeatedly warn Ringer that he won't have traps set in the park—far too dangerous."

The man sniffed, then mumbled, "'Twere me own. It's your fault, though, comin' at a man like a bat outa 'ell."

"Yours? So you're one of these poachers I've been hearing about." Danvers grabbed the man by the scruff of his collar even though he was unlikely to bolt on his injured ankle.

"*Ow.* No need a that, gov'nor. Don't get rough. I ain't hurt nuffin but meself."

Danvers gave him a rough shake, which produced another howl. "Have you seen Jack Boileau tonight? Don't try to lie to me, or I'll turn you over to the authorities. They'd be only too happy to get their hands on a poacher. There's probably a reward out for you. There's been enough going on in this neighborhood blamed on poachers—and maybe they aren't so far wrong."

"No, no, gov'nor. Old Buckby never hurt nuffin. Friend of the animals, I am."

"You expect me to believe that? You sitting there sniveling with pain from your own trap, and you tell me you don't hurt anything?"

"A'right, a'right. But I hain't trespassin'. I got permission from the 'eir 'isself."

Danvers smiled. So this was Buckby. Here was his chance to check Jack's alibi. "So, it's true, is it? You've been taking Jack out poaching with you?"

"Tha's right. I give 'im lessons, like. Right lot I taught 'im. Bright lad, learns quick."

"And the night of his coming of age—did you give him a lesson that night?"

Buckby rocked back and forth a few more times. "Oh, aye. The night of all them fireworks. Not a good night for poachin'. All that poppin' and blastin' scarin' the game—and people trampin' about in the woods. Later though, after it quieted down a bit, we 'ad a rare treat. Two 'ares apiece we caught. And I taught 'im 'ow to skin 'em on the spot. But I ain't seen 'ide nor 'air of 'im tonight, and that's the gospel."

"All right, let's take a look at that leg of yours." The cloud cover was spotty, and at the moment there was enough moonlight for Danvers to see to wrap his handkerchief around the poacher's ankle as a makeshift bandage. "Be sure you wash that out good when you get home. Hot water and lye soap."

Buckby nodded.

"Do you have any iodine?"

He nodded again.

"Well, swab it out good. You don't want an infection setting in."

Buckby skulked off through the woods.

Danvers worked at the metal stake until it came up from the ground. The poacher was sure to have more traps, but at least he'd dispose of this one and save an animal a painful death. Maybe the experience would convince Buckby to stick to the use of guns that killed quickly and cleanly. Then Danvers recrossed the stile and retrieved his extinguished lantern.

So. He had found back-up for Jack's story—of a sort. Buckby had been vague enough that there could have been time for a visit to Stanfield first. But Danvers would choose to accept Jack's alibi as long as he could. Even though the heir's lapse tonight made it harder than ever to have faith in him.

Danvers had taken a lighted lantern from the gardener and started toward the gamekeeper's lodge in renewed search when he saw a shadowy figure on the path ahead. For only a moment did he wonder why anyone was searching without a lantern. From experience he recognized Caroline.

Staying well behind, he watched as she slipped up the path toward the church. He started to follow, then stopped short as another figure came to meet her. There was no mistaking the tall, gaunt figure that looked severe even in silhouette. Caroline was not slipping out to meet the curate, but the vicar.

Danvers's mind boggled. A liaison with Andrews? Carry? He shook his head. Impossible. Each explanation was more unthinkable than the last.

But at the end of the search, there was not even an unthinkable explanation for the heir's whereabouts. Jack had disappeared.

10

In spite of the tedium of sitting through family prayers again the next morning, Danvers found his own company sufficiently unpleasant to make him decide against taking breakfast in his room. The trouble was, his thoughts came with him, and being with the family simply focused his uneasy questions. What was going on in this seeming bastion of respectability?

"Hide thy face from my sins, and blot out all mine iniquities . . ." Sir John continued yesterday's reading from Psalm 51.

Danvers looked around. Caroline sat across from him, her pale head bowed, her hands quiet in her lap, betraying not the least evidence of discomfort. Indeed, had he not seen her at her tryst, Danvers would have thought—so far as another can judge such things—that Caroline was worshiping with the truest devotion of any in the room.

"A broken and a contrite heart, O God, thou wilt not despise . . ."

Far more worrying than the question of Carry's secret, however, was Jack's empty seat to his father's left. Try as he might to put it out of his mind, Danvers could not dismiss the fact that Jack had disappeared immediately after the payment book—if indeed that was what it was—

145

had been found. Did that mean the book was the heir's? Were they his gambling debts? Was the list payments made to Jermy? Or, worse yet, amounts owing?

Danvers thought of Sir John's wrath over the disclosure of the earlier debts. Were there yet more? Even if Danvers accepted Jack's alibi for the night of the murder—and he struggled to do so—the disclosure of more debt would cause enormous discord. Just when he thought he'd found daylight, the clouds rolled in again.

"As it was in the beginning, is now, and ever shall be, world without end. Amen," Danvers intoned with the others. Then he had to restrain himself from jumping to his feet and rushing from the breakfast parlor. He must search Jack's room.

He had barely touched his hand to the doorknob when Dalling emerged from the dressing room. "May I help you, my lord?" Morning light from the window reflected on his bald head.

"That's all right, Dalling. I'm just going to see if I can find some clue to Jack's whereabouts. You're quite sure he said nothing to you about where he was going?"

"Quite sure, sir. I should have told Sir John immediately if I had any information." His perpetually concerned look deepened.

"Yes, of course. And you have no idea what time he left?"

"None at all. Staff was given the afternoon off yesterday, what with the whole family going over to Tacolneston. I went into Norwich to visit my brother."

"What about Jack's clothes? Can you tell what he was wearing, or if he packed a valise?"

"Certainly." Here the lanky Dalling straightened his shoulders. He knew his job. "Four linen shirts have been taken from the press, his brown silk and worsted frock coat with the cut silk velvet collar—"

"Dash it, man! I don't require the pattern cards. Just tell me what he took."

"I was attempting to do so, sir. His blue-black wool dress coat, his gray and black houndstooth trousers, his tan trousers, his heavy cloak with shoulder cape, top hat—"

"That will do. It would appear he has gone to the city and plans a stay of several days' duration."

"Precisely what I should surmise, sir. Although why he should pack his own bags is more than I can guess. As if I wouldn't have missed my afternoon off to be of service. And why he should not ask me to accompany him—his boots are certain to return in unspeakable condition."

"Thank you, Dalling. That will do." Danvers's relief left him almost weak. He had not realized until now how much effort he had put into blocking out thoughts of Jack's having been abducted or worse. If he had packed a portmanteau of city clothes, he may have done a bunker, but apparently it was of his own free will.

He paused. He wasn't grasping at straws again, was he? It wasn't possible that if someone involved in the Jermys' demise had turned on Jack he would have allowed Jack to pack a bag first, was it? The idea was patently absurd. Far more likely that Jack was freely keeping an appointment of his own—with fellow conspirators?—to divide undiscovered spoils of their crime?

But if of his own will, why hadn't he left a note? Danvers turned to search the room. The mantel was lined with invitations giving evidence of nothing more sinister than ambitious mamas who would be happy to snare the heir to Ketteringham for their daughters. The shelves were stacked helter-skelter with books that reflected Jack's interest in guns and hunting. There was nothing that offered a clue as to his whereabouts.

At first glance, Jack's writing table was such a clutter it appeared hopeless. But Danvers set himself to work through it. And amid the assortment of papers, letters, bills, notes from friends, and messages apparently written in reply but not delivered, he found an answer: two half-finished love poems and a tender note to Sarah, finished then ripped in half in lover's despair.

A slow smile spread over Danvers's face. He felt such a positive relief he pushed back in his chair and ran both hands through his hair. Of course! What could be more obvious than that Jack had been caught in the violent throes of love? Under the impulse of passion he had packed his most respectable wardrobe and rushed off to London to seek permission from the Mellors to pay his addresses to their daughter.

It was not surprising that Sarah had said nothing. She didn't know. Danvers admired the boy's scrupulousness. Sarah was just out of the classroom. It would be most improper to speak to her without her parents' permission. And Jack was clever too. What better way to circumvent Nigel Langston's competition than by winning her parents to his own side?

Yes, the lad showed remarkable resourcefulness and restraint toward Sarah if he were so in the grip of love that he would rush off to London on such an errand without letting his mother know. He had probably even forgotten all about the bonfire party that night.

Danvers smiled. He had been similarly gripped with the pangs of love at twenty-one. The smile faded. Charlotte. Lovely, beloved, lost Charlotte. For the first time in many days he was washed anew with the combination of mourning and guilt that accompanied his every thought of Charlotte.

Danvers was about to leave the desk when his own name, scrawled across a folded sheet of paper, stopped him. Ah, Jack had thought to leave a note of explanation.

But the three lines he found there sent a chill down his spine:

"£1250
Blackmail inescapable
3 or 4 days"

The note was undated. Was this another of the many Jack had written over apparently several weeks but failed to post? The papers were so rearranged and scattered it was impossible to garner any meaning from its position on the desk. And what did it mean?

Was someone blackmailing Jack? Or was Jack confessing to blackmailing someone else? If Jack was the victim, what had he done? Was it not really just a simple loan Jermy had been trying to collect, but rather extortion? Or had it nothing to do with Jermy? Perhaps someone else, such as Nigel?

Danvers stood long, the note between his fingers. If Nigel had been doing the extorting, perhaps the book had fallen from Nigel's pocket. Perhaps it was an account of blackmail payments. Perhaps Nigel had been blackmailing Jack for something, and Jack shot Hickling and then blamed the death on Nigel to get rid of him. Or if Hickling had been the blackmailer . . .

Danvers crumpled the note and stuffed it in his pocket. This was all useless speculation. He was sick of playing blindman's bluff—especially when he was the blind man.

"Ah, there you are, Danvers. Dalling said I might find you here. Still want to go to Stanfield today?"

Danvers couldn't believe Sir John sounded so hale. "You're going—" He looked helplessly around Jack's room to indicate its owner's absence.

"Certainly. No reason for me to shirk my duty just because that young rake decides to run off to London. You can be sure I'll give him whatfor when he returns for upsetting his mother like that."

"You're satisfied he's gone to London?" Danvers had reached that conclusion as well, but he wanted reassurance.

"Not a doubt. Dalling tells me he took his city clothes. The groom reported finding his horse and phaeton stabled at Wymondham station. Obvious he caught the train to London. Shame we raised such a hue and cry last

149

night, but it was a bit of a facer finding he missed his own celebration. How I'll ever meet Sir Sidney again, I can't say."

Sir John delivered his monologue while leading the way to the entrance hall. The footman there handed both men their heaviest coats as well as top hats and gloves.

They drove to Stanfield under a sky the color of a bruise. It was as if the weather, having turned the calendar page to November, had decided to drop the last leaf from the trees, lower the temperature ten degrees, and cover the countryside with a heavy frost.

They found Stanfield Hall with its curtains drawn, black crepe on the windows, and a wreath on the door. The mousy-haired, bespeckled Watson opened the door with a solemnity that would have befitted the doorkeeper of an actual tomb. The black and white of the marble floor was repeated in the black-draped hall mirror and the vase of long-stemmed white lilies.

The sickly-sweet smell of the lilies followed them across the staircase hall. Danvers had to restrain a shudder as they passed almost directly over the spot where Mr. Jermy, Jr.'s, body had lain. He hoped the bloodstains had come out of the carpet, but the somber light in the room revealed nothing.

Watson opened the door on the library and stood aside. The room was a model of proper fashion. Every table and both mantels were draped with fringed velvet scarves. Potted palms and dried flower arrangements filled every corner. The furniture was heavy, carved black oak— proof of the occupants' stability and respectability. This was not a family that could be brutally murdered in its own home. And yet it had been.

Sir John frowned at Watson. "I trust you received my note that we'd be calling on official business. Please be so good as to light a fire in here. Or better yet, both of them. And turn up all the lamps, man. Can't perform my duty in the dark."

"Yes, sir." Watson turned on his heel so fast his spectacles slipped on his beaky nose, and in a few minutes a housemaid was fanning a flame on the hearth.

Danvers was glad of the warmth. He found the job of going through a dead man's papers a chilling one at best. An intensely private person himself, Danvers had considerable trouble justifying his own desire for privacy with all the snooping he was doing into the affairs of others.

"You take the desk, Charles. I'll do the file cabinet," Boileau directed.

Danvers was glad for official orders to salve his conscience. For some time the only sound in the room was the rustling of papers and a crackling on the hearth.

At last Boileau held up a sheet of foolscap. "Ah, yes. Here are some notes Jermy made before he was examined on the bankruptcy fiat against Rush in London in May. That can't have produced any good feelings between them. I suppose this had better go into evidence." He laid the paper on a side table, then turned to examine another file.

Charles finished one drawer without finding anything of importance and banged it shut with a sigh of annoyance.

The magistrate was having better luck. "Listen to this letter Rush sent Jermy last April." Boileau leaned back in his chair and read. "'You have completely ruined me, so far as my own property goes. If you think I shall not take steps to ruin you and your family, you never were more deceived in your life. You do not know me yet. Hitherto I have done nothing but what I have told you of, but unless you answer this letter satisfactorily, nothing on earth shall prevent me treading in your steps, and paying you off in the same most villainous and base coin as you have me.'"

"Good heavens, did the man write a confession of his crime before he committed it?"

"Afraid it isn't quite that simple. He gets rather muddled here and runs on a bit about what he terms his own weakness regarding Jermy. Then he says, 'Don't take this letter in the wrong light, for you may believe me when I tell you that such is my weak and foolish way of looking at what has taken place that, after bringing your dear old father in my mind's eye, I feel as great reluctance to commence hostilities against you as if you had never wronged me in the way you have. And I do believe, if you were now to propose fair and reasonable terms to what I have mentioned, I could go on as if nothing had ever gone wrong with us.'"

"Fair and reasonable terms?" Danvers asked.

"Apparently Rush's mother's lease on the Felmingham farm and his own debt to Jermy."

"Strange man. He sounds so violent one moment and soft as a baby the next."

"Yes, listen to this: 'I am quite sure no one ever had my interest at heart more than your father. I am sure if he could have been told what would have taken place between us or had the least idea of it, I should have been well protected from anything you or anyone else could have done, to have brought me to the state you have. For I will defy you or anyone else to say that I ever asked him for a favor in my life, but it was granted. And when I consider the hundreds of happy hours I have spent in his company, I could almost say to you—do as you like, and behave as bad as you can, I cannot do anything against a son of his.

"'Therefore, for his sake, think of my children and my dear, dear mother, and do not let me loose every tie that still links my best wishes for your family's welfare, for, if you do, God only knows what will be the consequences.'"

Danvers sat silent for a moment. "It almost sounds like a cry for help—as if he knew his own capacity for violence but didn't want to give in to it."

Boileau was still shaking his head over the letter when Danvers opened the bottom drawer on the desk, one filled the length of it with files. The name *Langston* on a tab made him put all other considerations out of his mind.

152

He spent a long time wading through leases, mortgages, contracts, bills of sale, letters from Langston and copies of Jermy's replies regarding dispositions of assets and all the normal transactions one would have through their man of business.

Danvers scanned a letter from Nigel instructing Jermy to pay some money owing him from a tenant directly into the St. James's branch of the Bank of England and to send notice of it to him. All very routine. Danvers tossed the letter aside.

Here was a copy of Nigel's father's will and the probate proceedings, when he died seven years before and Nigel succeeded to the estate. The property had been heavily encumbered, due largely to his father's gaming debts, but not so much so that careful management couldn't have brought it right again. Unfortunately, as Danvers continued through the file, he could find no evidence that Nigel had provided the careful husbandry that would have produced this happy state of affairs. Indeed, the notices from creditors threatening bankruptcy proceedings became more and more numerous the farther he worked into the file.

But it was the next section of correspondence that made Danvers catch his breath. The date of the first letter made his blood rise so fast his ears rang. 16 September 1847. The day after Charlotte's death. Her body could hardly have been cold yet when her second cousin wrote to his lawyer about her estate.

When Danvers recalled his own pain at that time, such crassness on the part of one of her family made him boil. But the anger was preferable. The moment it began to lessen, the agony he thought he had put behind him returned with the fresh recalling of the event.

He forced himself to read the letter. " . . . And as I believe myself to be a legatee of my cousin, the late Charlotte Auchincloss, I hereby request that you file notice of my claim with the probate court . . ."

Danvers, who was only now emerging from mourning, recalled that Nigel's had lasted until barely after the funeral.

The file told the complete story. In response to his client's letter, Jermy had sent a pleading to the probate court requesting notice of its proceedings in the estate of Charlotte Auchincloss. At the probate of the estate, notice went to all heirs, legatees, and bevisees. Charlotte's Uncle Edward had inherited the real estate that had belonged to the orphaned girl. But the property that had been her mother's, and all cash, stocks, and bonds—nearly £15,000 worth annually—had gone to Charlotte's cousin, Nigel Langston.

Danvers was astounded. He had no idea he had been affianced to such a wealthy woman. Not that that would have mattered to him in the least. His own wealth left him completely free to marry for love. But somehow knowing this about Charlotte made her dearer yet. That with so much wealth at her fingertips she could have been so unspoiled, so gentle and kind, have cared so little about making a splash in the great world of London society . . .

That was not a helpful road of thought for him to follow.

"Find anything, Charles?" Sir John called him back to the matter at hand.

"Nothing relevant to the Rush case." Danvers returned the file and continued his investigation, but the deep furrows remained in his forehead. None of the theories he and Jack had postulated in the shooting field seemed to hold up. There was nothing here to suggest that Jermy might have had reason to blackmail his client or that Langston might have blackmailed and murdered his attorney.

Nigel's pushing to collect Charlotte's money was the height of bad taste but hardly a matter for blackmail. Apparently all the proceedings had been perfectly legal and aboveboard. Charles had always known that Charlotte and Nigel were cousins, of course, and the fact that Charlotte, who had lived with an elderly aunt from the time her parents died several years ago, had left an inheritance to some cousins or relatives was no secret. The size of the inheritance, however, and Nigel's haste were startling news. How was it possible for Nigel to be so shockingly debt-ridden after coming into money like that?

Sir John's stack of documents to be submitted to the coroner's jury had grown considerably by the time he closed the bottom file drawer and turned to Danvers. "Finished?"

"Almost. Just this little drawer left." He pulled it open and took out a flat box containing a few odds and ends of papers. "Doesn't look like much here." Danvers started to close the lid, then stopped.

"Find something?"

Danvers reluctantly handed the paper to Sir John. An agreement that Jack's debt to Jermy Jermy would double to £1250 if not paid by the end of October. Less than two weeks after Jermy was murdered.

"Thank you." The squire slipped the note in his pocket.

£1250 was the amount named in the note Danvers found in Jack's room. Was it just coincidence? Or did the fact that Danvers had seen the book make Jack bolt while Danvers followed up the straw man Jack had erected by suggesting Nigel as the guilty party?

After the warmth of the library, the entrance hall seemed to have chilled several degrees. Watson was holding Danvers's coat for him when there was a knock at the door. Danvers quickly shrugged into the coat, and the butler, with his accustomed gravity, opened the door.

The new chill in the hall had nothing to do with the temperature of the outside air as Caroline Boileau and the vicar entered.

"I did not expect to find you here, Caroline," Sir John said.

"I am calling on Mrs. Jermy, Papa. Surely you would not have me neglect my Christian duty to visit the sick and the bereaved."

Sir John bowed his head in stiffest assent.

"I am much relieved to hear that the festivities have come to an end, Sir John." Andrews handed his low-crowned black hat to Watson. "Sinful drunkenness ought not to be allowed even for the sake of family celebrations. An outing for the Sunday school children was all very well, but I understand that there was dancing at the next event and that one of the kitchen maids was taken with hysterics from overfatigue. Such levity must not go unchecked."

"Indeed, Vicar. I am sure we can all count on you to remind us of our duty." Boileau was in the carriage before he spoke again. "Blasted long-faced legalist. My Bible says God is love. Don't know what that man's been reading to think religion has to be sour to be true. Don't want him contaminating my family with his holier-than-thouism."

Danvers remained silent, but the image in his mind of a dark form slipping toward the vicarage would not go away.

11

Two days later there was still no word from Jack, and efforts of the family not to look at his empty place during family prayers and meals were so loud it was as if an alarm went off each time someone's eyes flicked past the gap in the seating. Now that the celebrations were concluded, most of the nonfamily guests took their leave. Tommy left the morning after the bonfire with barely a "Fare thee well" from Carry.

Sarah, whose springlike freshness seemed to fade a little each day—was it from concern for Antonia? worry over Jack's disappearance? or missing Nigel's company?—accepted Sir John's offer of a carriage and the escort of his second son, Frank, to the residence of the Baron of Barston in the hopes that she could now be of comfort to Antonia.

Danvers couldn't help noting the alacrity with which Frank undertook the task. He had never seen the freckled face of the eighteen-year-old curve in a broader grin—even brighter than when he had done such an enthusiastic job of lighting the bonfire in Jack's absence.

For the first time it occurred to Danvers how overshadowed Frank was by his older brother. One seemed to forget Frank existed when Jack was around. Was it possible this ruddy, seemingly open-faced boy harbored deep resentments that could have in some way contributed to the heir's disappearance? The viscount berated himself for having fallen into such a suspicious manner of thinking.

Danvers and the dowager duchess remained the only guests. He wondered if the decent thing to do would be to take himself off and let the family be private. But Sir John seemed to encourage his company, and Danvers had no desire to leave with so many questions unanswered.

"Coroner's jury in Norwich today," Sir John said as he returned the large family Bible to its place of prominence on the sideboard. "Care to go with me, Danvers?"

Charles accepted readily. He hadn't been following this case closer than an investigating officer only to be left out now.

"Don't wait meals for us, my dear." Boileau gave Lady Catherine a good-bye kiss somewhere near her cheek. "This may run on a bit."

It was fortunate that seats had been saved for magistrates, or Sir John and his guest might have been obliged to stand out in the hall with the flock of the curious who gathered at the Castle.

Danvers was shocked by the number of apparently upper middle-class women who came, heavily veiled and accompanied by their maids, to hear firsthand the bloody details at which they would have fainted if forced to hear them in their own drawing rooms. He wondered how many men knew their wives were indulging in such entertainment. Few husbands would allow their wives or daughters to read newspapers—beyond the society and fashion pages, which they handed over to them. Surely they would have ordered these women home if they had any idea of their presence at court where an accused cold-blooded murderer would be in full view.

"Please rise for Her Majesty's coroner."

Danvers stood, then sat again with the rest. The early stages of the hearing may well have titillated the interest of the properly repressed ladies in the room, but Danvers found it repetitively boring. Officer after officer swore to what he had seen and done on the night of the murder. Then magistrates began going through the endless documents produced by searches of Potash Farm and Stanfield Hall, including a repetition of the testimony concerning the authenticity—and lack thereof—of the papers.

The only item of interest to Danvers was the account books Sergeant Pont produced—its end papers matching the note the murderer dropped in Stanfield Hall. These books, which Pont had found at Potash, were intact, but they were part of a set of three, and the missing volume had not been found. Had it not turned up because Rush had burned it after ripping out the sheet for his forgery?

But then the mood became charged with drama. The bailiff and two assistants approached the witness box, removed the railing, and positioned a heavy plank to serve as a ramp up to the dais. All rustling stopped in the gallery. Everyone in the room leaned forward for a better look as Eliza Chastney was wheeled in, recumbent on a carriage made especially for the purpose. It appeared much like a crib used for the repose of an oversize infant. Danvers noted that Rush dropped his head, seemingly overcome by the maid's suffering.

"In consequence of her wound, which has not healed, and the weak state of health induced by her injury, Miss Chastney will give her evidence lying down. Mr. Nichols, the Jermy family physician whose evidence you heard earlier, will attend his patient." The long-faced, white-haired coroner punctuated this announcement with a rap from the gavel and a nod to Mr. Nichols. "I appreciate your coming here at such considerable inconvenience to yourself, Miss Chastney. Please tell the court what happened on the night of the shooting."

Eliza attempted to raise herself on one elbow. Mr. Nichols moved to lay her down again but arranged her pillows to elevate her head. A few brown, corkscrew curls untucked themselves from under her lace cap and made shadows on her thin face.

"I heard a gun, then another, and then a groan. I went to the passage and saw my mistress, Mrs. Jermy. I threw my arm around her and took her hand in mine and said, 'My dear mistress, what is the matter?' Then I saw Mr. Jermy Jermy on the floor. A man came from the dining room door. He had a short gun or pistol up to his shoulder. He leveled it with both hands and shot me."

The witness gasped and beads of sweat stood out on her forehead. The physician wiped her face with a cloth that smelled pungently of vinegar, felt her pulse, then nodded that she could continue.

"I did not fall directly. Another shot followed at once. I saw my mistress's arm twirl about. I twisted round and fell down. *I am going to die and no one will come and help me,* I thought. Then the butler, Watson, came. I remember no more until I awoke and found myself wounded in the hip."

"And did you get a good look at your assailant before he shot you, Miss Chastney?"

"I saw the head and shoulders of the man who shot me. There was something remarkable in the head. It was flat on the top—the hair set out bushy—and he was wide shouldered."

Every head in the courtroom turned to view Rush's burly head and shoulders.

"And did you form an opinion as to who the man was?"

"I formed a belief immediately who the man was. I still have no doubt in my own mind about it."

"Who do you believe it to be?"

"The prisoner."

Eliza was pushed from the room in her outsized perambulator, one wheel squeaking all the way down the aisle.

A hush held over the courtroom until the double doors at the rear swung shut behind her. Then a buzz of female voices, equal to that at any afternoon soiree, filled the room.

The coroner's face grew longer yet. He gaveled. "I will remind those in attendance that this is a court established under Her Majesty's direct authority. Anyone creating interruptions will suffer immediate penalties."

The room was quiet.

Although the testimonies wore on—servants, surgeons, villagers, and tenants—nothing could match the drama of Eliza's evidence until the final witness. Emily Sandford entered the room, and the accompanying murmurs and twitters grew so loud the coroner gaveled them down with another warning. "I'll have it quiet in here, or I'll order the bailiff to clear the courtroom."

The room was silent, but one could feel the straining attention as Emily Sandford took the witness stand, in black gown and small white collar, huddled as usual beneath her black knit shawl.

"Miss Sandford." The coroner nodded his hoary head. "Mr. Andrews has told me that you are a God-fearing woman."

"Oh, yes, your lordship!" She hesitated. "I won't say I've never done wrong." She looked at her swollen abdomen. "I know there's many as call my taking up with Mr. Rush living in sin, but—"

"Quite so. It won't be necessary to go into that. It was another commandment I had in mind."

"Sir?"

"'Thou shalt not bear false witness.' Now, Emily, you wouldn't want to stand before your Maker someday with a lie on your conscience?"

Emily's eyes grew wide. "Indeed I wouldn't, sir—and that's God's truth."

"Then, in full awareness of the danger to your immortal soul, Emily Sandford, I want you to tell me what occurred at Potash Farm on the night of the shooting at Stanfield Hall."

161

Emily was quiet. Her eyes never lifted.

"With God as your judge, Miss Sandford."

Her first words were inaudible.

"Speak up, please, Miss Sandford."

"Mr. Andrews, the vicar, warned me that if I do not speak the truth, I will be subject to the penalty of perjury in this life and punishment in the next. It has preyed mightily on my mind."

"As well it should. What do you have to tell us now? Did you speak the truth when you gave witness before?"

"No." Emily burst into tears.

A wave of excited murmurs washed through the gallery, and again the coroner gaveled for silence. "You will now tell us what really happened, Miss Sandford."

Emily took one fleeting glance at the prisoner sitting on the front bench below her, gave a loud sniff, and took a gulp of air. "Mr. Rush was out for about an hour. I did not see him come in. He went upstairs into his own room. After a short while he came down again carrying his boots, with his stockings about his heels and I think with his coat off."

She paused for another sniff and gulp of air. "He said, 'If any inquiry should be made, you say that I was not out more than ten minutes. Now make haste and put out your light and go to bed as soon as you can.' I asked him where I should sleep, and he told me I was to sleep in my own room—for the first time for a considerable length of time."

It required three sharp raps of the gavel to silence the tittering in the room. "That will be all, Miss Sandford. You may stand down."

As she took her seat, Rush caught her eye. "You have done all you can to hang me."

The coroner turned to the jury. "Do you wish to adjourn to consider the evidence you have heard?"

The jurymen put their heads together, then the foreman turned to the coroner. "No need, your honor. We think he should be tried for murder."

162

The coroner rapped sharply three times, and the bailiff hustled Rush to his feet.

"As this jury has brought in an indictment, James Blomfield Rush, you will be bound over to stand trial for the willful murder of Mr. Isaac Jermy and Mr. Jermy Jermy."

Above the final rapping of the gavel and the buzz of the crowd, Rush's voice could be heard clearly. "My lord, I am innocent of that, thank God Almighty."

The way from the Castle was jammed, and the noise and excitement on the street in front so turbulent as to make Danvers wonder if another murder had been committed. On closer inspection, however, he discovered the crowds were gathered around various street hawkers, who were promoting their wares at the top of their lungs.

"Ruddy patterers—should be run in," Sir John growled. "As if the populace wasn't stirred up enough about this affair."

Danvers noted that the genteel ladies emerging from the courtroom would not be seen purchasing a broadside but opened their reticules to supply their maids with pennies to secure the scandal sheets for them while they were handed demurely into their carriages. He approached the patterer who was attracting the largest crowd by the use of pictorial boards illustrating the contents of the merchandise he was hawking.

"Ladies and gents, read all the details of the 'orrible crimes committed by this one man." He adjusted his brown cloth cap and held up the brightest of his picture boards. Painted in garish colors and wholly negligent of perspective or background, each board was divided into compartments and graphically depicted a series of blood-splashed murders Rush was said to have committed.

A young boy, in cap, muffler, and fingerless gloves, stood at the patterer's feet, dispensing broadsheets in exchange for pennies.

The hawker himself was too busy with his spiel to

pause even to take money. "You won't believe it—but it's God's honest truth. All right 'ere in Norfolk . . ."

Danvers held out his copper and took a sheet. Its smudged print evidenced that it had been brought to market before the ink was dry.

MONSTER MURDERER CONFESSES!!

The Chilling Confessions of James B. Rush

The numerous monstrosities committed by that fiendish, brutal murderer James Rush were disclosed today at the Castle. The heinous Rush confessed before coroner and jury to committing no fewer than five murders, including that of his old grandmother fourteen years ago, whom he ignominiously buried under an apple tree in the garden, and more recently to the murder of his wife whom he lasciviously replaced with an innocent young governess and successively ravished . . .

The details bore on. Danvers didn't know whether to laugh or to be outraged. "This is monstrous!"

"Murder is always monstrous." Sir John signaled his coachman to pull to the curb.

"I mean this broadsheet. Not a word in it is true. No such murders were even hinted at, much less confessed to. Rush even maintains his innocence of the Jermy charge."

"Take me home, man. I've missed my tea," the squire ordered his driver. "No one expects truth. They want excitement. Reporting that an accused murderer claimed he was innocent wouldn't sell newspapers."

"But it's all a hoax."

Boileau shrugged. "Good for the publishers. I understand that printer fellow Mayhew was deep in dun territory before this murder. Now has all his bills paid. By the time of the actual trial and hanging he'll have a tidy savings."

"And no one tries to stop it?"

"Why should they? One of those Greek fellows (Aristotle, wasn't it? You should remember—your Oxford days aren't so far behind you) said the populace needs their share of violence, and if they don't get it vicariously by public hangings and the like, they'll turn more violent themselves. I suppose it's what Andrews would call original sin."

"I daresay he might be right. But that's no reason to pander to it."

"What he's sure to say is that's why man needs Divine forgiveness—I fear we'll never hear the end of it from the pulpit. It's enough to make me think we might remove to London early this year."

Danvers laughed and shook his head. "And yet you never miss a service."

Boileau shrugged. "One has a duty. It is my responsibility to do the right thing, no matter what my opinion of another fellow's actions—or his theology."

12

It was far more than duty or theology, however, that filled Ketteringham Church to overflowing on Sunday. Perhaps word of Andrews's influence on Emily Sandford had spread through the parish, or perhaps it was the same love of spectacle as affected the buyers of broadsheets and the gentlewomen who slipped off heavily veiled to trials. Whatever the impetus, there was no doubt of the stir caused by Andrews's announcement that he would express his views on the Rush matter from the pulpit.

The church was crowded before the morning service began. Only those possessing locked pews were able to take their accustomed seats. The vicar looked out over the congregation, then shook his head. "You are mistaken. I intend to speak of Rush in the afternoon service."

A total stranger sitting in the fourth row spoke up. "We are come to secure seats for the afternoon."

Throughout the next hours, carriages continued to arrive from all over Norfolk. When the squire's party returned for afternoon service they found hundreds crowded in the churchyard. And inside, people were stuffed like figs in a cask. Even the windows were darkened from faces trying to peer through the obscure glass. Many of the locked pews had been scaled, and people were sitting two deep.

The squire gave a snort of satisfaction that his position had been awarded sufficient respect to keep his pew inviolate. "Good job Lady Catherine and the duchess didn't care to attend—they'd have been overcome in this squeeze."

Danvers doubted there was much that could overset the Dowager Duchess of Aethelbert, who traced her title back to the ruler of Kent in 500 A.D. But since the curate, Mr. Parnell, had begun the hymn singing, he was spared a reply. After the singing of three hymns—all five verses of each—there was a stir as Andrews entered at the back of the church.

He had just begun to press his way through the crowd when a woman, unable to force her way in on her own, grabbed his arm. "May I lay hold of you?"

Andrews did not reply but did not shake her off as he inched forward. She clung to him, and he dragged her with him to a front position by the reading desk. All that was left, Danvers thought, was for someone to remove the slates from the church roof and lower a member by ropes.

Andrews's gaze swept the throng before him, and he raised his arm in a gesture to address them. Then he stopped. His arm froze in mid-sweep before him, his mouth opened, but no sound came out.

Danvers and the amazed vicar were perhaps the only ones in the room who noticed—Andrews had forgotten to put on his gown. He lowered his arm, shook his grizzled head as if to shake off the embarrassment of appearing in the pulpit without proper vestment, and began again.

He directed his voice not to the congregation before him but toward the little lancet window that stood open at the side. As Andrews projected to the thousand listeners in the churchyard, Danvers felt his ears ring with the force of the preacher's voice.

"I have been asked by many, Why has not Rush confessed his crime in penitence? And my answer is that Rush, as we all must, made his choice. Rush not only had a liberal education but also sat under a gospel ministry.

167

He was for several years accustomed to sit in a pew exactly opposite to me." Andrews swung around and pointed to a seat just four rows back in the center of the church.

A shiver appeared to pass through those sitting in that area. Even as crowded as they were, it seemed they shrank from the spot.

Andrews lowered his thatched-roof eyebrows. "Was Rush a hypocrite? Were his religious impressions artificial? I do not believe so. I have many times seen him weeping as if his heart would break. Would a man thus weep in hypocrisy? No! It was God's Word bruising the conscience but not breaking the heart—the Spirit enlightening the understanding but not influencing the will and the affections. Rush felt remorse for having done wrong, but refused a Savior's love constraining him to what was right. There is a great gulf between canting religious forms and a personal faith."

Danvers blinked. *Andrews* preaching against canting piousness?

"Like Faustus, James Blomfield Rush was presented with a clear possibility of redemption. And he turned his back. On the fateful day when James Blomfield Rush approaches the scaffold, as in the course of justice he surely will, he will have his arms bound with cord to make it impossible for him to escape. But those cords will only be an emblem of the manner in which he was bound by the cords of his sin.

"This miserable man believed a delusion. Satan deluded him with vain hopes, and he deluded himself with the idea that he could make others believe him innocent."

Danvers shifted uncomfortably. There was truth to what Andrews was saying. Danvers himself had certainly believed for some time in the possibility of Rush's innocence. Even now, although he was convinced Rush had a hand in the murder, a tiny part of his mind wished the police had at least given some credence to the two-men theory—and that they could find the murder weapon.

The monstrous proportions of the atrocity made it absolutely essential that every loose end be tied. If Rush had been brought to this by allowing himself to believe a lie, Danvers was determined to struggle on for the last shred of truth.

The honest mind demanded judicial truth and philosophical truth. As usual, Danvers's mind turned to a recently read article by Mill. The utilitarian had argued that, when belief becomes only a hereditary creed, there is a tendency to forget all the belief except the formulas. Then the belief ceases to connect itself at all with the inner life of the human being.

The creed, Mill had argued, remained outside the mind, encrusting and petrifying it—doing nothing for the intellect or heart.

Danvers recalled the imperturbable Rush in court. Had Rush so believed in the power of external religion he had failed entirely to make the gospel a living force that could guide his life? And thus go so far astray from its precepts as to commit a terrible murder?

Danvers stopped. Had a similar thing happened to his own faith?

The thundering from the pulpit brought the viscount's mind back to the preacher.

"Men do not consider that all Rush's black deeds were caused by one thing—a bad heart—and that their own natural heart is no better than his. What a thought! Your heart or mine, left to itself, is ready for any of the crimes laid to this man.

"But do not despair. God did not intend that you be left in the pit of your own wickedness. Your redemption rests upon the free grace of Christ. I call upon you to search your own hearts and to beware of the world and its temptations—the ballroom, the theater, the Sunday newspaper . . ."

The list went on, but Danvers refused to listen. Love and grace made very nice sermon topics, but he would not be ranted at with a list of Thou Shalt Nots. He slipped his gold timepiece from his waistcoat pocket. Andrews had been preaching upwards of two hours. Surely his voice couldn't hold out much longer at that pitch.

"And if you are different from Rush, consider—who made you to differ? Whence comes our change? Did it begin with ourselves? No! We are helpless to make ourselves good. It was grace—the sovereign grace of a Triune Jehovah." Andrews dropped his arm.

Danvers relaxed as quiet replaced the blast.

The crowd seemed in no hurry to disperse, though, and Sir John's party was required to measure their exit to the slow drift of those who would live for many days on the gossip of this event. When they finally reached the churchyard, Danvers saw part of the reason for the snail's pace. Reporters, conspicuous with their scrawl-covered notebooks, were interviewing those who had been so fortunate as to acquire inside seats.

Sir John brushed past a fellow in a brown-and-yellow checked suit and shut the gate to the Hall behind him with a click.

Lady Catherine had a tea tray ready to revive them in the drawing room, and the duchess was as eager for an account as any London reporter. "I shall never forgive myself for missing it. I had no idea there should be such a brouhaha. If it hadn't been so cold I could have sat on the terrace and likely got every word. That vicar of yours has amazing stamina."

"I expect he should have preferred to preach outside, as there were more out than in." Caroline took a cup of tea from her mother. "But Papa would have disapproved."

Boileau's eyes widened, and his eyebrows rose. "Preach outside? I most certainly *would* have disapproved! I would have written to the bishop immediately. The parish church should be a parish church, and none of this catering to outsiders. Takes them away from their own churches. Disorderly. Such helter-skelter practices could disrupt the whole order of things."

The duchess rapped impatiently with her walking stick. "I am not interested in your views of churchmanship, Sir John. I want to know Andrews's views of Rush."

Here was Danvers's opportunity to express the uneasiness he felt. "It appears that Andrews and all the congregation have convicted and hanged Rush months before his trial. Its all very efficient, of course—could save the Crown an incalculable amount of money. But indictment by a coroner's jury is not the final step in the process of justice. I thought the whole affair premature."

Caroline was quick with an answer. "But this is when some good may yet be done. Once Rush is hanged, it will be too late for his soul. Reverend Andrews referred to Faustus, most appropriately, I thought. You will recall that until the moment Faustus leaves the stage with Mephistopheles, the Good Angel continues to wrestle for his soul. So may even one as black as Rush be redeemed."

Danvers was interested in Caroline's warm defense of the vicar. Could he lead her to betray herself in the heat of the moment? "I'll grant you that. A most appropriate topic for a prison visit, and I don't doubt that Andrews has used it on Rush. But proclaiming it to all of Norfolk seems little better than the fabrications of the penny broadsheets."

Caroline set her cup aside with a clatter. "There is no comparison! Those scandalmongers print outrageous lies for their own monetary gain. Reverend Andrews is using the opportunity to warn people of the eternal peril of their souls. It is his calling to prevent others being deceived by the enemy as Rush was. The Scripture admonishes us to be ready to give an answer to all men. The vicar has done that."

"And so it would seem have you, my dear." Lady Catherine's soft voice recalled her daughter to her proper place.

Ama and Frank, by turns, gave the duchess an account of the substance of the vicar's sermon. But Danvers had no desire to hear it again. He drifted inconspicuously to the hallway, then paused, considering going to the library to find something to read. In his room was the vellum-bound volume of Milton's sonnets that had been Charlotte's last gift to him. But he shrank from returning to the poem he had read only last night of the lover who had dreamed of his departed one:

> Love, sweetness, goodness, in her person shined
> So clear as in no face with more delight
> But, oh! as to embrace me she inclined,
> I waked, she fled, and day brought back my night.

He shook himself and turned toward the library. Dwelling on such thoughts wouldn't do. Recalling Milton and Mill led to depression. He needed some lighter reading. Perhaps he could find a recent edition of *Household Words* and catch up on the latest installment of Mr. Dickens's "Dombey and Son." Then the soft swish of silk on the stairs took his attention.

Caroline slipped up the steps and across the gallery above his head. Perhaps the time had come to discover what all her furtiveness was about. He followed her with light step and found her seated in a small sitting room that opened off her bedroom.

"Oh!" She started at his entrance and shoved some small pieces of paper under a book on the table before her.

"Forgive me. I didn't mean to frighten you."

Caroline's resemblance to a mouse had never seemed so apparent before. He had the distinct impression that if it had been possible she would have scuttled under the floor skirting.

Now that he was there he couldn't imagine what to say. He could hardly ask her outright if she were having an affair with the vicar. But no subtle approach occurred to him. Then he caught her uneasy glance in the direction of the papers she had hidden. "I daresay I'm interrupting something of importance. Might I be so bold as to guess that you are indulging a literary interest?"

"Literary interest?"

"I am told that Jane Austen wrote all her books on small pieces of paper, which she hid under a book if anyone should enter her room. Am I committing such an interruption?"

"Oh, no, no. My only literary pretentions are to the diary I keep. Although I suppose it is a little vain of me to keep a journal which I mean to be read by others. It is merely an account of our daily comings and goings, entertainments, the weather—I hope it might be of some use to my sisters. That is all."

Danvers mentally dismissed the diary. A journal written for others to read would hardly include accounts of secret rendezvous. "Then I can only suppose you are writing a letter now, for surely you do not keep your diary on loose sheets of paper. Carry, if you are writing to Jack, will you tell me? I am greatly concerned about him."

Caroline looked startled again. "But is he not at his club? Papa said he had gone to London. I didn't think there was any question. Oh"—her forehead creased in worry—"he isn't gambling, is he? Papa will be so angry. It is a great burden to Papa that he must provide dowrys for five daughters. He cannot bear to have money squandered."

Danvers was startled at the turn the conversation had taken. "No, no. I'm sure Jack is at his club—silly of me not to think of it." He squared his shoulders for one final attempt. "Caroline, won't you tell me what you're writing?"

She blushed.

Silently Danvers berated himself. It suddenly occurred to him that she was writing a love letter. Surely, it was no affair of his. Whatever Caroline was doing, his interest in it could only be one of curiosity—that emotion he so abhorred in others. Whatever Carry Boileau might be up to, it could have no bearing on the mysteries surrounding Rush, Hickling, and the notebook from the park. "Forgive me for asking. It was unpardonable prying." He started to leave.

"Lord Danvers—" Her soft voice called him back. "I am not at all offended. I am pleased by your interest." She drew out the papers. "I was merely writing down notes on today's sermon. I'm afraid hiding them was a reflex. You know how strongly Papa disapproves of Reverend Andrews. I do not want him to know for fear he might forbid it."

"Forbid your taking notes on sermons?"

"Papa does not wish us to form independent religious opinions. He says it might lead to an entire derangement of the family, with every child and every servant saying they had 'a feeling' that some habit or wish of Papa's as head of the family was wrong and they could not join in it. Then all should become confusion, and he would forfeit his place and the duty God has given him as head of the home."

Danvers could only bow before such irrefutable logic. And yet, why did he feel that Carry was not telling him the whole truth? He had little time to puzzle over that though. The most astounding idea to come from the conversation was one Carry had taken as a matter of course. If Jack had gone to London, surely it was obvious he would be at his club. Danvers started to take his leave, then turned back. "And what is Jack's club?"

"Boodle's." Her quill was making quick marks across the paper before he was out of the room.

Again he cursed himself for being a fool. Boodles, one of the clubs to which he himself belonged. How many times must he have seen Jack there himself and paid no attention?

Danvers thrust open the door of his suite. "Hardy, pack a valise. One for each of us. We're going to London."

13

The black-caped, top-hatted lamplighter had just finished illuminating the gaslamps before 28 St. James Street, when the travelers arrived there late Monday evening, chilled to the bone and in no improved humor over having had their journey slowed by dense fog. Disliking the noise and dirt of trains that belched black soot from their smokestacks, Danvers had chosen to set out in a borrowed phaeton. But now he regretted his impetuosity.

Boodle's was famed for the excellence of its dinners. Good food by a hearty fire was the most welcomed prospect imaginable. "Hurry and unpack my evening clothes, Hardy. Then you may relax downstairs. I shan't require your services further this evening."

Hardy pulled himself up with a primness worthy of Dalling, even though it little suited one of his rotund stature and rosy appearance. "Yes, m'lord." He even went so far as to sketch a bow, an irony lost on the preoccupied viscount.

An hour later Danvers entered the dark-paneled, red-velvet-upholstered dining room to be greeted by many friends indulging in the convivial atmosphere for which the club was famous. But the face he most hoped to see was not among them.

Charles was just starting on his second glass of port when Tommy Frane came in. "Frane, care to take a glass with me?" Danvers signaled the waiter. "Have you seen Jack Boileau around town lately?" He tried to keep his voice casual. If he had driven all the way to London in a dripping fog on a fool's errand he would not know enough ways to curse himself for being an imbecile.

"Course I have. No one in town just now. Absurd time to be here. Can't think why he came. Or why I did, for that matter. That's the trouble with having one's estate in Cornwall. Being in one of the home counties where one has hounds to ride to and hunt balls to attend is all very well to fill the time before the season begins. But Cornwall is quite another matter." He took an appreciative sip of the port. "Good cellar here."

Danvers attempted to hide his irritation at Tommy's rambling. "Haven't seen him this evening, have you?"

"Who?"

"Boileau!"

"Oh. No, can't say as I have. But I have two tickets for the show at the Haymarket. Care for a spot of opera? Haymarket's not what it was since Brisi and the others went over to Covenant Garden last year, but I daresay you may still find it amusing. Chorus is every bit as fancy as before, if you take my meaning."

Indeed, Danvers did. The truth was, however, he was one of that rare breed—a true opera lover who enjoyed the art for the sake of the music itself and not for a showplace to be seen by society nor for a stable to select a bit of skirt. And not for any reason tonight. "No thanks, Tommy. Think I'll try to find Jack. Want to talk to him."

"I should try the gaming room if I were you. If not here, at White's. Or maybe some private establishment. Sure to be at the tables somewhere though."

Danvers felt chilled as if the windows had been opened to the fog. "Been playing deep, has he?"

Tommy laughed. "You know Boileau. Always one for a flutter."

Having a flutter was all very well but not an adequate explanation for disappearing from one's own birthday celebration without a word to anyone, Danvers thought a short time later as he sat at a particularly desultory game of 21. He took a third card and cursed when it took his count to 23. He paid his shot and moved on.

The gaming rooms at Boodle's, White's, and Traveller's all failed to yield his quarry, but he found a spot of luck at Watier's in the form of a mutual acquaintance who had seen Jack earlier in the day. He thought Jack had mentioned something about a new house in the Strand that night. "Going there myself at any rate. This place is dead. Care to come along?"

Outside the club, Danvers stopped to adjust his cape while his friend signaled a cab.

"Penny for a posey, sir?" A ragged flower girl with a dirt-streaked face beneath her flat-crowned, black straw hat, held out a small nosegay of Michaelmas daisies in a hand red with cold.

Danvers gave her a copper with his own silk-gloved hand. Then he reached into his pocket again for a two penny piece. "Get yourself some gloves, child. It'll snow soon."

Her startled smile was the brightest spot in his dismal evening. And five hours and three houses later, when a depressed Danvers with a wilted boutonniere and considerably lighter pockets caught a hackney back to Boodle's, he had found no further cause for smiling. In the gloom of his own thoughts and the equally murky fog, he paid no attention to the top-hatted figure emerging from a cab just ahead of him until a familiar voice called out.

"I say, is that you, Danvers? Frane told me you were in town. Didn't think I could handle it myself, huh?"

"Boileau! Are you foxed? I came to find you. Didn't think you could handle what?"

"Why, sleuthing out the mystery of your little book, of course. I say, let's get out of this wet."

"Come up to my room." Danvers took Jack's arm as if he might escape him again and signaled the hall porter. "Franklin, send a bottle of your best to my room."

In the room Danvers poked up the banked fire but didn't bother lighting any of the gaslamps. He didn't even wait for Jack to sit down. "Now, do you mean to tell me you've been in London, going the rounds all this time while I've been up in Norwich covering for you at *your* birthday celebrations and with *your* family? I've been half out of my mind expecting to find your bullet-riddled body behind every haystack. What is the idea of this?"

With half a provocation he could have shaken the boy by his lapels. And if this was a grand charade to cover a darker intrigue, Danvers vowed he'd uncover it and perform the hangman's duties with his own hand.

"You mean to say you didn't find my note?"

"I found something all right. Making sense of it was another matter entirely. What I found looked suspiciously like a blackmail note, although whether it was blackmailing you or you had determined to blackmail someone else was left entirely to conjecture." Danvers wished the port he had ordered would arrive. He felt sorely in need of fortification. "Jack, I can't help feeling we've had this conversation before—but if you're in any kind of trouble—"

"And you accused *me* of being foxed! What blackmail note are you talking about?"

Danvers pulled the crumpled sheet of paper from the side pocket of his valise and held it out.

The effect was alarming. Jack grabbed the note, gave a strangled shout, and flung himself back in his chair. At last he caught his breath, and laughter burst forth. "It's too much to believe! First you thought I shot Jermy, and now you think I'm a blackmailer. Where you formed your opinion of my character, I can't think."

Danvers ran his hand through his hair. If he were as wrong as Jack said, he had to give the lad credit for being remarkably good-tempered about his misjudgment.

"Look. This should have been very clear to you—" Jack held out the note so they could both read it. "*£1250*—that's the amount the sums in the notebook add up to—a very healthy amount. *Blackmail inevitable*—the regularity and size of the payments look like an account of blackmail payments—but the fact that the amounts vary make them appear tied to something else—like gaming debts—that's what I hoped to solve. *3 or 4 days*—sorry about that, should have realized I couldn't travel to London and learn anything quite that quickly. But I did think I'd have something by now."

"Do you mean to tell me I was supposed to understand all you've just said from that blasted cipher scrawled on a scrap of paper without so much as your name signed?"

The anger in Danvers's voice appeared to sober Jack. He straightened in his chair. "I do see it was rather cryptic. I was in a hurry, though, and I thought—"

"You thought it unnecessary to so much as bid your mother farewell or make your excuses to your father for missing the celebration at Tacolneston?"

"I thought you'd explain it to them—" Now completely serious, Jack lowered his eyes. "No, the truth of the matter is I didn't think at all. I completely forgot that dashed affair at Tacolneston. I knew I'd miss the train at Wymondham if I didn't hurry. But if I'd had any idea I'd be so long, I certainly wouldn't have come without Dalling." He looked at the scuffs on his shoes. "Was Father livid?"

"At first. When he thought you were off in a haystack with the dairymaid. But he was genuinely worried when we discovered you'd disappeared. At least Dalling told us your city clothes were gone, so it looked as though you hadn't been abducted."

"And my mother?"

"Oh, Lady Catherine and your sisters accepted that you'd gone to London."

"And Sarah? Oh, blast!" He struck his forehead. "Why didn't I think? Did I frighten her too?"

"Miss Mellors seems to have kept her head." Whether it was because she was extremely sensible or because she had been too busy thinking about Nigel, Danvers couldn't say and chose not to pose that complication at the moment.

Jack smiled. "Yes, she wouldn't make a fuss. But do you, er—think she missed me?"

Danvers tossed his driving gloves on the bed. "I'll not be drawn into *that* speculation. She's gone to Barston with Antonia. You must look to your own defenses." He shifted the direction of the conversation. "It was Carry who told me I'd find you at Boodle's."

"Yes, and so you have. But you find me none the wiser—and certainly no richer. What a complete ass I've been. Do you think we should give it over to the Metropolitan Police?"

"I doubt they'd accept our suspicions as reason for action. Besides, we have no idea that anything occurred within their jurisdiction—Norwich seems more likely."

Jack nodded glumly.

"Well, at least tell me what you've tried," Danvers said.

"I assumed the key was Nigel's debts—probably gaming debts. I thought I could get a line on his wins and losses at the tables. Only trouble is, no one will talk about a matter of honor like a gaming debt—or admit to a deep loss—so the only way I could learn anything was to make a big win or loss myself and have an excuse to enter it in the club's gaming book, then create some sort of diversion and take a peek at Nigel's account."

"And what have you learned?"

"That its far easier to lose big than to win big. What

180

the squire will say I can't imagine . . . well, I can, but I'd rather not."

Danvers tried to look severe, knowing the firelight would give added harshness to his strong-boned face. "And so you've lost heavily and learned nothing to the point." But he couldn't hold the pose, and his black eyes relaxed in humor. "Well, truth to tell, I didn't do so well myself—"

Just then the door burst open, and the raucous strains of a music hall song filled the room. " . . . I plucked the bloom in my garden of love and found . . ."

"Hardy!" Danvers jumped to his feet. "What in blazes do you mean by coming in like this? I gave you the evening off."

The manservant turned to stone. The final word of the song hung in his gaping mouth, and a sheaf of bills fell from his hand. "M'lord—" His voice broke. He swallowed and tried again. "It's begging your pardon I am, m'lord. The room was dark. Didn't realize you were here. I—"

"Very well, man. Close the door and pick up your blunt. I see I must be paying you extravagantly well if you have such excess to flaunt about."

Hardy fell to his knees to recover his money. "Yes, m'lord. Er—that is, no, m'lord—if you must be knowing, it's my winnings—er—"

To everyone's relief, a footman arrived with Danvers's port. "You may pour three glasses," Danvers directed. "And make them big ones." The servant obeyed and departed.

"Am I to take it you've spent the night at play, Hardy? Most successfully, it appears?" Before Hardy could answer, Danvers went on. "How is that possible? I thought I put in an appearance at every club in town."

"You wouldn't be knowing this one, m'lord." Hardy accepted the glass Danvers held out to him. "A very common sort of place, it is, if you take my meaning. But a far sight easier to get information there, I'll wager."

"Yes, apparently you've done very well with that—wagering, that is. I never suspected your Irish grandmother was so strong in you."

Hardy grinned. "The luck of the Irish, sir?"

"And did you learn anything about Langston?"

"No, sir."

"Blast!" Danvers groaned and so unmercifully ruffled his hair that the action brought an outcry from his valet.

"But, m'lord, it's learning about Hickling I was."

"Hickling?"

"I did say it wasn't your sort of place. Six shillings would be buying a look at their records. If my memory's right, his losses were matching the numbers in that book Pip found."

Jack drew the notebook from his pocket and tossed it to Hardy. "Care to refresh your memory?"

Hardy nodded and reviewed the page for a moment. "The very same, for certain."

"So we've got a list of *Hickling's* gaming debts. Where does that get us?" Jack asked.

Danvers was quiet for a moment. Then, "Hardy, would the class of establishment you patronized be likely to extend credit to the amount of £1250?"

Hardy shook his head. "That's more than most of their clients would be earning in a lifetime."

"So if Hickling continued to play and run up losses, it must have meant that the old bills were paid."

"Certain it is. I was thinking it too obvious to mention. They were all paid but the last one." He glanced at the book. "£163."

"How could a servant pay debts like that?" Danvers asked.

"Suppose Nigel was paying them."

The room went silent at Jack's suggestion. The log crackled in the fire.

"One of the letters I saw in Jermy's file mentioned Langston's bank as being Bank of England, St. James's

Branch." Danvers said. "Between the two of us, Boileau, we must know one of the officers who could take a peek at Langston's accounts."

"How official do we have to be? Maybe I could claim to be representing my father as magistrate."

The furrows in Danvers's brow deepened. "Might work. Worth a try at any rate. Why don't you toddle off to bed now? I'm going to have my man sing me to sleep. Always was unaccountably fond of music hall songs done with an Irish lilt. Do you know 'The Lightening Express'?"

Hardy had the grace to blush.

It wasn't until after lunch the next day that Danvers felt he had a sufficiently clear head to tackle an officer of the Bank of England. And the watery November sunshine and blustery wind did nothing to add further encouragement.

At least Freeson, the accounts officer, did not seem inclined to have them thrown out at first glance, in spite of his thin-lipped smile. Then Danvers let slip a reference to his father, the Earl of Norville ("I say, is that sword on your wall from the Rifle Brigade? You weren't by any chance in my father's regiment?") and Jack was able to extend his signet ring of the pelican in her piety as the badge of Sir John Boileau. After that, Danvers felt quite sure they would have been given a tour of the sacred vaults had they requested it.

"Just a list of withdrawals over £100 from Langston's account and their dates for the past year. A private investigation." Danvers refrained from referring to the affair at Stanfield Hall for fear of overplaying his hand.

"Certainly, your lordship. I'll do my best. If you'd care to call back in three quarters of an hour." Freeson left them with a stiff bow and sent a clerk for the information.

To pass the time, the three men—Danvers and Boileau in the lead, Hardy following a respectful pace behind—walked along Green Park toward Piccadilly. As they neared the main thoroughfare the noise of traffic increased. Metal-wheeled omnibuses rattled by on the paving amid hackneys, cabriolets, and private carriages of every description.

At Piccadilly they turned toward the Circus. The cries of street vendors blended with the sounds of the vehicles. If the gentlemen had been tempted by pastries there was a wealth of choices: tarts of currant, gooseberry, or apple; plum cake; gingerbreadnuts; Chelsea buns; muffins; crumpets.

"Ginger beer, the best drink out!" a white-aproned vendor called, extending a glass at arm's length.

"Oranges, tuppence apiece," offered an old woman with a wooden tray of fruit suspended from a rope across her shoulders.

But the offering they finally succumbed to was that of the oysterman. Behind his folding table he plucked fresh oysters from a large wooden bowl, slit the shells open with a deft turn of a penknife, and presented oysters on the half-shell for a penny apiece. "A shake of salt, sir?"

Danvers was savoring his third when he became aware of two pair of eyes looking up at him from under the table. Two more coppers found their way to the oysterman's palm, and the urchins ran off with their delicacies.

The end of their forty-five minutes nearing, by common consent the men turned toward the bank with long strides, and Danvers led the way into Freeson's office.

Immediately he noticed a change in the atmosphere. The dark walls and the clutter of account books on the oak desk seemed more oppressive than they had in his earlier optimism.

Freeson's pinched features were unsmiling as he squinted at them from behind his wire-rimmed spectacles. The bank officer cleared his throat and tugged at his black tie. "I am afraid, my lord . . ." He came to his feet and sketched a bow.

Danvers frowned. Was the man going to be obstreperous, when victory seemed within grasp? What could have happened to change his earlier cooperative mood? Where could they get their answers now?

"I am afraid," Freeson continued, "the account in question has been closed. Most precipitously, it would appear. And after the Langston family accounts have been with us for three generations." He shook his head, then was obliged to remove his spectacles in his agitation. "I cannot imagine where our society is headed, when the young show such blatant disrespect for tradition." He shook his head again. "Three generations."

"Shocking," Danvers agreed with emphasis. "Still, it's incumbent on those of us who remain to carry on. Our information—it was still available? I wonder if we might . . ."

Freeson recalled himself with a start. "Oh, quite so, quite so. Yes, yes. I have it right here." He began shifting papers on his desk. "Yes, yes, right here." He held out a slick, dun-colored envelope sealed with a blob of red wax. "So glad to be of service to your lordship. St. James always strives to be the best."

"I have always been most happy with your service." The envelope firmly in his grip, Danvers left Freeson in the middle of the banker's third bow.

A few minutes later Danvers, Boileau, and Hardy emerged from the bank with triumphant grins on their faces.

Danvers didn't remove the paper from its sealed envelope until they were back in his rooms and the brown leather notebook was open before them for comparison. He slit open the envelope and read: "16 November 1847, £105; 28 December, £217—the Christmas season doesn't seem to have brought good cheer to everyone; 8 January '48, £137—"

"Yes, yes! That's it!" Jack took the paper from his hands and laid the two accounts side by side.

Hardy whistled. "By Jove, look at that. Exact matching it is."

"Looks like the only thing Langston withdrew money for was to pay Hickling's gaming debts." Jack stopped.

"Suppose Hickling had some powerful hold on Nigel," Danvers mused. "And Langston shot him to get out from under it . . ." He began pacing the room. "Hickling wrote down his monthly gaming losses, and his already debt-ridden employer paid them. Why? What could Hickling have known that was worth all that?"

Jack frowned. "It must have been as serious as murder for Nigel to risk murdering to cover it up."

"And why was he waiting so long?" Hardy asked.

Danvers looked at his man.

"What I'm meaning is, why pay for a whole year and then be murdering him? Surely he could have been finding plenty of opportunities better than the shooting party to kill a servant—" Hardy stopped and looked around uncomfortably.

"Don't worry, Hardy. I'm entirely satisfied with your service." Danvers grinned at him. "But that is a very good question."

14

On Thursday morning Danvers arrived back at Ketteringham with the mixed emotions of having worked his way to the end of one labyrinth only to find it opened onto one yet more complicated. Before a welcome fire in the rosewood paneled library, Jack and Danvers told the squire all they had learned.

Boileau listened with careful attention, then shook his head. "An interesting story, but I doubt it's one Superintendent Yarrington would care to hear. He'll say Langston was an uncommonly thoughtful employer to pay his man's gaming debts, and that you have no evidence of extortion—or anything worse. Besides, the police are working like beavers preparing for the Rush trial. Now that they have a coroner's indictment, they have no intention of losing the big show."

"Have they found the murder weapon yet?" Danvers asked.

"No, and I'd guess Yarrington would give a pretty to the man who could bring it in. It's the only hole in his case."

Danvers nodded imperceptively. He shared the superintendent's feeling.

"I've been thinking about Emily Sandford—wondering what will become of her when this is all over." Sir John brushed his bristly mustache in thought. "The only option for a fallen woman is to take to the streets. And even if one didn't care about her, by then there'll be a child to consider." The squire tapped his fingertips together in front of him.

"Did you have anything in mind, Father?" Jack asked. "Maybe Andrews would take her on as a maid."

"There's nothing that man wouldn't do if he believed it his Christian duty. But I can't imagine Mrs. Andrews allowing Emily Sandford in the house—the vicar's wife is far more straight-laced than her husband."

Danvers's mind boggled at the thought.

Jack smiled. "Oh, I can imagine they'd both be delighted to take her in—then make her life a misery preaching to her day and night."

"How about her brother in Australia?" Danvers stretched out his long legs before the fire.

"Haven't heard she had one." Sir John's voice rose in question.

"Right after the shooting I went to Potash to look at some papers. She had a letter—I assumed it was a brother, could be a cousin or something, I suppose."

"Most interesting. I'll inquire about that." Sir John made a note.

"I must call on Mother to let her see that the prodigal has returned unscathed—and to apologize for distressing her over that Tacolneston affair." Jack stood. He had already apologized to his father, and the fact that he was willing to refer to his behavior openly evidenced that the squire had forgiven his helter-skelter son yet again.

But Jack's exit was blocked by Huntley, whose sour expression showed that he disapproved heartily of the message direst duty required him to deliver. "There is a person asking to see you, sir."

"To see me?" Boileau looked up.

"To see the young master, as it were, sir." The butler's back became stiffer yet.

"For me? What sort of a person, Huntley?"

"A person who smells, sir."

"A beggar? Well, tell Cook to give him a sandwich, and he can apply to Andrews for something from the poor box. What does he need with me?"

"He was most insistent, sir. Gave the name of Buckby."

"Did he, by Jove? Well, why didn't you say so? Where is he?"

"In the servant's hall, sir. But Cook is most anxious that he be removed quickly." Huntley's nostrils pinched closer together.

"Quite so. Let's go see what the fellow wants, Danvers." When they had gained the privacy of the passage, Jack let out his laughter. "Imagine that old poacher having the nerve to call at the Hall and ask to see me. He must have discovered a mighty remarkable covey of quail."

"Maybe the law's on his back, and he wants help."

"Well, if that's it, I'll pay his fine. I owe him."

Danvers didn't ask why Jack felt indebted to the poacher—in spite of all his commitment to the truth, he still feared learning something he didn't want to know at this late date, when it was so easy to believe wholeheartedly in Jack's innocence.

Huntley was right. Danvers smelled the poacher before he saw him. The last time, they had met in the open air, and that had been distinctly more pleasant.

Buckby's gap-toothed grin spread all over his bristly face. "Found it, Master Jack, sir. Near the 'ole where we cotched them first 'ares, it were." He pointed a grubby finger to a brass-tipped oak rod lying on the table.

"My ramrod!" Jack seized the stick. "Well done, Buckby! I'll see you are well rewarded. Would you care for a reason to roam the park with authority? I'll tell Ringer to take you on as assistant gamekeeper—then you can hunt here as of right. You would be invaluable in protecting the park, seeing as you know all your fellows' ways."

"I'd be right grateful, Mr. Jack, sir. It do seem, though, like bein' the law, as it were, might sorter take the spice outa 'untin', if you see what I mean."

Jack grinned. "Indeed, I do. Perhaps if we continue to go out together at nights you won't lose all your—er— irregular skills." Jack strode to the door between the hall and the kitchen. "Cook, do you have a nice meat pie for Buckby here?" In response to her scowl he added, "Wrap it up for him. I'm sure he'd prefer to eat it in the park."

When Buckby was gone with a heavy meat pie under his arm, Jack turned to Danvers with a glimmer in his eye. "Relieved?"

Danvers grinned back. "Foolish is what I feel. But it's worth it." He was quiet for a moment. "I say, Jack. I'm most awfully sorry—"

"What? Oh, that you suspected me? Not a bit of it— since I got in on a spot of the detecting. This is great fun. And an excuse to go off to London saved me the blooming boredom of another party with toasts and speeches."

Danvers clapped the heir on the back but didn't reply. He was too busy thinking that the truth was better than fear. He was profoundly grateful that the answers hadn't been unpleasant ones—but even if they had been, reality was less painful than one's dreadful imaginings.

That afternoon Jack and Danvers, in heavily caped greatcoats, accompanied Sir John, likewise bundled against the chill November air, to Potash for his interview with Emily regarding her future.

"Do you think her trustworthy, sir?" Danvers asked the squire as they drove down the lane lined with leafless trees.

"Trustworthy? Indeed not. I have the lowest opinion of her character. But I pity her. Her plight distresses me. If it's possible for an unmarried woman to be a widow, she will soon qualify, and her child shall be fatherless in every sense of the word. How will a woman who is notorious throughout the land as the mistress of a monster live if no one helps her?"

Danvers reflected that Andrews was not the only one ready to respond whenever duty called. "Has she no family in England?"

"I've made a few inquiries. It appears her father is a lawyer's copying clerk who married above himself. They gave their daughter a good education but completely cut her off when she fell into bad company with Rush. Your suggestion that she go to her relation in Australia seems the most practical plan."

Emily was playing the piano when they arrived at Potash, a Schumann air, Danvers thought. She seemed ill at ease but invited her callers in, offered them seats, and excused herself to fix tea for them.

When they were served, she folded her hands in front of her rounded stomach and looked at Sir John. It was impossible to tell whether the look was one of patient waiting or of hostility at being invaded by authority.

"Miss Sandford"—Sir John set his cup aside—"your testimony showed you to be a courageous woman."

"He's guilty. I'm sure of it. He would have murdered me next if he could have—to insure that my evidence should remain hidden."

Danvers gave a sardonic smile behind his teacup. So it was self-preservation, not love of justice or fear of God, that had prompted Emily's "courageous" testimony.

"Be that as it may," Sir John continued, "it will now take a great deal of courage for you to make a life for yourself and your child. Have you any plans?"

"Mr. Rush, Jr., and his wife make no secret that they want me out of here as soon as possible. I have a friend in Kensington. I've written to ask if she'll take me in until the child is born. Then . . ." She spread her hands.

Boileau nodded. "Sounds an excellent plan. Of course you'll have to stay in England until after the trial

191

next spring. Then, I wonder if you've given any thought to emigrating. Perhaps to your—brother, is it?—in Australia."

Emily looked surprised that the squire should know so much about her. "Tickets to Australia are expensive. Henry's a good brother, but he's a dockworker. He wouldn't have money to send to me." She shook her head.

"I was not suggesting that. If you agree to the plan, you may leave it all to me. I shall plan your voyage, pay your bills, see to your accounts." He paused. "Yes, I think a letter of introduction to the Bishop of Melbourne—and if I make arrangements to buy you a piano there, you will be able to earn a living in Australia by teaching music."

Danvers wasn't sure whether he was more amazed by such generosity from one who forever fretted over his son's debts, or by the lack of any show of gratitude on the part of the recipient. Emily simply submitted to the squire's plan. Sir John, in return, seemed satisfied that his charity had been accepted. Neither apparently felt a need for more.

Upon arrival, Savory, Rush's farmhand, had taken Sir John's carriage to the stable. Savory was now nowhere in sight, so Danvers offered to bring the gig around.

He was approaching the stable when a familiar young voice called to him. "Oh, I say, gov'nor! Just see where my balloon's come down today!" Pip the aspiring aeronaut was sitting in his mother's laundry basket, this time attached by tangled strings to an assortment of pinned-together rags.

"Better take care, Pip. That bullpen's knee-deep of mud. Your mother will skin you if you ruin her basket."

"Right you are, sir. But the wind changed just as I was comin' down, like."

Danvers grinned at the child's active imagination and started to turn to the stable. Then he stopped, remembering James Rush's warning. "Pip! You mustn't play in there. Rush's bull is a mean one." He strode to the pole fence and reached over. "Here, just walk quietly as you can to me. We'll have you out of there before the creature discovers he's been disturbed."

Pip didn't move.

"Leave the basket, Pip. Savory can get it out for you. I'll buy your mother a new one if I have to." Danvers fought to keep his voice calm, but he felt his forehead getting damp in his desperation to remove the child from the danger of trampling feet and goring horns.

Pip laughed. "Gorm, sir, you ain't spent much time on a farm, 'ave ye? The old bull's as content as a kitten."

"Pip! Don't argue with me. Come out at once!"

Pip responded to the voice of authority.

Danvers boosted the child over the fence. Once his feet were on the side of safety, Charles felt free to deliver his lecture. "Now look here, young man. This bull is notoriously dangerous. Even Sergeant Pont and his men from the Norwich police wouldn't go in that pen. I want you to promise me you won't go anywhere near him again, or I shall warn your father. Grown men have been killed by angry bulls." Infuriated by the child's complacency, Danvers turned graphic. "I once saw a man with a hole this big gored in his stomach and his back broken. He only lived—"

The viscount stopped in the face of Pip's grin. Was he going to have to shake the child to make him listen? Then his eyes followed the direction Pip was pointing.

Around the corner of the shed came the enormous, red Gurnsey bull, his head down, his long, sharp horns curved forward. Walking by his side was a cow about half his size, making eyes at him, and looking for all the world like a maiden on a Sunday afternoon stroll.

Danvers choked, but he wouldn't concede the point. "That's all very well, Pip. He looks docile, but he might be even more ferocious if he's interrupted when he's with a cow."

Pip laughed. Darting just beyond Danvers's grasp, he slipped under the fence. He pulled two handfuls of dried weeds from the basket and extended his arms. The bull ate out of the child's hand. With a triumphant grin, Pip picked up his gondola and balloon and walked from the bullpen.

Danvers was still standing there considering when Boileau and his son joined him. "What's taking you so long, Danvers? Trouble with the horses?"

"What? Oh, no, no—I've just seen the most amazing thing." He recounted the incident for them.

The squire at once saw the significance. "But young Rush told Sergeant Pont—"

"Precisely what I was thinking. And yet he must have known how easily the bull could be pacified. So why didn't he want the bullpen to be searched?"

Sir John looked first at the mud, then at his gleaming boots and spotless trouser legs, but Danvers was over the fence before his sentence was finished. Jack and Pip were right behind him.

"Do you think you could find us some shovels, Father?" Jack asked as the stick he was using to probe a pile of hay broke in his hand.

The squire returned from the barn in a few minutes, laden with shovels, hoe, and pitchfork. Sergeant Pont and his constables had dug up the whole of Potash farm—pierced the pastures, examined ditches, pits, and hedgerows. This was the one spot on the land that had escaped scrutiny. But now they probed every inch.

Pip was the first to tire. He leaned against the wall of the bullock shed and shoved his pitchfork into the muck. "Might 'elp if I knowed what I was searchin' for, gov'nor."

Danvers grinned at him. "The gun that shot Jermy—a rifle or a pistol, we aren't sure. But you can pretend its buried pirate treasure if that helps."

"Yo 'o 'o and a bottle o' rum!" Pip cried and gave a mighty thrust with his pitchfork. The fork stuck in the mud. Pip vaulted across the pen more as if on a punt than on a pirate ship.

Imagination appeared to fire his flagging energy. The despicable pirate Pip now inched his way across the pen, pitchfork thrust by pitchfork thrust. He was almost halfway on his third crossing when he cried, "What's this, mateys? I've struck gold!"

After less than a minute's digging, Danvers dropped to his knees in the stinking mud. With a shout he pulled up a blunderbuss.

He washed it in the bull's drinking tank, then left the pen to examine it more carefully. The double-barreled gun was a short, but exceedingly heavy, instrument.

Sir John nodded. "Matches Eliza Chastney's description. She said he leveled it with both hands. This would require that."

Jack ran his hand over the stock. "In spite of the damage from the mud, I'd say it's quite new. First-rate workmanship—"

"Yes," Danvers agreed. "And I'll wager anything you'd care to name that its bore and ramrod pipe will fit exactly the rod they found in Stanfield Hall."

He and Jack exchanged looks over the squire's bent head.

"I found the treasure, didn't I?" Pip was jumping up and down at Danvers's elbow.

"Indeed you did—I'd say you've earned another balloon ride."

Pip turned a series of handsprings in reply. "When can we go?"

"Soon as the weather allows. Maybe tomorrow, even. You come to the Hall on our first fine day."

Pip started to turn another cartwheel, but Danvers stopped him with a stern warning. "Now see that you wash the mud off your mother's basket. And stay out of bullpens!"

"Yes sir, yer lordship, sir." Pip's answer was obedient enough, but the gleam of mischief in his eye was undimmed as he scampered off toward the gamekeeper's lodge with his aerostat.

Sir John leaped into the carriage. "Duty calls. We must drive directly to Norwich castle and deliver our evidence."

Danvers, who had not been so forgetful of himself in the presence of mud since he was Pip's age, was appalled at the thought of driving into town caked from boot to knee and from cuff to elbow. "Perhaps just a quick bath?" he began.

But the magistrate had already gathered the reins, and the others were barely in the carriage before the horses were off at a brisk trot.

On the drive to Norwich, Danvers realized that the final piece of the Rush case had fallen into place. All the external questions were answered. Yet he found it impossible to understand. "Do you really think Rush expected to get away with it?" he asked Sir John.

"I don't think he ever for a minute truly believed he would be convicted. He had so convinced himself that he had been ill-used by Jermy that he felt justified in his act, and, of course, he really thought all that evidence he'd concocted about Joe Clarke and the Jermy cousins would stand up to scrutiny."

"Do you think he's insane—should he be sent to Bedlam?"

"No. At times he seemed close to raving, but everything was coldly calculated. Low intelligence, I should say, and an incredible conceit and capacity for self-deception. Add to it his failure to accept responsibility for his own actions—a fatal combination." Boileau shook his head.

Danvers considered for a moment. "What about the peace of conscience he claims to feel?"

Boileau gave a rueful smile. "A conscience dulled by a lifetime of disuse isn't likely to cause undue disturbance over even the most heinous crime."

"And all the tears he shed? Simple-minded sentimentality perhaps?"

"Perhaps," Boileau agreed. "Or perhaps Andrews was correct—a sort of spiritual conviction. Who's to say?" Sir John clucked to his horses to speed their pace.

By the time their statements had been copied down and duly signed, the gun examined, and indeed the ramrod returned to the case made for it, the mud had dried to the consistency of plaster—an exceedingly odoriferous plaster.

"I can't think what Huntley will say to this." Jack picked bits of mud off his cuff and dropped them over the side of the carriage as they drove back to Ketteringham.

Danvers laughed. "Well, I know what Cook would say—she'd send us out in the park to eat game pie with Buckby."

When they arrived at Ketteringham, however, it wasn't the reaction of the servants they had to face but that of a very elegant, auburn-haired lady, who was being handed out of her landau when the Boileau carriage swept around the circle drive in front of the Hall.

"My dears, how lovely to see you all again. I've just come to call upon Lady Catherine and her daughters. How fortunate to find—" Lady Antonia stopped mid-sentence. "Have you been in an accident?"

"It's all good news, Tonia," Danvers assured her. "The only damage done was to Rush's defense."

When he continued, Antonia burst into trills of laughter over the story of the viscount, baronet, and heir digging in the muck of a bullpen, watched over by the bull and his enamorata. "But that's too marvelous! I simply must go straight to London. I can't bear the idea of anyone telling the story before me."

Danvers winced, but protesting would only add spice to the story, so he chose instead to change the subject. "And are you quite recovered from the—er—unpleasant shock you received here?"

"It seems there is no end to the surprises Ketteringham has in store." She flicked a ball of mud from his coat sleeve. "But yes, thank you, I am quite recovered."

Glancing at the others, who seemed not to be listening, she added quietly, "I have something to tell you. I'm not sure what to do about it—" Sir John looked their way, and Antonia raised her voice—"I'd give a pretty to see Hardy's face when you walk in like that. Would you care to borrow my smelling salts for him?"

"Hardy's a stout fellow. I don't think that'll be necessary."

Jack, however, had more pressing concerns than the reaction of a manservant. "Sarah. How is she? Did she not come with you?"

Antonia gave him a knowing smile from under the deep brim of her bonnet. "The child is fine. I invited her to accompany me, but she had plans to take tea with a friend this afternoon."

"Oh." Jack was obviously dashed that Sarah had rejected an invitation to Ketteringham.

A few minutes later Danvers saw that he had underestimated the impact his appearance would make on his man. Hardy was very nearly overset. "M'lord! And is it ruffians you've been battling? I shouldn't have let you out of my sight. And now you'll be saying it's all my fault." Hardy began tugging at the encrusted jacket, then stopped in distress when his action caused a shower of dried mud flakes.

By now, though, Danvers had had quite enough fuss about the mud. "Just deal with it, man, and have water for a bath sent up." What could Antonia have meant by her whispered sentence? Whatever it was, he hoped it wasn't some affair of the heart. He was in no mood for more entanglements. The leap his own heart had taken at her unexpected appearance was quite enough discomfort to add to his other worries.

An hour later, however, when a freshly washed Danvers, his hair sleeked to near precision and his shirt cuffs gleaming white accented by their gold links, appeared in the library, he was met by a thoroughly sensible Antonia.

"You must think me the most weak-witted creature in the world after my performance on the shooting field."

"Please, you must put such distressing scenes out of your mind."

Antonia smiled. "Don't fear, I shan't go into hysterics. I never do." Danvers's eyebrows shot to his hairline. She gave a self-deprecating chuckle. "Well, hardly ever." Then she sobered instantly. "The truth is, my initial reaction was genuine enough. Then I realized it was a convenient excuse to escape. Nigel could hardly fake an accident for me if I stayed well out of his way."

Danvers gripped her shoulder and spun her around to face him. "What are you saying?"

"I was hysterical all right, but not over the sight of blood. I was terrified for my own safety. I realized that of all the people there, I was the only one who knew Hickling had been shot on purpose. And I knew why."

15

ntonia! What do you mean?"

"I mean that I heard Nigel tell Hickling to go get the ramrod. And I saw him deliberately aim at his servant."

"You heard?"

"Yes. I was standing right behind him. He didn't know I was there, and no one else was close enough to hear over all the shooting and flapping and barking. But when Nigel looked up at me, I knew he realized what had happened. And I knew I'd be next."

"And you know why he shot Hickling?"

"Well, not exactly. But I know Hickling had been afraid for his life for more than a year."

"And how do you know that?"

"He gave me a letter."

"A letter? Well—what did it say?"

"I don't know. I didn't read it." Before Danvers could ask, she went on. "It wasn't to me. It was to Jermy. Isaac Jermy."

"Hickling gave you a letter for Nigel's lawyer?"

Antonia nodded. "For me to post in case Hickling died in—er—unusual circumstances."

"My word. Does Nigel know you have this?"

"I don't suppose I'd be in a condition to be telling

you so now if he did. But I've stayed well away while I thought what to do, just in case he suspected."

"And what have you done?"

"Come to talk to you and Sir John. It would hardly do any good to post the letter now that Jermy's dead."

Just then Jack, also looking immeasurably more like himself, entered the library.

"You don't mind if I tell Jack, do you? He's been helping me work some things out. What you've said just confirms our suspicions."

Antonia was delighted to have a wider audience for her story. Sitting before the fire, she told it with dramatic embellishments.

Then it was Jack's and Danvers's turn to tell her all they'd discovered. "Not that we really needed any more proof that Hickling was blackmailing Nigel," Jack said.

"*We* didn't, but now maybe we have enough to take to the police." Danvers jumped to his feet. "Antonia, give the letter to Sir John. As local magistrate he's the proper person to deal with it." His dark eyes snapped with excitement. "This may be the last piece to the puzzle. We could have the whole matter solved tonight."

Jack shook his head. "Afraid not. Father just left for a county council meeting in Wymondham. Said he'd be late."

Danvers slammed a fist into his hand. "Well, we'll wait up."

"I say, Lady Antonia—" Jack paused and reddened slightly. "Speaking of letters, if I wrote a bit of a note to Sarah, would you—er—would you mind taking it to her?"

Antonia gave him an encouraging smile. "I'd be delighted, Jack. And I'm sure she would be too. I'll either return tonight or in the morning, depending on how late Sir John is."

"Right. Thank you!" Jack started to hurry from the room, then caught himself in time to make his bow before leaving.

Antonia turned to Danvers. "Such a nice young man. I so hope Sarah will see sense. It's hard at her age. I myself failed to see so much that was right under my nose, but then . . ." Her voice trailed off. Both sat silent for several moments, gazing at the fire.

At first Tonia's touch on his sleeve was so slight that Danvers wasn't sure he felt it. He looked at her and smiled.

"Forgive me for interrupting your reverie, Charles, but it seems we have so little time alone to talk. I did want to ask how you are—how you really are."

It was the sincerity in her voice rather than anything in her words that made Danvers know he was talking to the real Antonia, the one he saw so seldom but would see more of if he could.

"I'm much better, Tonia. But let's talk of you." Suddenly he realized that was something they had never done. From a lifetime acquaintanceship, how much did he really know about this woman beyond her beauty and her brightness? "Antonia, why have I never seen you like this? Just now—and that early morning we met in church—why don't you let the world see you so—so intelligent, so caring, so . . ." He almost said "spiritual," but he feared she would laugh at him. "I had long suspected—" He had meant it all as a compliment, but he could see from the look on her face that she was horrified.

"Oh, no." She turned her face away. "I tried so hard to please them both."

"Both?"

"Both Father and Aunt Emma." As if for comfort, she reached down and picked up Tinker, who had curled himself before the fire. "When Mother died, Father took charge of my education and made rather thorough work of it. But Aunt Emma, his sister who took over the direction of the household for him, was horrified. She said he had turned me into a bluestocking and I'd be left on the shelf as she was. Besides, they both made clear I must fill the family's place in society."

202

She gave full attention to scratching Tinker's ears. "I don't know—it all sounds very complicated and like I'm blaming them for my failure."

"What failure?"

"My failure to please you."

Danvers couldn't believe it when her green eyes shimmered with tears. Could she really care so much about him?

"I could bear it when you had Charlotte, because she was a lovely person and I knew you were happy. So I carried on in my society role. But since you've been alone and unhappy, and I could still do nothing for you . . ."

One tear spilled over and ran down her cheek. Danvers caught it with his white silk handkerchief.

"You haven't failed to please me, Antonia. But I think you've failed to please yourself."

Danvers spent the next three hours wondering where that conversation might have led had not the dowager duchess announced her entrance with three sharp raps of her walking stick on the parquet floor.

"The tea tray has gone in to the drawing room. You may escort me, Lord Danvers."

Charles sprang to his feet, bowed deeply, and offered his arm before the duchess could note Antonia's unsettled state.

As the evening wore on, Danvers began to doubt the wisdom of his decision to wait up for Sir John. He had drunk all the tea he could hold, and even the incisive observations of the dowager duchess no longer amused him.

"Won't one of you girls give us some music?" Lady Catherine sounded doubtful of her own suggestion. Carry looked pained but rose obediently to sing the Scotch ballad Ama began playing at the piano.

By the second number Danvers was fighting mounting frustration over his powerlessness to pursue the questions that plagued him. He had to grip the carved rosewood arms of his chair to restrain himself from rising and pacing rudely around the room. Much as he would have liked to continue his conversation with Antonia, he felt he must settle some of the more immediate concerns of the Boileau family before he gave himself to personal matters.

At the end of the fourth song the musicians changed places. Carry played for Ama, and Wesleyan hymns took precedence on the program.

Danvers's impatience was now enough that he was willing to give way to vulgar curiosity and pursue the question of Carry's after-hours trysts, since he was blocked on every side in pursuing answers to Nigel's secret. He looked at the pale head bent over the piano keys. Well, she had said her diary was meant to be read. It was as good as an invitation—almost.

With the strains of "Love Divine, All Loves Excelling" following him up the staircase, Danvers opened the door to Caroline's sitting room. The volume, bound in green vellum, lay open on a side table, welcoming the reader. Danvers lighted a lamp with a stick from the fireplace, adjusted the wick to a bright, steady flame, and looked through Carry's record of the past days.

As he had earlier suspected, the writer gave no hint of secret rendezvous. If anything, the only surprises he found were more references than he would have expected to time she spent in Bible reading and prayer. He shook his head and started to lay the volume aside, when a new thought occurred to him. If the meetings had been going on for a long time, perhaps when they began the diarist might have recorded something that an informed reader would recognize as significant.

He turned back to the beginning of the book. It was marked in Carry's fine copperplate hand as "Volume the Second" and began when the family returned from a seaside holiday in August of the previous year. Danvers scanned the pages quickly, not taking in anything of importance. Then he stopped. Nigel's name caught his attention, and he read with care. He looked back at the date at the top of the page, thought a moment, and read again:

10 September 1847

> Nigel Langston stopped in to see Papa about some matter of business on his way to Northamptonshire. Most likely tried to borrow money, because I heard him say he expected to come into some soon. I hope he does. It's not good for the neighborhood to have an estate so rundown as he has allowed Aylsham to become.

Nigel was going to Northamptonshire—where Charlotte lived—on the tenth of September? And he said *then* he expected to come into some money soon? But that was two days before Danvers took Charlotte on that ill-fated picnic. How could Nigel count on an inheritance before his cousin was even ill?

He recalled his mild surprise at the time, when Nigel arrived at Charlotte's bedside so quickly. Dr. Boothe had made no suggestion of calling in the family—as a matter of fact, just before Nigel's arrival he had told Danvers the situation looked entirely hopeful. That was what had made the shock so dreadful the next morning.

Danvers recalled dressing cheerfully, hoping to see Charlotte sitting up in bed before he took his leave of her. Then Hardy had ushered Dr. Boothe into his room. It seemed as if black crepe had hung between himself and the sun ever since.

He returned the diary to its table and went to his room. Hardy was there, preparing for his master to retire. "Hardy, do you recall—the night Charlotte died—did you see Nigel or Hickling after everyone else retired?"

Hardy laid Danvers's linen nightshirt on the bed and thought for a moment. "No, m'lord. Only person I was seeing that night was that maid of Miss Auchincloss's—what was her name?"

"Millicent?"

"Yes, that's her. Silly name for a maid, if I may be saying so."

"But where did you see her? She was supposed to be sitting with her mistress all night."

"Aye, that's right. That's what she was telling me. Just slipping to the servants' hall for a cup of tea about 2:00 A.M. Having trouble staying awake, she was."

"What were you doing in the servants' hall at that hour, Hardy?"

"Making a cup of cocoa for you, m'lord. If you'll be remembering you had trouble sleeping, and us planning an early start back to Norwood Park the next morning."

"Yes, I remember. If only I could forget."

Danvers turned his back on his man and stood staring blindly out the window whose drapes Hardy had not yet closed.

When he saw a shadowy form slip down the path, he didn't even stop to question who it was or where she was going. He muttered an excuse to Hardy and left the house by the nearest exit.

His long-legged stride quickly closed the distance behind Caroline. This time he would learn the truth about her rendezvous. The crinolined silhouette led him past the church and directly to the vicarage. The door opened to Caroline before she had time to knock, and Danvers could see Mrs. Andrews in the parlor behind the vicar.

Danvers slipped along the side of the house to where a lamp had just been lit in Andrews's study. Fortunately, the maid who pulled the heavy velvet curtains had left a gap Danvers could see through.

Caroline sat, feet together, hands folded, on the black horsehair sofa. Andrews sat stiffly upright in a straight-backed wooden chair. The parson had a large Bible open on his knees and appeared to be expounding a passage from it. The scene was more astounding to Danvers than if he had caught them in flagrante delicto. He was fully aware of Sir John's views on children who chose to obey their own ideas of God rather than be guided by their parents. That Carry should violate her father's wishes to this extent seemed unthinkable.

The pair before him slipped to their knees, and Danvers turned away. Then he stopped. Sir John, his driving cape billowing behind him, strode down the path. It was too late to avoid him. The men nearly collided.

"What? That you, Danvers? You know about Carry, do you? I suppose the whole county knows. Saw Bishop Stanley at the meeting—he told me my own daughter was taking spiritual counsel from Andrews. From the *vicar*—not from her father. I'll be a laughingstock." He barely bothered knocking before marching into the vicarage. "I've come for my daughter, Andrews."

Danvers slipped into the room behind Boileau. The vicar emerged from his study. "Sir John—"

"Is this the way you teach the duties of children towards their parents? Subverting my own daughter against me? To think I've harbored a viper in my own church—"

"It is not your church, Sir John. It is God's church, and I am His minister."

"Then why is it you do the devil's work? That so intelligent and coherent a girl as Carry should be lured from her father's home to the influence of a man so unworthy and so unfitted to be the guide of her soul is incomprehensible—"

Caroline emerged from the study and stood before her father, her hands clenched at her side, her eyes regarding him levelly. "I come to be led in prayer and Bible study, Father. How can that be wrong?"

"You were sneaking out. Expressly disobeying my orders. What may have begun nominally for religious purposes is easily perverted to domestic disturbance. I suspect that it is due to a dislike of parental control that you claim a belief in the authority of religion—or of the minister—to justify your opposition to my wishes."

"Father—"

"At the least, your behavior has been the height of indiscretion."

Caroline bowed her head at the truth of that thrust. "Forgive me, Father. I know I am only a woman and must submit to authority. I have no desire to be disloyal to you—or to the vicar or to God. But should I not also be loyal to myself? Should I not have enough faith to do what I know is right? Can I not do so without being disloyal to you?"

Sir John sought refuge in quoting Scripture. "Servants should be obedient unto their own masters—showing good fidelity."

"Just so, Father. God is my master; you are my master. Who must I obey?"

Here was a question Sir John could handle with authority. He squared his shoulders. "God speaks to me. I speak to you. That is the order of things. Return to your mother, Caroline."

She turned to go.

"And I forbid you to have further conversation with this man." He banged the door closed between himself and Andrews.

Danvers remained inside the vicarage. It was an awkward moment, but no occasion seemed graceful with Andrews. And yet the man at times showed a depth of wisdom Danvers envied.

"I have received word that Rush's trial has been set for the April assizes." The vicar opened a new topic, apparently to clear the air of the vibrations still hanging there from Boileau's banged door.

"It is the Rush affair I would speak to you on." Danvers took a chair at Andrews's leading.

"I have given the matter much thought, but I can find no satisfactory answers. I cannot understand how such evil can exist in the presence of a loving, all-powerful God such as you preach and such as I would believe in if I could."

Andrews cleared his throat. "The evil in the world is not God's fault. It is man's."

"You're saying man created evil?"

"No. I am saying man chose evil. God allowed man free choice because the Almighty didn't want to be served by puppets. How much would our love mean if we didn't have any choice in the matter?"

Danvers nodded to indicate he was listening.

"So because man first chose to rebel against God, we now all have a fallen nature—all as fallen as Rush's—which prevents us from being able to choose good over evil."

"Then there is no hope." Danvers had come to the same conclusion on his own. But in the face of despair he had hoped Andrews would have an answer. He should have known better.

"Ah, but here's the good news." Andrews leaned forward, fervor lighting his austere features. "There is no hope on our own—there is none good, no, not one." He shook a bony finger at Danvers. "But God offers free grace—He helps us choose good over evil if we allow Him in our life."

Danvers was quiet a moment. "And if we don't, any of us is capable of such an act as Rush's?" He shuddered. Surely not. He was forgetting about the progress of man and society. True, progress had passed some by—some such as Rush. But those of education, of breeding, those of his own class—they had risen above such barbarianism.

He moved forward in his chair to take his leave. Then another thought struck him, and he sat back. He thought of Nigel. Langston was of his own class. Social progress had not passed him by. And yet he lived in extravagance and debauchery.

"Then what hope exists for mankind?"

"None!"

Until Andrews thundered his answer, Danvers didn't realize he had voiced his question aloud.

The vicar's face looked longer, his wrinkles more severe than ever as his eyebrows cast shadows in the dim light. "None, aside from the grace of God. Good is God's gift, but too often man substitutes an evil of his own choice."

When he returned to the Hall, Danvers learned that Antonia had retired, taking Nigel's letter to her room with her. He sighed in irritation at having to wait yet again to learn the secrets of the envelope's contents. But this gave him more time to think on Andrews's words.

16

The next morning Danvers opened one eye to peer at Hardy bringing in his tea. His vision cleared just in time to fling himself across the bed and avoid sustaining a fierce blow to his stomach as a tow-headed projectile hurtled toward him.

The missile collapsed on his bed with a shriek of giggles and a wild flailing of small arms and legs. "There's sunshine and a right brisk breeze, gov'nor. We can go, just like yer said!"

"Pip! What are you doing in my room! And at the crack of dawn?" No matter how fond he might be of children at other times, that emotion did not emerge before breakfast.

"You said so, sir. Said we'd go today if it's fine. And it is!" He began bouncing up and down on the enormous fourposter.

"Stop that! Get off my bed, brat!" Danvers flung up his arms as much to protect himself from being bounced on as to push the child off the bed.

Pip landed on his feet, then turned a somersault across the thick turkey work carpet. Unfortunately, at that moment Hardy was crossing the room with the viscount's steaming teacup. He tripped over Pip and landed in the center of the carpet, surrounded by a puddle of tea and broken china.

Danvers groaned and flung the bedclothes over his head.

"Ooow, I'm orful sorry, gov'nor! Truly, I—"

"Shut up, brat! Hardy, will the Norwich main supply us with gas to float that blasted overgrown bladder again?"

Hardy was gathering bits of china and his dignity. "The balloon? Indeed, m'lord."

"Well, get about it then. Seems I made a rash promise to this infernal pest, and the only protection for our peace and our host's china is to get it over with."

There was nothing Danvers wanted to do less than go ballooning today. But a promise to a child was a sacred commitment, and, after all, the brat *had* found the gun.

Pip started to turn another handspring, then appeared to think better of it. "Can the old lady go too?"

"Who?"

"The one with the silver 'air and sparkles on 'er dress—her who went up before."

"That is the Dowager Duchess of Aethelbert, young man—Her Grace to you."

"Ya, that's 'er. She's a right 'un."

Danvers shook his head in surrender. "Hardy, would you be so good as to inquire if Her Grace would care to make an ascent this morning?"

Little more than an hour later, in the remarkably crisp November air of Ketteringham Park, Danvers decided the whole idea wasn't such a bad one—at least he had escaped sitting through family prayers. With a grin he wondered if that thought had had anything to do with the duchess's quick acceptance of his invitation.

Hardy attached the last sand-filled ballast bag to the side of the gondola, and the balloon tugged on its tether ropes like a racehorse at the gate, its pennants whipping in the breeze.

"Now this won't be a long ride this morning, Pip. I

have some very important matters to deal with today. Can't spend the whole day floating about the sky daydreaming."

"Oh, yes, sir. Oooh, she's just ready to go, ain't she?" Pip gazed upward, and his eyes shone as bright as the sun reflecting off the red-and-gold ball over his head.

With a yip of excitement, he bounded into the gondola, then stood, proper as any footman, with his hand extended, to help the duchess. She had arrived in Jack's gig, and the heir handed her from carriage to balloon.

"Very nice of you to invite me along, Pip."

"Oh, I knew you wouldn't want to miss it. I mean, at your age you might not get many more chances—er—I mean—"

"I know very well what you mean, young man. Please do not attempt an explanation. Do you mean to dwaddle here all morning, Danvers? I thought I'd been invited to an ascent, and as Pip pointed out, I'm not getting any younger."

"Right, Your Grace." Danvers bit his lip to restrain his mirth, and he and Hardy began undoing the tethers.

He was loosening the last one when he was interrupted by a somber figure in a clerical collar, black coat and low-crowned hat. Andrews had never looked so chastened. Apparently he, too, had spent much of the night in thought.

"I beg your pardon, I was told I could find Sir John here. I am afraid I owe him an apology. I spent the night meditating on 'Children, obey your parents,' and I fear that in my zeal for Miss Caroline's soul—"

As he warmed to his topic he flung out his arm in a pulpit gesture toward the balloon. Unfortunately, his gaze followed his action, and his eyes lighted on the bottle of champagne stowed in the basket. "What's this? Spirits! When you are taking a child up? Lord Danvers, I fear duty requires me to protest. Have you given no thought to the tender conscience in your care?" His ardor carried him into the gondola to seize the offending intoxicant.

Danvers rushed to appease the clergyman's wounded sensibilities. "It is merely a tradition of the sport, sir. Begun as a necessity to placate the tempers of French peasants whose fields—"

"I am not concerned with the history of your hobby, my lord. I am concerned with the guiding of immortal souls—"

The duchess had no interest in being conciliatory. "Put that down, Vicar. If there is anything I cannot abide it is a rigamarolist."

"By your leave, madam, our Lord—"

"Our Lord had more humor in His little finger than you—"

"Humor? Madam, I will not listen to blasphemy!"

"You will listen to whatever I care to say to you, Vicar." She stamped her walking stick on his toe. "When I can see this personal relationship to the Divine you're always ranting on about producing some love and joy rather than more pharisaical rules, I might choose to stay awake through one of your sermons."

"Joy? What can you mean? It is our duty . . ." Andrews pulled a heavy, black Bible from his pocket and began flipping pages.

A rustle in the park made Danvers turn. Antonia came running, her bonnet thrust back, the sun on her auburn hair and russet skirts a most pleasant sight against the background of brown leaves.

"Charles, whatever can you be thinking of? Jaunting off in a balloon when we must take this to Sir John first thing?" She waved Hickling's letter at him.

Before Danvers could reply, there was a sharp cracking of dry underbrush in the other direction, and Nigel emerged from the thicket.

"I've come to talk to you, Antonia," he said through clenched teeth.

Antonia struggled to slip the letter into her pocket unnoticed. "Nigel. How did you know I was here?"

214

"Your obliging little cousin told me when she accepted my invitation to tea yesterday."

"Your invitation? Sarah went to Aylsham? Ridiculous. I would never have allowed it."

"That was why I suggested we keep our little party a secret. I told her how jealous you would be because you wanted my attentions for yourself." As skillfully as the best Yorkshire sheepdog, Nigel was cutting Antonia off from the others.

"You despicable scoundrel. You leave that child alone."

"Oh, I promise you, Tonia, I'll take the best possible care of her when I get back to Aylsham."

"What, you mean she's still there?"

Langston advanced, and Antonia was obliged to take another step backwards.

Danvers started to move protectively toward her when Sir John's carriage pulled up, and the squire and Carry stepped out. "I say, Danvers, what's all this then? Huntley said you left an urgent message—something about some letter Hickling wrote to Jermy?"

"Ah, so! Just as I thought!" Nigel's harsh words took everyone's attention. "Antonia, I must ask you to deliver my servant's correspondence to me."

Antonia turned to run toward the balloon.

"Stop!" Nigel drew a small pistol from his pocket. "The letter, please."

Andrews leaped out of the basket and stood beside her.

"No one move. The letter, Antonia." Nigel held out his hand. In the breathless silence, the click as he cocked the hammer was as loud as a shot.

"I came to deliver the letter to Sir John." She thrust the letter toward the squire.

Sir John stepped toward her.

The shot exploded in a flash of fire and ear-shattering noise.

Antonia screamed and fell backwards against the basket.

Danvers stepped forward but got no farther as Caroline fainted in his arms. A blur of rust silk caught his eye as the duchess and Pip pulled Antonia into the gondola.

With no time to reload, Nigel dropped his flintlock and leaped into the basket after her. With the repeated jarring, the already-loosened final tether knot slipped free. The balloon surged heavenward.

"Antonia!" Danvers struggled forward, still hampered by the unconscious Caroline. It was too late. They were far beyond reach. "Hardy!" He thrust Carry into the valet's arms and attempted to quiet his own mounting alarm. "Did anyone see? Was there much blood? Do you think—is there any chance?"

"Thy word is a shield and a buckler." Andrews turned to him, holding out a bullet-torn Bible. A lump of lead was buried deep in its pages. "Flung it out when the villain shot. Couldn't think of anything else." He examined the ruined pages in consternation. "Oh, Lord, forgive me."

Danvers clapped him on the back. "I'm sure He will, Vicar."

"Best work you've ever done, Andrews. Maybe you're learning." Sir John grinned. "Supposed to be saving people, aren't you?"

"M'lord, the balloon!" Hardy yelled.

The golden ball was a rapidly shrinking dot as it moved eastward. Danvers grabbed the telescope, which hadn't yet been stowed in the basket. "Come on!" He sprang into Sir John's carriage. The squire and vicar were right behind him.

"Take care of Carry, Jack," Boileau called. He looked around. "Where *is* that boy? He leave his own party again?"

But no one had time to locate Jack, and Danvers sprang the horses.

Once on the Norwich road Danvers made better time. The carriage was soon nearly below the balloon. The fact that the basket contained the weight of three adults and a child kept them low, and the steady wind made following easy. But that would only help until they reached Great Yarmouth. The brisk westerly wind was carrying the balloon directly toward the North Sea. Once they were over the water there would be no place to bring the balloon down until they reached the Netherlands—if Pip sufficiently remembered the instruction Hardy had given him. If not, who knew where the balloon might wind up?

The most important consideration was that on the continent Nigel would be free. Danvers refused to consider what Langston might choose to do to Antonia and the others then.

"Pray, Vicar." He spoke against his will and yet he repeated it. "Pray."

The carriage drew closer to the balloon. Danvers handed the reins to Sir John and drew out his telescope. There must be something he could do. He longed for a bow and arrow to make a hole that would force the balloon down. Even if he had a rifle, he wouldn't dare shoot with two women and a child in the basket.

A glint of sunlight on metal made him blink. The sheath knife, used for cutting off sandbags. He shuddered at the thought of Nigel's holding the razor-sharp, ten-inch blade to Antonia's throat. Suddenly he realized how very precious her life was to him.

Then an action in the balloon brought Danvers to his feet.

"Sit down, man!" Boileau bellowed.

Danvers sat but never took his eye off the scene now being played almost directly above him: Antonia bent backwards over the basket, her red-gold hair whipping in the wind, her right arm extended just beyond Nigel's grasp. The flash of white paper in her hand told what they were struggling over. For a moment he closed his eyes, and his mind was filled with the horror of imagining Antonia's coppery figure hurtling to the ground while Nigel triumphantly brandished the letter.

Danvers forced his eyes open. Antonia was still in the basket but bent even more precariously over the side. At least the balloon was not rising higher, as he would expect with the sun warming the gas inside. If anything, it seemed a bit closer to the ground. Then another flash of silver riveted his attention. Nigel slashed the blade toward Antonia's hand.

His heart gave a lurch as he saw a white object fall toward the earth and thought of the slim white fingers that had held his arm so lightly. Then he realized. It was the letter.

"Stop!" He sprang from the carriage before the horses had halted and darted across the rough field in the direction he had seen the paper fall. Seconds later Danvers held the vital document.

He arrived back at the carriage out of breath. "Here, Sir John, you read this. I'll drive." He vaulted onto the seat and cracked the whip over the horses' heads to make up the lost distance.

Boileau broke the wax seal and read quietly, then folded the document and put it in his pocket. "Well, that makes it all very clear. When Langston couldn't get his hands on his cousin's money by persuading her to marry him—apparently she had the bad taste to prefer you—he decided to get it by murdering her and inheriting it. Only trouble was, he didn't know his man saw him hold a pillow over her face in the middle of the night."

Danvers froze. The reins slipped in his hands as the scene played in his mind: the dim sickroom, Charlotte's pale face on the white bolster framed in the lace cap covering her hair . . .

Sir John took the reins once more. Danvers slipped a finger up to loosen his collar as he seemed to see the suffocating pillow descend over Charlotte's face and felt his own air supply shut off.

"No!" He shook his head to stop the choking and realized his cheeks were wet. Yet, even as he protested, one small part of his mind realized that the suspicion had been growing. Ever since he learned Millicent had left her mistress unattended, he had suspected that the sudden tragedy had not been entirely natural.

Still he protested. "But no one suspected."

Boileau shook his head. "Well, the girl was ill already. Amazingly convenient, as he apparently meant to see her off anyway."

Danvers sat in silence for a time. He couldn't really take it all in. Then he nodded in dawning understanding. "Jermy's death was the key to bring it all to a head." Once he said it, the pieces fell into place. "Yes, I see. Hickling told Nigel he had written the letter to his attorney, and Nigel was helpless—until Rush was so obliging as to murder Jermy and remove that threat. When the document failed to show up in Jermy's papers, Nigel thought he was free."

"Oh, the darkness of which the human heart is capable." Both men turned at the sound of Andrews's voice. Danvers had forgotten that he was in the carriage, but the vicar had apparently not taken his eyes off the balloon. He now pointed to it, veering to the left.

Sir John turned all his attention to his driving. He had almost a mile of distance to make up to reach the balloon.

As the carriage jostled over the frozen, rutted ground, Danvers's shock at this newest revelation began to wear off, and Andrews's words echoed in his mind. Man's heart was capable of great darkness.

But Danvers's heart didn't feel dark. For the first time since Charlotte's death the glorious sun broke in on it. His spirit soared higher than the balloon. He had not caused Charlotte's death. He was free.

The release from guilt was the headiest thing he had ever felt. He had had no idea of the weight of the burden he had carried for the past year. He felt he must grip the side of the carriage in order to keep his seat.

The sudden light that poured in upon his soul with such blinding revelation was so sharp a contrast to the darkness he had lived with that he now heard Andrews's words in an entirely new way—as if he had just learned the language. Man's heart was indeed dark. Look at Rush, look at Nigel, the dark deeds they had committed, spurred on by greed, lust, and pride.

The words of Andrews's sermon came back to him: *Without God's grace we are all capable of such.* From the blatant evils of Rush and Langston, he turned to thoughts of the darknesses in his own heart—angers, hatreds, lacks of charity. Perhaps in spite of his legalistic nonsense, Andrews's theology did hold the root of truth.

As impossible as he would have thought it a few minutes before, a new freedom, a greater lightness than before filled him. The light of hope. Perhaps he *could* find answers. Perhaps his life *could* have a purpose that he had not found by escaping in a balloon.

Suddenly the vicar brought his attention back to the present.

"Oh! He's mad! He'll kill them all!" Andrews, who had been watching the balloon through the telescope, dropped it and clasped his hands in prayer. "O most powerful and glorious Lord God, at whose command the winds blow and lift up the waves of the sea, we Thy creatures, but miserable sinners, do in this our great distress cry unto Thee for help . . ."

As the vicar continued, Danvers seized the glass and took it all in with a single glance: Nigel held the occupants of the gondola all at bay with the lethal-bladed sheath knife. The lifeline of the valve rope dangled in front of Pip, but he dared not pull it. The duchess seemed to be holding something behind her skirt but couldn't move.

Antonia . . . Antonia was blocked from his clear view, but Danvers was overwhelmed with a need to reach out to her, to let her know what was in his heart.

The winter sun flashed icily on the steel blade.

Danvers must act. He jumped to his feet, flung out his arms and, in tones that thundered bass and shrilled a high tenor in almost the same note, gave voice to the entire chorus of the "Ride of the Valkyries." Within seconds, Boileau and Andrews joined in with equally off-key fervor.

The startling ruckus reflected from the balloon took Nigel's attention for only a moment. But it was enough.

And the crack heard was not that of a Rhine-maiden wielding a staff but of the duchess whacking the champagne bottle across Nigel's forearm.

Danvers saw Nigel grab for the falling knife as Pip pulled on the valve rope. The combined actions caused Nigel to overbalance. He plunged headfirst over the side of the basket.

With a wild grab at a ballast bag Nigel checked his plummet and dangled two hundred feet above the fallow Norwich fields. In the distance, Danvers glimpsed just a sparkle of the North Sea, which would have spelled freedom to Nigel.

Shouting triumphantly, Pip hauled again on the valve rope. The balloon descended.

"Got no rope, gov'nor!" Pip shouted.

"No problem. Langston'll do!" Danvers yelled back and grabbed Nigel's legs to pull the balloon to the ground.

As Langston's feet touched earth he let go of the basket, and the balloon surged upward again. Instinctively, Danvers lunged for the gondola, loosening his grip on Langston. With a quick movement Nigel shoved his knee at Danvers's stomach and wrenched free.

Nigel took out across the field of wheat stubble at a run, his speed only slightly hindered from having clung for his life to the outside of a descending balloon. But Danvers, now knowing he was pursuing Charlotte's murderer, was spurred by an even swifter fire than Nigel's desire for self-preservation.

At first it seemed Nigel's head start was too great, no matter how strong Charles's determination. If the man made it to the thicket, he might still escape. The distance was short, but the exertion required was great.

Sweat dripped into Danvers's eyes, and his heart pounded as his feet thudded across the stubble. His throat was on fire, and his chest ready to burst. His pace slowed, and his vision blurred.

Then, it seemed, Antonia and Charlotte appeared before him, cheering him on. He took a great gulp of air and plunged forward.

Langston was only yards from the woods when he stumbled. He barely dropped to one knee before he found his feet again, but the few seconds' delay was enough.

Danvers lunged. His first blow fell on Nigel's shoulder, spun him around, sent him reeling backwards.

Danvers threw himself on top. The two men rolled on the stubble, fists thrashing. Langston landed a jab at Danvers's throat that loosened his grip and allowed Nigel to stumble to his feet. Danvers sprang upward, grabbed Nigel's arm, and scored a facer that gave the satisfying sound of knuckle hitting bone.

Nigel struck with his left. Danvers blocked. His next blow bloodied Langston's eye.

Danvers grabbed his opponent's cravat and drew back to administer the leveler that would finish the fight. But Langston sank to the ground before Charles could punch. Antonia, a triumphant gleam in her eye, brandished the ballast bag she had just swung at Nigel. The blow of the sandbag was followed in quick order by a crack from the duchess's walking stick.

"Such impertinence, young man. In my day gentlemen did not behave like that. Didn't your mother teach you any manners?"

Danvers hauled Nigel's crumpled form to his feet. "I'm afraid she didn't, duchess. But Her Majesty's courts will see to that now." He bound Langston's hands with his belt, then shoved the defeated man ahead of them as the three returned triumphant to the carriage. "Watch him, Andrews."

Danvers started to turn to Antonia, but Pip said, "I say, I'm sorry I called you old, duchess—you was great!"

"Thank you, young man. And when you get your own aerostat, I shall expect you to take me up in it."

"Right you are!" Pip turned to Danvers. "Did you see, gov'nor? I pulled the valve like you showed me. I opened it everytime 'e warn't lookin'. Thought it best to keep us low. Did I do right?"

Danvers ruffled the flaxen hair. "Indeed you did—first class airmanship, Pip."

Pip turned a handspring, narrowly avoiding crashing into the duchess.

Sir John joined them, bearing glasses and the traditional champagne to Danvers and Antonia. He started to raise his glass with them, then paused and grinned. "Think I'll just see if the vicar will join me in a drop."

From the carriage they could hear Andrews's voice —preaching repentance to Langston. Then they all turned at the sound of an arriving carriage. Jack pulled his winded horses to a stop. With him was Sarah, looking prettier than ever. Her black curls were disarranged under her bonnet, and her blue eyes were wide in her white face. She held tightly to her maid's hand until she released it to fall into Antonia's arms.

"Oh, I'm so sorry, Tonia. I shouldn't have deceived you. He asked me to tea. I thought it would be such fun. Then he wouldn't let me go. Jack rescued me. He made the servants open my door." Her eyes shone as she looked back at Jack, and Danvers thought she was seeing much more clearly now.

"Nigel didn't love me at all. He only wanted my fortune. He said I'd be ruined, and I'd *have* to marry him." She paused and looked from one face to the other.

The duchess voiced the question that Danvers, as a gentleman, couldn't ask. "And are you all right, girl?"

Sarah blushed. "Oh, yes. Yes. Samantha was with me all the time." Her maid nodded.

"Quite proper." The duchess sniffed. "If any such hugger-mugger could be said to be proper." She glared at Danvers. "Hand me into the carriage. I shall take this girl under my protection. It's quite clear Antonia is far too much in need of chaperonage herself to stand guardian for another. And *you,* sir,"—she turned her attentions to Jack —"may not speak for her for at least a year." She planted herself firmly on the carriage seat. "Not until she's eighteen. What this generation is coming to doesn't bear thinking on. Take me to Ketteringham."

She was still instructing Jack on his courtship of Sarah as the iron wheels of the carriage rolled over the rutted road. Danvers turned to Antonia. "Are you truly all right? You did give me such a fright."

"Truly. But there is a look in your eye that's definitely not fright, Charles. I think detecting suits you."

He took both her hands in his. "Antonia, I have suddenly found there is so much that suits me. I have a great deal to tell you—to ask you. And now that I'm truly free, living is going to suit me." He broke into the liberation aria from *Flying Dutchman*, which he had not sung since Charlotte's death because it had been her particular favorite.

> "Star of misfortune, wane!
> Light of hope, rekindle!"

Antonia regarded him for several moments. "Definitely an improvement, Charles. You're almost on tune. But, you know, I even like it when you aren't."

Arm in arm they walked over the rough field, singing together.

Afterword

On Saturday, 21st April, 1849, James Blomfield Rush was executed by hanging. The prisoner was dressed in black with black patent boots and a scrupulously clean shirt collar. Andrews attended him and solemnly urged the duties of repentance and confession, which Rush refused. "Thank God Almighty, all is right," he said.

As he walked to the scaffold, Rush asked the governor what the words were with which the burial service ended. He was told that it was with the benediction "The grace of our Lord Jesus Christ, and the love of God, and the fellowship of the Holy Ghost, be with you all evermore. Amen." Rush requested that the drop might fall when the chaplain came to those words.

Rush mounted the scaffold and turned his face to the Castle walls. The executioner threw the white nightcap over his head, fastened the rope to the beam, and adjusted the noose to Rush's neck. "This does not go easy," Rush said. "Put the thing a little higher—take your time—don't be in a hurry."

Those were his last words.

My special appreciation goes to Miss Jean Kennedy, County Archivist, and her excellent staff at the Norfolk Record Office, who were so efficient and gracious in providing research materials.

Thank you, John Debliech of Alpine Sports, who knows antique guns; Ada County Coroner Erwin Sonnenberg, who fortunately uses his knowledge of how to commit murder for lawful purposes; and Curt Pengelly, whose balloon trip was a real high.

Major References

W. Teignmouth Shore, ed. *The Trial of James Blomfield Rush*. *Notable British Trials*. Edinburgh and London: William Hodge & Company, Ltd., 1928. Used by permission.

George Perry and Nicholas Mason, eds. *The Victorians, a World Built to Last*. New York: Viking, 1974.

W. J. Reader. *Victorian England*. London: B. T. Batsford, Ltd., 1964.

Owen Chadwick. *Victorian Miniature*. London: Hodder & Stoughton, 1960.

Richard D. Altick. *Victorian Studies in Scarlet*. New York: W. W. Norton, 1970.

Moody Press, a ministry of the Moody Bible Institute,
is designed for education, evangelization, and edification.
If we may assist you in knowing more about Christ
and the Christian life, please write us without obligation:
Moody Press, c/o MLM, Chicago, Illinois 60610.